# THE FIRST YEAR

Rose Standing, probationer nurse at St Martin's Hospital, London, knows what it is like to work under an exacting Sister, to be so busy that hunger and tiredness are forgotten, to lose count of the days in the hectic routine.

Even so, there is still time for romance. There are the usual overtures from the students, not to be taken too seriously, and the real thing: a shy, frustrated love for the senior member of the surgical staff, hedged about by hospital etiquette.

But love has a way of conquering such difficulties in this vivid, true-to-life hospital romance.

# THE FIRST YEAR

## Lucilla Andrews

This edition published in Great Britain 1995 by
SEVERN HOUSE PUBLISHERS LTD of
9–15 High Street, Sutton, Surrey SM1 1DF.
First published in Great Britain 1957 by
George G Harrap & Co. Ltd.

British Library Cataloguing in Publication Data
Andrews, Lucilla
    The First Year. – new ed
    I. Title
    823.914 [F]

ISBN 0-7278-4752-x

Another for Poosie

Typeset by Hewer Text Composition Services, Edinburgh.
Printed and bound in Great Britain by
Hartnolls Ltd, Bodmin, Cornwall.

# Contents

# 1

## A Dummy Patient and a Live Surgeon

THE cranial nerves," said Sister Preliminary Training School, "radiate from——" She stopped her lecture and sighed impatiently. "Nurse Standing, wake up! How many more times am I going to have to remind you that you are in my classroom and not in bed?"

I shot up from my seat in the third row of desks. "I'm sorry, Sister."

Sister P.T.S. looked me over. "Since you have been good enough to rouse yourself from slumber, Nurse, you had better go out to the changing-room and do something about your cap. It is about to descend upon your right ear. Then you will have to return and copy down the notes you will thus miss in your break period. I cannot expect the whole class to wait while you see to your hair-dressing."

I said, "No, Sister. I'm sorry, Sister."

Her expression was coldly resigned. "So am I, Nurse. This is not the first occasion upon which I have discovered you day-dreaming in a lecture; nor is it the first occasion upon which I have had to inform you that your cap is intended to cover your hair and not be worn as a hair or ear ornament. I hope, Nurse Standing," she added awe-fully, "not to have to refer to either of these matters again."

I said, "No, Sister. I mean—yes, Sister."

She dismissed me with a brief nod, and I left the classroom quickly. I had actually been listening to Sister; but I knew that I had also been gazing out of the window by my desk, watching the main hospital building that stood on the other side of the park. I had a perfect view of the whole hospital from my desk, and that view fascinated me. It was like watching a silent movie; I could see the white caps and aprons of the nurses flitting past the long, wide ward windows; the white-coated figures of the doctors; the careful ambulances nosing their way over the paved yard outside Casualty; the constant in- and out-going stream of tweed-jacketed students carrying armfuls of books; a stream that was matched by the steady trickle of up-patients and relatives all going to or coming out of the great long stone building that was St Martin's Hospital, London. And I was soon going to be a character in that movie, as I was going to spend the next four years of my life in Martin's.

But I was not, I reminded myself gloomily as I fixed my cap, going to get into Martin's unless I survived the final P.T.S. exam. next week. That exam. loomed blackly ahead; a far more difficult obstacle to overcome than the present minor obstacle of discovering how to keep my stiff, slippery cap in the correct position on my very fine, straight hair.

Sister P.T.S. was right when she said she had had occasion to talk to me about my cap previously. As far as I could recollect, in my last ten weeks in the School she had never met me without discussing my cap or my absent-mindedness. I was trying to cure myself of the latter—so far without much success. My cap had been equally resistant to my efforts and the efforts of the girls in my set. We had tried pins, brilliantine, hair-grips; nothing worked. The wretched little scrap of starched linen rose on my head two minutes after I had fixed it impeccably in place, and Sister P.T.S. continued to sigh impatiently.

I fixed four hair-grips in a row down the back of my cap; they were pinching my scalp, so I thought they might do the trick and returned to the class-room as the break-bell rang. Sister dismissed the class, but remained at her desk. As the girls filed out one girl, called Josephine Forbes, lingered by my desk.

"I've got it all down, Rose," she murmured. "Want to borrow my book?"

Sister's head jerked up from the notebook she was correcting. "Nurse Forbes, if you are offering to assist Nurse Standing with the notes she has missed, kindly refrain from so doing. I do not approve of young nurses borrowing each other's books or brains. When you get into the wards you will have to stand on your own feet; so you must allow me to teach you to do that in this School. Get off to your break, Nurse Forbes, and leave Nurse Standing to find out for herself what she has missed through her untidiness." She glanced at the board behind her. "The notes are all there, Nurse Standing. If you hurry you should be done in time to have some break yourself."

Josephine and I chanted, "Yes, Sister; sorry, Sister"; then she vanished to the refectory, and I copied Sister's neat drawings into my notebook. I labelled each cranial nerve rapidly, checked once to see I had missed nothing, then went out to break, chanting the cranial nerves under my breath. Sister did not look my way again.

I helped myself to a cup of cool cocoa and a pile of bread and dripping, and joined Josephine at one of the long tables. She raised her eyebrows at my stack of bread and dripping.

"Rose, did they starve you at home? How can you eat all that and not grow fat?"

"I'm just always hungry," I apologized, "and, anyway, worry keeps me thin. I'm scared stiff about that exam. I feel in my bones that something ghastly is going to happen to me. If by any miracle I get through the written either my cap'll drop off in the practical or I'll spill something on Matron in the viva."

Josephine, being a practical girl, said I would not have anything in my hands to spill during the viva. "You just have to hold your hands behind you and answer questions. But, for goodness' sake, don't go off into one of your comas like you did this morning. I saw Sister looking at you several times before she bawled you out. You just weren't with us, Rose. I did try to catch your eye, but it wasn't any good. You kept gaping out of the window and then closing your eyes as if settling down for a nice little snooze."

"But I always close my eyes when doing heavy thinking," I protested, "and I really was listening to Sister. I can quite well listen with my ears and watch something else with my eyes at the same time. And, Josephine," I turned to her, "I

was watching Cas. yard. You can't think how exciting it
looked this morning; there was something big going on, and
the yard was simply stiff with cops, bodies on stretchers,
doctors—the lot! Just like watching the curtain go up on
the first act of a play—or a movie," and I went on to tell her
about my silent movie.

"Rose"—she shook her head—"if you don't keep your
cap on your head and your eyes on Sister P.T.S. you almost
certainly won't get into the act. You've got to concentrate on
the present; let the future and the hospital take care of itself.
Unless you get through the P.T.S. exam. your nursing career
will end next week; and unless you get through your practical
try-out with Sister this afternoon you may not even get to
the exam. Remember, they do throw us out before that exam.
if they think we are no good. So do be careful with your
blanket-bath and don't spill your water all over the bed like
you did last time."

I swallowed my last piece of bread and dripping. "Not to
worry, Josephine. I'll be so careful and professional that Sister
won't know me."

I was careful with my water during that blanket-bath; I
did not spill a drop or drop the soap; and my cap miraculously
stayed in place. But Sister was furious with me when I
finished. The reason she was furious was that just after I
had finished bathing my life-size dummy patient I inadvertently pushed her out of bed. The dummy dropped on to the
floor with an ugly thud and cracked one of its knees.

Sister's foot beat a positive tattoo of irritation on the
wooden floor. "Nurse Standing, what will you do next? Poor
Mrs Clark!" Her voice softened at that name, and she helped
me lift the large, heavy, placid-faced doll back into bed. "My
poor Mrs Clark! You have survived three decades of pupil-
nurses without ever having such a dreadful accident occur to
you before. Now you will have to go to the carpenters' shop
to have that knee mended." She straightened the bedclothes,
then frowned at me. "Settle her on her pillows comfortably,
Nurse Standing—using care this time—and then prepare to
bath Janet. As Janet is fortunately made of rubber," she added
drily, "not even you can do any damage to her."

We had a whole hierarchy of dummies in the P.T.S. Mrs Clark was the senior member, but both she and her daughter Lady Smith (no one knew why she was titled) had been in use for thirty-odd years. Lady Smith had a son, Tom, who was an eternal twelve-year-old; and there was a grand-daughter Janet. Janet's parents had both vanished at some period, and the empty bed in the practical class-room was always called unofficially 'The Missing Link.' Janet was a lovely baby doll, life-size like all the other dummies and a joy to bath. I tidied the broken Mrs Clark, avoided her wide, staring blue eyes, and rushed off thankfully to do the baby. For once I managed without mishap.

Sister watched me in silence. When Janet was back in her cot she said, " It appears I have at least taught you the correct manner in which to bath a baby, Nurse Standing. I suppose I must be grateful if only for that. That will be all your nursing practice for this afternoon; but before you go off duty for the evening I want you to wheel Mrs Clark to the carpenters' shop. We must have her back for the examination, and I do not wish anyone to touch her until she has been properly repaired. Go and fetch your cloak and a wheel-chair while I write up a request-form."

The wheel-chairs and our cloaks were kept in the changing-room. Several of the other girls were in that room, sitting on the wheel-chairs waiting for us all to come off duty. " I've got a hunch," I told them as I found my cloak, " that I'll get that wretched doll in the exam. I'll bet she'll topple out of bed again in front of Matron."

Josephine said I really must take life more seriously. " How would you like that to happen to you if you were ill, Rose? "

" It wouldn't have happened with an ill person," announced a girl called Angela Black. " Real patients can co-operate. They're much easier to wash than dummies."

Angela always knew the answers. She had been a part-time nursing cadet in Martin's for two years, and consequently was able to give us an endless fund of inside information on nursing.

" Is that really a fact, Angela? I've been panicking about

that ever since it happened, for all Josephine says I don't take life seriously. I've been worrying just what would have happened if the patient hadn't been made of wood and papier mâché like Mrs Clark."

Angela said all that would have happened would have been that my patient would have felt herself slipping and told me so. "Then you would have known what to do."

I said, "But supposing she was too ill to tell me?"

Angela smiled knowingly. "Then you wouldn't have been allowed to touch her. Junior pros. don't get near very ill people. You don't wash the really ill until you are in your second or third year."

I sighed with relief and swung my cloak round my shoulders. "Thank goodness for that." I buttoned the collar quickly. "I must get moving or Sister'll send me to Matron for dawdling. Out of that chair, Angela! Thanks." I pushed down the footstand and tested the chair. It ran easily on the polished wooden floor. "Be seeing you, girls!" I put one foot on the rail of the chair and scooted to the door. "I rather like this form of transport."

"Rose!" Josephine rushed after me. "Rose, you mustn't do that. You'll snap that rail. It isn't made of cast-iron."

Angela drifted over to us. "And you've knocked your cap sideways, too. Here." She adjusted it for me, straightened my cloak collar, then dusted me down as if I was one of Mrs Clark's family. "That's better. But do walk slowly, like a proper nurse."

"Proper nurses bustle—like this—" I waddled across the room at a jog-trot. "I know. I've watched 'em out of the classroom window."

"Not across the park," said Angela importantly. "You can bustle up and down a ward, but you must walk across the park with—with——"

"Decorum?" I suggested.

Josephine said she was surprised I knew that word. "But that's the idea, Rose. You mustn't scoot or jog-trot or sway or run. Nurses only run——"

We all interrupted her with the chant: "—in case of hæmorrhage or fire!"

Josephine smiled. "So something has actually penetrated through to you at last, Rose. Jolly good. There may be hope after all. Good luck with the carpenter."

I spun the wheel-chair round and stood primly behind it. "Mrs Clark's the object that needs the luck."

"And what makes you think," asked Josephine smoothly, "that Mrs Clark is the only one with the loose screws?"

I laughed. "I walked straight into that one."

She held open the door. "Well, don't walk into anything else, Rose."

Sister P.T.S.'s lips were a thin line of disapproval as she tucked the red blanket firmly round Mrs Clark.

"That should hold the poor doll securely in place. Now, Nurse Standing, I have explained where you are to go. Are you quite clear of the way?"

"I think so, Sister. Thank you."

She gave me a shrewd look. "And which way are you to go?"

I took a deep breath. "Straight across the park, along the yard that runs by Casualty, turn left at the main Dispensary, keep on to the Medical School, then turn right; there I will see a side turning that leads down into the basement—I go down there, take the left fork of the corridor, and it is the third door on the left once I pass the laundry."

Sister's lips twitched slightly, then she controlled them. "Quite correct, Nurse." She looked down at the doll. "If," she went on, "you ever succeed in becoming a St Martin's trained nurse, Nurse Standing, I suspect you will have your memory to thank for your certificate. It appears to be your greatest ally."

I was so shaken by the hidden compliment in her words that I blushed. "Thank you, Sister."

She glanced up at me. "Off you go, Nurse."

It was a lovely evening. It was one of those evenings you sometimes get towards the end of an English summer, when the whole world is golden. The sun was still quite high in the sky; it shone on the old grey stone of which the hospital was built, softening the corners and plating the windows with gold. The grass in the park had dried after the unusually hot summer we had just had; this evening the withered patches were a warm, glowing rusty yellow. The lack of rain had affected the plane-trees too, and some of their leaves had already turned; several were a brilliant yellow, and here and there one was scarlet. The park was sprinkled with up-patients in wheel-chairs enjoying the late sunshine. Like Mrs Clark, these patients were wrapped in red blankets which made vivid splashes of colour against the dying grass. The patients' hands and faces were all tanned by the sun, and to me they appeared incredibly and uniformly healthy. They smiled at me as I walked by with my wheel-chair; then, as they recognized what it was I was pushing, their smiles vanished momentarily, then reappeared more widely.

"I thought she was real, duck!" called one woman. "Proper life-like, ain't she? She from the School over there? And are you one of the new nurses what's learning to be a nurse?"

I stopped beside her. "Yes. This is one of our dolls. We learn on dolls."

"There now!" She surveyed Mrs Clark with admiration. "Think of everything, don't they, duck, to teach you girls proper? And how you getting on?"

I smiled at her. "Not very well, I'm afraid. I'm always doing the wrong thing."

"There now," she said comfortingly, "you don't want to let that fret you—not that you look the fretting type, duck. But you'll learn. We all got to make mistakes afore we learn not to. And this here"—she nodded at Martin's—"is a lovely hospital, and they learn you nurses to nurse real lovely. Mind you, it's hard work; and they do say as you have to be born to it." She looked up at me curiously. "How do you feel about it? Think you're going to like it?"

I looked over her head at the hospital. "If I ever get into it, yes, I do. But there's an exam. to be got through first."

She said she would keep her fingers crossed for me. "I expect you'll be all right, duck. Expect I'll be seeing you in Margaret one of these fine days."

"Are you in Margaret? Have you been in long? How are you getting on?"

She said she was getting on lovely, real lovely. "I comes into Margaret twice a year, like. For me treatment. Takes about two weeks, then I goes home again. I'm due back just after Christmas, the doctor was telling me this morning; so perhaps I'll see you next time I'm in."

I smiled at her pleasant, homely old face. "I hope so, too. Thank you."

"So just you ask after Mrs Jannings next time you are in Margaret. All know Mrs Jannings in Margaret, they do," she added proudly. "And what might be your name, duck?"

"Rose Standing."

She nodded. "That's ever such a nice name, duck; but, if you'll not mind my saying so, you didn't ought to have told me your name was Rose. That's not proper, duck. You should just say Nurse Standing, or you'll have the Sister carrying on at you."

I thanked her again. "So I should. Oh, dear. That's the sort of thing I forget."

"Never you mind, duck." She took up her knitting. "You'll learn in time. Ta-ta for now, Nurse—and good luck for your exam."

I wished her good luck, and said I hoped we meet in Margaret, then wondered if I ought to wish her back in hospital. However, she seemed to think I had said the right thing, as she beamed, gave me a friendly wave, and went on with her knitting.

I trundled on. Despite Sister P.T.S.'s perpetual disapproval of my conduct and the presence of Mrs Clark to remind me of my carelessness, I felt very happy. I thought about Mrs Jannings and how friendly she had been; I hoped the other patients with whom I came into contact would be equally approachable; it had never occurred to me before that nursing, as well as being hard work and interesting, might be fun too. But a ward filled, or even sprinkled, with Mrs Jannings's could hardly fail to be anything else.

I crossed the rest of the park while I thought this out, pushed the chair over Casualty yard, read a sign that said "Main Dispensary," and turned left. The Dispensary was still open, and a number of people carrying medicine bottles and pill-boxes came down the steps from the department as I went by. Those close to the bottom step kindly waited to let me precede them with my wheel-chair. I felt very guilty at being given this priority with my present cargo, since the out-patients must almost certainly be in far more of a hurry than I was; but I did not like to stop and explain, so I pushed on as quickly as I dared, smiling and bowing slightly as I did so, and now feeling exactly like Royalty, since the people anxious to go up the steps were also waiting for me, and I was bowing to left and right.

The Medical School looked closed for the day. I was relieved about that. I knew no students there, but, like all new pros. at St Martin's, I had already been told of their hair-raising habits. I did not doubt that under present circumstances I was a moving target for any student wit or rag; as the School was shut, and there was now no hurry, I slowed down, dawdled along the concrete path beside the building, enjoying the sunshine before I vanished into the basement.

The small side turning was easy to find. The ground there sloped gently downward. I guessed that this was to facilitate the wheeling of chairs, oxygen cylinders, and stretchers into the basement, then felt very smug about my knowledge of hospital life. It was dark in that alley after the sunshine outside, but once my eyes grew accustomed to the dimmer light I saw that the long, straight, scrubbed-stone corridor was empty. The slope was also sharper than I had thought, and the chair was running of its own accord. I held it back for a few feet, then, without conscious thought, I put one of my feet on the back rung as Josephine had warned me not to do. My weight provided the added impetus that made the chair quite unmanageable. I had either to hang on and let it take me or let it go. I thought quickly, no good nurse would abandon her patient even if made of wood and papier mâché —lifted my other foot from the ground, and hung on. The chair carrying Mrs Clark and myself shot down that sloping corridor as if it was jet-propelled. It was an exhilarating sensation, and, as there was no one about to object, I enjoyed it immensely. I went on enjoying it until we reached the end of the corridor and I found it was not the end but only a sharp corner. Round that corner the ground sloped upward; at the end of the up-gradient the chair came to an abrupt stop. Mrs Clark pitched forward in her seat, and I pitched forward over her head. Neither of us was hurt, because we both fell soft. We fell soft, because by then we had run into a little group of men in white coats, and they broke our fall.

There was absolute silence as, with the help of one of the men, I got unsteadily on to my feet.

I said breathlessly, "I am so sorry. I hope I didn't hurt you." I bent forward to look at Mrs Clark, whom the other men had lifted back into her chair. "Oh, dear! Do you suppose her other leg's come off this time? "

The large man with the serious face who had stood me rather grimly on my feet moved me aside as he bent over the chair. Some one behind me made an odd sound that seemed to be a cross between a grunt and a cough. The large man touched Mrs Clark's shoulder. " Her other—Nurse, what do you mean? And what were you doing pushing a patient——" he broke off as he recognized my ' patient.' " Good God. It's Mrs Clark." He patted her head as if they were old pals. " Haven't seen you for a long time." Then he looked back at me, and his attitude changed. " Are you from the P.T.S., Nurse? " he asked severely.

I said weakly, "Yes, I'm afraid so," and forgot to add, Doctor.

His eyes rested on my face. His expression reminded me of the one Sister P.T.S. always wore when she looked at me. " Were you—a nurse in St Martin's uniform—scooting on a chair in the hospital building? "

I felt about two inches high and six years old. I also felt my face growing red. " I was taking Mrs Clark to the carpenters' shop."

" At that speed? And scooting, weren't you? "

I clutched my hands behind my back. " Yes, I was. I'm sorry."

He looked me up and down. " You know this is not the type of behaviour we expect from our nurses? "

I said yes. Then, as the fact that he was wearing a long

white coat eventually penetrated through my shocked senses, I added helpfully, " Yes, Doctor."

I had said the wrong thing. " I'm a surgeon," he replied curtly. " Surgeons are called Mister."

I knew quite well that he meant Mr So-and-So, but was far too rattled to be coherent about anything. I said, " Yes, Mister."

" The name is Waring." He turned from me to Mrs Clark. " Why is she going to the carpenter? I've never heard of her being hospitalized before. And what was that you mentioned about her other leg? Has she broken something? "

There was nothing for it, so I showed him her damaged knee. The other men had melted into the shadows against the wall; I knew they were still there, because I could hear their careful breathing; none of them had spoken a word.

The surgeon who said he was Mr Waring tucked the blanket back into position. " How did that get broken? "

I said, " She fell out of bed."

" A dummy? How? "

I swallowed. " I was blanket-bathing her. I pushed her out."

He said, " Oh! " and smoothed his hair. His hair was very fair; so fair that in the artificial light that lit the second corridor I thought it to be white. He looked down at his feet and told his feet that nursing was an occupation for adults, and that young women who proposed taking it up as a career would be well advised to grow up before they entered the hospital. Then he turned and walked away down the corridor.

The three men by the wall came to life. They looked younger than the fair man, and they wore short white coats. One of them, a tall, very dark young man, with an attractive voice, asked if I was hurt. " Quite an impact you made just then, Nurse. No fractures? Not even a laceration? " He wagged his head. " How about acute shock setting in? " He glanced at his companions. " But I must say it makes a change, eh, chaps? Been mown down by many things in my day, but never before by a P.T.S. pro. pushing a dolly."

His colleagues agreed that there was never a dull moment at Martin's.

I was too concerned to be amused and, since they seemed more human than the man who had just left, I asked anxiously, "Is he very angry?"

They exchanged glances.

"It's this way," explained the dark one; "our nurses don't make a sort of habit of scooting round the basement—pity, I agree—but there you are. And if they did," he shrugged, "well, it's the sort of racket a chap in his position would have to create about. Must take a serious view if you're an S.S.O. A chap has to be on the ball all the time. Bad for discipline and moral fibre and what-not, if not."

I closed my eyes in despair. This was worse than I thought. I opened my eyes again. "Is he very important? And are you important too?"

They guffawed. "We, dear Nurse," replied the dark man, jerking his thumb downward, "are less than the dust. Student men. The scum of the hospital earth."

But Angela had told us that students never wore white coats, and that was how you could tell a doctor from a student. "You're wearing white coats."

He flicked at his cuff. "Senior students attending P.M. demonstrations, for the use of. But note the length of the jacket, Nurse." He held his pockets out from his body. "Behold. And therein lies the secret of identification. Students —to here. Housemen have sort of reach-me-downs to the hips; and the big bosses, the senior residents, wear them right down between the knee and the ankle."

I felt sick. "That Mr Waring? His was long?" They nodded like three mandarins. "So he is important?" They nodded again. "And you said he was S.—something? What's that?"

They all fell on their knees. "The Senior Surgical Officer." They bent forward and swept the floor with their foreheads. "The big white boss of resident surgery," they chorused in mock deference, "ace high." They salaamed for a third time, then stood up.

"Of—the whole hospital?" I gasped.

"Have a heart, love," said the talkative student kindly, brushing the dust from his knees, "Martin's is a biggish place. It's got around twelve hundred beds. Say half of those are surgical. Jake Waring is boss of the surgical side." They fell on their knees again, and when they were on their feet the dark man went on brushing his legs absently. "But don't get the wrong idea, Nurse. Even if Jake is only boss of half the hospital that's still not as easy a job as falling off a log or "—he grinned at Mrs Clark—"being pitched out of a chair. A chap not only has to be a Master of Surgery to hold it down; he also has to be a cut above every other surgical character in his era to be chosen. There are other hospitals, I believe?" He looked at his friends, who murmured that they had also heard tell of other places. "Of no account, naturally."

"Of no account," he agreed, "to any Martin's man. Which whittles the thing down a lot; only one Martin's, and every surgeon at Martin's wants the job which at present is held by our golden boy. So, for your further information, Nurse, the chap you just bunged in the small of the back with yon dolly is Mr John Arthur Kevin Edward Waring, M.Ch., F.R.C.S., S.S.O. at St Martin's Hospital, London, known to one and all, for obvious reasons, as Jake—only not to his face unless you mix in exalted circles."

I felt not only sick, but dizzy, after all those letters. "Do you think he'll report me? To Sister P.T.S.? Or—Matron?" I shuddered. "Is there anything I can do to improve the set-up? Apologize or something?"

The smallest man, who had up to now only spoken in chorus, suggested I resign instantly. "Much simpler than being chucked out. More dignified. A woman should always be dignified."

The third man mildly remarked that there was always the river. "Quite handy. Not half a mile off. Only problem there is that the water will be so cold when we have to dive in and rescue you. I hate bathing at the end of the season. No, skip the river." He brightened. "I've got it. You go into a decent decline, Nurse. Pine away—take the green sickness. And when they ask you what ails you, before you turn your face to the wall for the last time, say you can't forget the shame of ploughing the S.S.O. down. Pro. bites Dust after making Pundit bite Dust." He beamed at us. "How's that for a coroner's headline?"

"Lousy," replied the dark student. "Now, you listen to Uncle, love," he told me, "and ignore these two heartless characters. I'll give you some words of wisdom. Never believe a word any student man ever tells you. Don't get in a state over this; it'll just make a good story—nothing worse. Jake's said all he's going to say. He may tear a character into little pieces himself when roused, but he never delegates the tearing. As far as he's concerned, the subject'll be closed— providing you don't make a come-back with another cracked dolly. And, since we can't offer you any more constructive advice, we can at least shove this character Clark along to the carpenter for you. So shall we get cracking?"

When I had returned the empty wheel-chair safely to the P.T.S. changing-room I went up to Josephine's room. Angela was there too. "How did you get on, Rose? All serene?"

"Very," I said grimly, and told them what had happened. Angela shouted with laughter, but Josephine was upset.

"Rose, how could you be so daft? And what a pity you didn't just run into those three students. Then no one would have heard about it."

Angela stopped laughing. "That shows how little you know about hospitals, Josephine. Every one," she assured us, "knows everything about every one else in a hospital. Everything gets round. The grapevine works like radar. You can't keep a thing dark."

"Oh, no." I stared at her. "You aren't telling me Sister P.T.S.'ll hear?"

"As you're in the P.T.S., she'll be the first person."

Josephine looked even more shocked than I felt. I said, "Well, girls, this is it. Write and tell me how you get on as nurses. I certainly won't be here to see. I'll be out by the morning after this."

I was not out by morning, although when Sister sent for me after Prayers I almost wished that I was. But Sister had only sent for me to tell me that the carpenter had told her that Mrs Clark was not seriously damaged and could be repaired easily. "I am sure it relieves your mind, Nurse, to know you have done no irreparable damage?"

I said it did, and thanked her very much.

" The carpenter is sending her back with one of his staff, so you need not go and fetch her." She looked at me calmly. " We would not wish to run any more risks with our oldest and most valued dummy, so possibly that arrangement will be for the best." Then, without any change in her voice or expression, she asked me if I had hurt myself when I inadvertently collided with Mr Waring.

I started. " Er—no, Sister. Thank you."

She said she was glad to hear it. " That corridor can be difficult to manœuvre with a heavy chair." She inclined her head. " That was all I had to say to you, Nurse."

In the classroom the girls were waiting for me. " Was she furious? What did she say? Have you got to go to Matron? "

I waved them down. " Relax. No panic. She only wanted to know if—— " Then Sister's voice from the doorway cut me short.

" Nurse Standing, do you propose to deliver the lecture this morning? Or will you be good enough to take your place at your desk and allow me to discuss the Central Nervous System? Thank you."

That last week flashed by. We practised bandaging on each other, feverishly; made endless beds in which we took turns to act as live patients; washed each other's heads in bed; read numberless books on anatomy, physiology, general nursing; chanted the names of the bones and muscles in every corner of the P.T.S. and its grounds; drew weird charts of the circulation of the blood and even weirder ones of the lymphatic system. And then there was no time to read another page or roll another bandage. The first day of our final P.T.S. exam. arrived, and by to-morrow evening we would know if we had passed into the hospital or whether we were not considered suitable candidates to become first-year students at Martin's.

The written examination, we all agreed, was bad enough; the prospect of the practical and viva-voce examinations was worse. With pale, set faces, spotless aprons and caps, clean dresses, and shining shoes, we waited outside the closed door of the classroom on that second morning. The examiners were Matron, the present Senior Sister Tutor to the hospital, Sister

Martha, the senior ward sister, and two retired Sister P.T.S.'s.

Angela lowered what morale we had by saying, "When I was part-timing the girls all said the viva and practical were what really mattered. It just hangs on to-day. That's why they line up this bunch of experts."

Josephine nudged me. "How do you feel, Rose?"

I said, "I still feel sick."

One of the junior Sister Tutors who had come to help Sister P.T.S. for the day overheard me. She stopped by us and smiled. "I actually was sick, Nurse—but I got through. If you try to remember what Sister has taught you, you will too. Sister P.T.S. is a wonderful teacher."

"She may be," I whispered to the other two when that Sister Tutor had gone, "but I can't remember a thing. My mind's gone blank. And I bet I get Mrs Clark."

I could have wept with relief, when as I stood before her table Matron said, "Nurse Standing, will you please blanket-bath Lady Smith? I will watch you from here."

Lady Smith stared at me with round, blank brown eyes and behaved beautifully. I did spill a little water on the floor, but none on the bed. I quickly hitched the locker forward with one foot and hoped that would cover the slight mess. The bedclothes remained neatly as I placed them, and when I rolled Lady Smith, decorously covered by a blanket, from side to side she never shifted an inch of her own accord.

Matron supervised me with an expressionless face. When the bath was over she told me to make an operation bed in the Missing Link, set a dry-dressing trolley, a trolley for tepid sponging, a tray for a hypodermic injection.

One of the other examiners stood at my elbow as I laid the trolleys. Once she stopped me. "The top of that trolley is supposed to be sterile, Nurse. You touched it with your un-sterile elbow."

My heart sank. I murmured, "I'm sorry, Sister," and wheeled the trolleys over to Matron for her inspection, and then noticed I had forgotten to put the ice-bucket on the tepid-sponge setting. I saw that Matron had noticed the mistake too. She wrote something on the piece of paper in front of her. Then she beckoned me. I was sure it was to tell me to stop wasting her time; but she only said, "Will you please make a starch poultice and apply it to my arm, Nurse?"

I answered mechanically, "Yes, Matron," and walked away in complete despair. There was now no doubt; this was the end. I had never yet been able to make a decent starch poultice, no matter how often I had practised. I had bought pounds and pounds of starch, and wasted the lot. I stood staring unhappily at the long table on which was arranged all the apparatus we might need, and wished and wished that I had never been so stupid as to think I wanted to be a nurse. How could I hope to be a nurse when I knew my starch would go lumpy? And how could I dare apply the inevitable mess of a result to Matron's arm?

A quiet voice beside me murmured, "You are, of course, looking for a suitable tray on which to set your poultice, Nurse Standing?" Sister P.T.S. looked thoughtfully at the dozens of enamel trays. "Yes, that one will not be required by anyone else," she added, although I was too dumbfounded to say a word; "so carry on with it, Nurse, and do not be discouraged if your starch congeals as previously. You merely have to continue stirring the boiling mixture and it will clear." She vanished as discreetly as she had arrived, but not before she had helped me pull my scattered wits together. But for her well-timed advice, when, as ever, the starch clung to my spoon in an ugly lump, I should certainly have burst into tears. Under the effect of her inspiration I stirred feverishly, and suddenly the liquid cleared to the right glassy consistency. I poured it on to the square of linen I had cut, and the starch set at once. My hands shook when I applied the finished poultice to Matron's arm, but she made no comment. When I had removed the poultice Matron nodded at Sister P.T.S. and wrote something else on her paper.

Sister touched my arm. "You may go now, Nurse. Wait outside with the other nurses."

I obeyed her thankfully and joined the post-mortem that was going on in the hall. My friends groaned with me. "Poor Rose! Starch! We all know what that means for you!"

I told them how Sister P.T.S. had helped me, and was very

relieved to find that she had done the same to all the others. "She kept popping up like the Demon King," whispered Angela, "and saying she was sure I was looking for just this —or just that—and handing me the very thing before I realized I hadn't got it. The old girl's human after all!"

The list of results was put up by Sister just before tea. She pinned it to the board, then stood back, and for once made no attempt to quell the small riot that followed her action.

Angela pushed her way to the front. "We've all passed, girls!" Then when the noise died down again she said, "Good Lord! Look who's top!" She thrust her body through the crowd and thumped my shoulder. "Good for you, Rose! But how ever did you do it?"

Josephine peered incredulously at the list. "I never would have thought it! Rose," she turned to me almost accusingly, "you must have stayed awake for once!"

The other girls were equally shocked, but I don't think any of them were as shocked as I was. I stared at the list blankly, feeling there must be a mistake somewhere; then I noticed Sister's amused expression. Sister said, "You have all done quite nicely, Nurses. And, Nurse Standing, I congratulate you. I agree with Nurse Forbes; you have stayed awake for once. May I suggest that you continue to do so for the next four years? By then it may well become a habit." She smiled at us. "Well, Nurses, this is where we part company. I wish you all every success in your training. Come back and see me when your training days are over, and tell me what you plan to do. I always like to follow the future nursing careers of the young nurses I have in my school."

"But, Sister," protested Angela, "that's four years off."

"And that you think," replied Sister quietly, "represents a near life-time?" She shook her head. "The years will pass before you are aware that they have started. They will be short, exciting years, in which you will certainly work harder, and possibly enjoy yourselves more, than in any other period in your lives. So do not waste your training-years, Nurses; make the most of every minute, because you can only train once. To quote your modern phraseology, you are going into the hospital on a one-way ticket; and you are now members of perhaps the most honourable profession for women in the world. We are very proud of our profession," she added sincerely, " and very proud of our hospital. I hope I shall always be able to be as proud of each one of you as I am this evening." Then, without another word, Sister P.T.S. walked out of the hall and out of our lives.

There was silence when she left us. It was Josephine who broke it. " She's not just human, Angela; she's a honey."

We had no time to discuss Sister P.T.S.'s heart of gold, as the senior Sister Tutor, who had now taken us in charge, appeared just then with another list. " You will no doubt wish to know in which wards you will be working when you return from your week's holiday, Nurses." She fixed her list to the board. " I have Matron's permission to show you this now."

Sister Tutor was a stranger and not the old friend we now considered Sister P.T.S., so we did not crowd round her to read the new list. When she left us Angela again appointed herself as official announcer. " I'm going to Martha—good! Sylvia—you're in Henry. Gill—you've got William Brown— watch out for Sister William Brown, she's a horror! Josephine and Rose, you are together, you lucky things! And you're both going to Francis Adams."

Josephine asked me what was Francis Adams. " Must be male—but surgical or medical? "

" I don't know. I'm still hazy which ward is which."

" Angela'll know." She raised her voice. " Angela! Come over here! What's Francis Adams? "

Angela squeezed a path to us. " Men's acute surgical." Then she looked at me and began to laugh. " Rose, dearie! Do you realize what that means? "

" Should I? " I could not see any joke, but I was so happy this evening that I was ready to smile at nothing. " Nice ward? "

" You may not think it," she spluttered, " but Josephine may like it. So let me warn you, Rose. Francis Adams takes all the acute surgical emergencies. Three guesses whose ward it is? "

" Oh, no! " I sat down on the window-sill behind me. " No,

Angela. It's not one of the S.S.O.'s own wards. Don't tell me that."

She said that was exactly what she was going to tell me. "Francis Adams and Susan are his babies. He's in and out of those two wards all the time. What do you think of that? "

I pushed my cap back on my head. " I think that's one of the most depressing bits of news I have heard in my life."

" Nurse! " Sister Tutor had materialized again and was standing in front of me. " What is your name, Nurse? Nurse Standing? Indeed. Well, allow me to tell you, Nurse Standing, that nurses do not perch on polished window-sills or allow their caps to slide down the backs of their necks. Kindly remember that from now on you are supposed to comport yourself with dignity."

I jumped to my feet and pulled my cap forward. " Sorry, Sister, yes, Sister." When she had gone on again I turned to the girls. " This is where we came in. She looks as bad as Sister P.T.S. has been until to-day."

Angela said not at all. " Sister P.T.S. wears velvet gloves compared to the ward sisters and the tutors. "Pros.," she assured us cheerfully, " get the iron-hand therapy."

I said I could hardly wait. " Somebody tell me just why we've bothered about this exam.! "

Josephine said she was past bothering about anything. " But I adore the prospect of you comporting yourself with dignity, Rose. I'd go through a lot to see that. Let's go and have some tea."

# 2

## *An Afternoon in Francis Adams*

THE Senior Probationer in Francis Adams was called Nurse Erith. On our first morning on duty she waited for us in the nurses' changing-room. "Which one is Forbes?"

Josephine said, "Me, Nurse."

"Right." Erith consulted a list. "You're to do meals and kitchen all this week. Standing, you are to be ward pro." She told Josephine the work she must do, then looked at me. "The left side of the ward is your concern; I do the right; but the extras and the outside bits are your responsibility. That means the sluices, bathrooms, clinical room, changing-room, duty-room; the cleaning of all the trolleys, sterilizers, screens, and wheel-chairs." She ticked the words off on her fingers—she had to use both hands. "Got that?"

"Just about, Nurse."

She nodded. "Good. And one more thing—the flowers. Whatever you do, Standing, don't forget to do the flowers."

I promised to remember the flowers. "What am I supposed to do with them? Just change their waters?"

"And see that they are fresh, take off the dead leaves, trim them—things like that. You do them in the clinical room, and they shouldn't take you long—see." She walked across to the clinical room and gestured to the rows of flowers in vases that would have stocked a well-sized florist's. "They shouldn't take you long," she said again; "you have ten minutes in which to get them done; that's from eight-fifty to nine each morning. Official flower-time. And they must be in by nine sharp. Don't forget that, either."

I gazed at the mass of flowers and felt a little weak. "No, Nurse."

"You had better not," she replied grimly. "Sister Francis Adams has a thing about flowers. Dead flowers send her right up the wall."

Josephine and I exchanged glances. I said, "Yes, Nurse."

"That reminds me," continued Erith, "something you must know, Forbes. Do see that every single glass, cup, and saucer is out of the ward by nine. We open then for the surgical and teaching rounds. I take the screen in front of the door down as nine strikes, and if there's another thing that sends Sister Francis Adams up the wall it's seeing a dirty glass in the ward when it's open. Sister Francis Adams," she repeated confidentially, "has a thing about used crockery."

Josephine and I exchanged another glance, as Josephine said, "Yes, Nurse."

Our thoughts must have been obvious from our expressions, because Erith added, "It's all right, girls. Don't get too worked up. Sister Francis Adams isn't at all bad really; she just has a few things." She considered us both and seemed to be making up her mind about something. Then, apparently reaching a decision, she went on, "Sister can be quite sweet at times, and the patients adore her; but the person you want to keep an eye on is our staff nurse. Sister is in charge, naturally; but the staff nurse does the actual running of the ward, and it's her job to keep an eye on the pros. So the person you girls have got to deal with is Staff Nurse Bennings."

Josephine asked warily, "What is Staff Nurse Bennings like, Nurse?"

Erith hesitated. "She's a—very good staff nurse. She's bright, too. Won the gold medal for her year. She's been staffing here for the past eight months. If she stays on at Martin's she'll certainly end up as a sister, if not as matron. She's a girl with a future." But she had not answered Josephine's question, and we all knew it.

I said, "Does Staff Nurse Bennings have 'things' too, Nurse?"

Erith smiled. "Does she not! But I won't waste time telling you what they are, as you couldn't keep count, and she'll certainly tell you herself! But take my tip, girls, and try to get on Bennings' good side. If you do that life in Francis Adams can be—quite peaceful."

"After which," I told Josephine, as we scurried off to our various jobs, "I really can hardly wait. I've not only got an irate S.S.O. to cope with—but a dragon of a staff nurse as well."

Josephine laughed. "Would you rather be back in the P.T.S. with Mrs Clark?"

"Dear Mrs Clark! I tell you, Jo, I'm really homesick for—— "

"Nurses!" A cold voice behind us made us spin round. A slight, very attractive, dark girl in a staff nurse's uniform stood watching us. "Nurses, since you are fresh from the P.T.S., you may possibly not be aware of the behaviour expected from probationers working in our wards—although I feel sure that Sister P.T.S. was at great pains to explain that behaviour to you. So will you allow me," continued Staff Nurse Bennings, "to remind you that we do not permit our nurses to laugh and chatter in the ward corridors. Do not let me catch either of you behaving like a couple of giggling schoolgirls again."

We chanted, "No, Nurse."

She looked us over. "Which is Nurse Standing?"

I said I was.

Her eyes dwelt reflectively on my face, but she merely murmured, "Your cap is crooked," and walked past us into the ward.

The day raced by, and after it the days that followed. The first week was over before we realized it had begun. Josephine rushed round and round the ward pushing breakfast, dinner, and tea trolleys; making porridge; cutting bread-and-butter; filling water-jugs; marking fluid-charts; collecting used crockery. I galloped up and down the long forty-bedded ward, made beds with Sister or Nurse Bennings, cleaned, dusted, polished, clicked castors straight, cleaned again, scrubbed more enamel bowls and kidney dishes than I would have thought necessary for the use of the whole hospital, scrubbed mountains of mackintoshes; changed flowers' waters, breathed heavily on the glass vases to aid my polishing, learned the trick of keeping the acid cupboard shining—you leave the door slightly ajar, and the vapour from the acid escapes into the atmosphere and does not cloud the polish—and became ruthless with semi-faded flowers. I chucked everything doubtful out. The vases were all numbered with bits of sticky labels, which I kept forgetting and rubbing off in my desire to make the vases gleam. I was equally bad at remembering who had given me which bunch to put in water. As it was a men's ward, this was not important—I discovered—as the men were not at all fussy about flowers and incredibly good-humoured. "That's all right, Nurse. I'll have them Michaelmas daisies even if they don't come from my missus. Look a treat, they do."

The men helped me with other things, too. They kept a keen eye on my routine. "You'll pardon my mentioning it, miss, but you ain't done those wheel-chairs and it's seven minutes to nine. You'll have that Staff Nurse creating at you again if you don't get 'em done afore nine."

One morning a new patient lit a cigarette after I had cleaned the ashtrays. His neighbours scolded him as smartly as Bennings scolded me. "You put that out, mate. Now! "

The poor man was surprised. "Why? It says we can smoke till nine."

"That," replied the old hands, "is as may be. But if you leave some ash on your ashtray and the Sister or that Nurse Bennings spots it our little Nurse Standing'll catch it good and proper. So we don't smoke after Nurse Standing done the trays—see, mate? "

The newcomer said he saw, and stubbed out his cigarette, put the butt away in his locker, and blew on the tray. "That looks good and clean, eh, Nurse? " he asked anxiously as I raced by with my duster. "Wouldn't want to get you young ladies into no trouble."

I thanked him gratefully. "I hope you don't mind? "

"Not me, Nurse. You got your work to do, and quite enough, too, if you was to ask me."

The other men nodded. Hard, they told each other, hard— that's what a young nurse's life was! On the go all day, and no mistake. And what with the Sister and that young Staff Nurse carrying on the way they did all the time—well, it just went to show that it was real hard for a young lady. "And that Nurse Bennings, she's only a slip of a girl herself—but you notice the way she never misses nothing?"

Higgins, a docker who had come in for an appendicectomy, scratched his head thoughtfully. "You mind what we used to say in the Army, mate? It was always's the young 'uns as made the worst N.C.O.'s. Talk about strict, eh? An old 'un might wink an eye; a good young 'un with his eye on the R.S.M.'s badge—never." He looked up the ward, then sat forward. "Nurse Standing, can you come here a tick?"

"Of course." I went over to his bed. "Something I can do for you, Higgins?"

"Not me, miss," he hissed in a stage whisper, "but you see that lampshade over Twenty-four. You missed it when you was doing the shades. It's got some soot on it, an' I just caught the Sister taking a look at it when she was taking Twenty-four's pulse. You best nip up and give it a wipe over, miss."

"I will. Bless you, Higgins. Thanks."

I went straight to the lampshade. Sister glanced up from her watch. She saw what I was doing and gave an approving little nod. "Good. I was afraid you had missed it, Nurse." She returned her attention to her pulse-taking. I went back to fetch more flower-vases and waved at Higgins as I passed his bed. He grinned. "Saved by the bell, eh, Nurse?"

I smiled back. "Thanks to you, yes."

"What I would do without the men," I told Josephine later as we drank our morning cocoa, "I can't bear to think. They keep me on the straight and narrow; tell me when my cap is crooked; when I've messed up my apron; what time it is; whether Sister or Bennings are blowing up for something; and what to do next. It's like having forty extra pairs of eyes and forty spare brains. I'm not nursing them—they're nursing me!"

"Don't I know it!" She promptly explained why. "If I forget the drinking-waters they say loudly, 'Nurse Forbes is just fetching them jugs in now, Sister,' and cover up and remind me at the same time. If some one asks for cocoa and I give him coffee by mistake he'll swear blind he never touches anything but coffee. And last night, when I over-cooked the rice-pudding, they must have heard Bennings storming on to me about wasting food as no one would touch it, for they all demanded dry rice-pudding and said it was ever so tasty! Higgins," she added lovingly, "was heaven. He said it reminded him of home, as his missus always burnt the rice-pudding—but he didn't let Bennings hear that. He told her in front of me that he'd had a lovely supper, ta very much, as he was always a one for rice-pudding!"

Erith bounced into the kitchen. "You girls shouldn't be drinking cocoa in here. It's after nine-thirty, and Sister's already chaperoning the first round."

Josephine explained that we had not hurried as our lecture was not until a quarter to ten and we were both off duty. "Does it matter if we take our time over our cocoa as we're off?"

Erith glanced anxiously at the door. "Not in most wards. But Bennings has got a thing about pros. lingering in kitchens. You girls had better drink up and go and get some air before your lecture—and before Bennings discovers you haven't gone."

It was too late. The door opened just then. Nurse Bennings frowned at us from the open doorway. "This is a ward kitchen, not a canteen! Will you two probationers get your cloaks and go off duty at once!"

Josephine put down her half-finished cocoa reluctantly. "Sorry, Nurse; yes, Nurse." She moved to the door, acci-dentally knocking my arm as she passed me. I had been determined to finish my drink, as I was hungry, and was just about to drink quickly. The jar to my arm made me relax my hold on the cup, and the cocoa spilled over and down on to the front of the clean white apron into which I had just changed to present a pristine appearance in our lecture. Josephine gasped, "Rose, I'm so sorry!"

Which annoyed Bennings on two more counts. "Really, Nurse Standing! Are you incapable of holding a cup without spilling it?" She turned on Josephine. "And, as for you, Nurse Forbes! How dare you use a Christian name in a ward? You know that is forbidden!"

Josephine apologized again. "I'm sorry, Nurse. I forgot. And I'm sorry about Nurse Standing's apron. It was my fault. I jogged her arm."

"Nurse Forbes," said Bennings calmly, "you do not have to make excuses for your friend. I have worked with Nurse Standing." She looked at my stained apron. "And I have already discovered that if there is anything to be spilt or dropped Nurse Standing will spill or drop it. The sooner——" but she broke off there, and her expression changed as she glanced down the corridor. She looked very attractive when she smiled like that. The tone in which she said, "Good morning, Mr Waring. How nice to see you back again! Have you had a pleasant holiday?" matched her smile.

The white-coated figure of the S.S.O. appeared at her side. He said he was glad to be back, had had a pleasant holiday, and had come to do a round. "Sister is with Sir Henry, I imagine?"

He glanced casually into the kitchen as he spoke, nodded at Erith, looked correctly through Josephine and myself. Every one looks through first-year pros.; they simply do not exist on the landscape. Unless they have ruined aprons. Consequently, although the S.S.O. avoided looking at my face, he looked for several seconds at my apron.

Bennings was purring at his elbow. "Sister is with Sir Henry, Mr Waring. But I could take you round if that will suit you?"

He said that would suit him very well, thank you, and they moved away from the doorway.

Erith closed the kitchen door quickly, leant against it, and began to laugh. Josephine asked what the joke was.

Erith shook her head weakly. "You wouldn't understand—you're too new. But you must have noticed how she changed into an angel of sweetness and light?"

I said I had. "She looked a different girl. She's daft. She ought to smile more often. It makes her quite lovely."

Erith, still grinning at her private joke, said Bennings would smile a lot now her beloved Jake was back from his fishing holiday.

"Is that where he's been?" I asked. Josephine and I had

discussed his absence a couple of times, but had been too busy by day, and too tired by night, to trouble to inquire of anyone why the S.S.O. never appeared in his ward.

Erith shot a keen look at me. " Do you know Jake Waring? Is that why he gave you the look he did just now? I must say, Standing," she smiled again, " you do look a sight, sprayed with cocoa."

" I'll bet I do. No—I don't know Jake Waring—only who he is." Which was perfectly true. Josephine said nothing; she just finished her illicit cocoa and watched Erith watching me.

Erith suddenly slapped her thigh. " That's who you are, Standing! Why didn't I get there before! Bill Martin's description absolutely fits you."

Josephine looked at me now. 'Angela was right,' was written all over her face. I decided to be dumb—and why not, being a blonde?

" What fits me, Nurse? "

As we expected, she repeated my basement encounter with surprisingly little exaggeration. " That P.T.S. pro. was you, wasn't it, Standing? " I nodded, and she laughed. " Was Sister P.T.S. livid? She always adored Mrs Clark. We all rocked when we heard about it—even Sister Francis was amused; all but Bennings, that is. She was not amused."

I said I supposed you had to take life seriously if you won a gold medal.

" It wasn't that. A P.T.S. pro. doesn't count as a nurse. No. It just happened that you bulldozed yourself and Mrs Clark into two of Bennings' private problems in that basement."

Josephine was as fascinated as I. " Which two, Nurse? "

Erith pulled open the door and looked up the ward. Then she shut it again and returned to her former position. " Both happy chaperoning, so I've got a moment. As I was saying— two problems. One, a dark lad called Bill Martin, who was running round with Bennings a while back. I'm not sure if they got as far as being engaged—it was when I was on nights last spring; but they certainly got around together, and then something seemed to happen, as Bill Martin wasn't around Bennings any more. But, for all that, when he comes in here, you'll see Bennings giving him the old green light she gave Jake Waring just now."

"What? Both of them at once?" I asked.

Erith said it was obvious I was very young. "Bennings collects scalps, my child. It's her favourite hobby. As Bill Martin isn't around much any more and the S.S.O. is, Bennings is busy trying to collect him. I assure you, she has a positive thing for him now; the whole hospital knows that."

"And has he got a thing for her?" I asked.

Erith said that was the 64,000-dollar question. "Could be. He's a quiet type, but he certainly smiles at her, and, like Bennings, Jake doesn't smile easy. So don't go knocking him down again, Standing. And stay clear of Bill Martin. Bennings doesn't encourage pros. to trespass on her preserves."

I said she was welcome to both of them. "Thanks for giving us all this inside information, Nurse. Now, I suppose I had better hare over to the Home and change my apron."

Josephine came across with me. She said she had been enchanted to hear all about Bennings' love-life. "She's dead lucky. That S.S.O.'s frightfully good-looking."

"Do you think so?" I buttoned a clean apron round my waist quickly. "I'd say he was too fair. And I don't go for that sort of my-work-is-my-all expression. I like men to look human, even if they are doctors."

Josephine was surprised. "Rose! I never thought you had any views on men. You're too much of a tomboy."

"Impossible not to be if you are brought up with brothers on either side of you. Question of self-defence. But, in theory, I'm all for the boys and a love-life. Only snag is, just when does a pro. have time for a love-life?"

I expected her to agree with me; it was a subject frequently bemoaned by our set. Instead, she said rather primly that she thought it was quite a good thing. "And after the dirty look the S.S.O. gave you this morning, Rose, I think it's another good thing that you like dark men. But do hurry up! We're going to be late for that lecture."

Angela was off duty that morning too, and after the lecture she asked Josephine and me to go shopping with her. "I want to go up West to buy a hat for a wedding. Come and help me choose one, girls."

I loved choosing other people's clothes and said so. "Only I've got very bad taste in hats, Angela. But if you buy what I don't like you'll probably do well; so I'll come and lend moral support in reverse."

Josephine declined the invitation. "My feet are killing me, and I must write up my lecture notes."

Angela said Josephine was making a great mistake. "A nurse needs relaxation and change in her off-duty. Do you far more good to come."

I laughed. "Angie, you sound exactly like Sister P.T.S.! But do come, Josephine. It'll be fun buying Angie a hat."

Josephine said, thank you, no. "I've shopped with Angie before. You're in for a Marathon, Rose. And you're tougher than I, even if you don't look it. I'm saving my feet for this afternoon."

"What's so special about this afternoon?" I asked. "We can't run any faster than we have on other afternoons, and, anyway, it doesn't matter how fast I run—I never get done. Even if I was jet-propelled Sister and Bennings would still chase me with their eternal, 'Get on, Nurse Standing.' So why worry?"

Josephine agreed that I was not the worrying type. "But we've got eleven men going down to the theatre this afternoon."

"Eleven!" I gaped at her. "Where are they coming from? We're full—and all with post-op. men."

She said Sister had come in to discuss the afternoon's list with Bennings when she was serving breakfasts. "There's to be a general post this morning. Our semi-convalescents like Higgins are moving to Albert, and we're taking the men who've been resting in Albert over the week-end."

"I'm not losing Higgins? Oh, no, Josephine! And I never even said good-bye to him."

She said she had meant to tell me over cocoa, but had forgotten. "I think Francis Adams this afternoon will be just like Piccadilly Circus in the rush-hour—so I'm going to rest my two feet."

I turned to Angela. "And you want to take me for a brisk morning's shopping? My love, I'd be nuts to come."

She said coolly, "So what? Every one knows you're nuts, Rose. Of course you'll come." And of course I did.

We had a frantic and hilarious morning in the West End. She bought not one, but two, hats, and promised to lend me either if ever I had a heavy date.

I thanked her warmly. "Though I can't see myself ever having time to be dated." And as we ran down the escalator to our tube train I told her about Bennings' love-life. "That's years ahead for us, and the hats'll be out of fashion then. Junior pros. don't exist. We may have to be seen"—we shot round the corner and galloped up the straight tunnel towards our platform—"but not noticed or heard."

Angela puffed slightly. "I've been thinking. Have you"—we leapt on to the train as the doors were closing—"stopped breaking things yet?"

"I'm getting better." I fanned myself with one of the bags containing a hat apiece. "I've not broken a vase for two days, and I only dropped the enamel bowls in the sluice this morning. No one was about, luckily, and they didn't break—one of them chipped."

"How's Josephine getting on? She breaking things?"

"Not she. She's really good. I'll bet our Josephine ends up with a medal. She's got only one thought in her head."

Angela looked at me a little curiously. "But, Rose, surely——" She could not go on, as we had to change trains then, and when we were in the next train we had forgotten that former subject. I remembered about it later, and meant to ask Angela what she had been about to say, then forgot directly and never asked her.

We arrived back in our Home with ten minutes to spare before we were due on duty. Home Sister was in the hall. "Have you nurses had lunch?"

Angela replied quickly, "Yes, thank you, Sister," and pushed me into the lift. "Coffee and buns at eleven," she murmured as she slammed the gates, "are called ' lunch ' in many circles. It was only a pale grey lie."

There was no time to discuss ethics; so I merely nodded and

pulled off my gloves and coat in preparation for the quick
change into uniform we were both about to perform. Five
minutes later we were back in the lift and sailing downward.
I reached the outer door of Francis Adams as the hospital
clock chimed one.

Josephine was waiting anxiously in the changing-room,
"Rose, what happened? You weren't at lunch."

I could not reply, as Bennings was behind me. "Do you
probationers intend to spend the entire afternoon chatting
in here, or are you considering coming on duty? If you are
may I remind you that it is two minutes past one o'clock and
you should have reported at one?"

We apologized, and she gave us our afternoon's work.
"Nurse Standing, will you do the ward routine? Nurse Forbes,
Sister wishes you to go down to the theatre with all our cases.
Come with me and I shall tell you what you must do."

Josephine had not been wrong when she said that that
afternoon in Francis Adams was going to resemble Piccadilly
Circus in the rush-hour. The traffic was phenomenal; but,
unlike street traffic, it never jammed. The theatre stretcher-
trolley came and went; one man was sent down; another
prepared; a third was ready waiting; the first man returned
to his bed again—and all before I realized that bed was
empty. Bennings moved like lightning from bed to bed. I had
never seen her working under pressure before; her brilliant
efficiency filled me with respect and admiration. She gave
pre-medication injections, filled hot-water bottles, made post-
operative beds, checked each man before he left for the
theatre, seeing that he was properly prepared, checked constantly each of the returned cases, supervised all I did, dealt
with all telephone inquiries, and throughout kept an eye on
Sister, who was escorting one of the constant teaching rounds
and might require something from her staff nurse.

These rounds I now accepted as so much a part of the
normal afternoon ward routine that I scarcely saw the crowd
of silent young men who moved so slowly from bed to bed.
Once I noticed them properly, because I had to wait behind
the trolley from which I was laying the afternoon teas, as I
could not push my trolley through the ranks, who were now

standing with their backs to me. As I waited for some one to notice my trolley I counted the heads for something to do. There were thirty-one students round that particular bed; but the ward was so silent that the sound of the consultant surgeon's lowered voice hummed round the ward with the hum of a drowsy bee on a summer's afternoon.

Some one touched my arm. Josephine was beside me. She looked very hot. Her face was pink, her dark hair plastered to her forehead.

"Bennings wants you—now."

I raised my eyebrows. "List over already?"

She shook her head. "I'm to do the routine instead of you. Get on."

Sister overheard our whispers and, turning, frowned us to silence; so I could not ask Josephine about the theatre. I had not yet seen any operation, and this was her first day there. I handed over my trolley; the young men noticed the movement and the trolley, and shifted to allow Josephine room to pass.

Bennings was waiting by Bed 18. She smiled at the man lying in that bed. "Back in a minute, Roberts." She jerked her head meaningly at the door. "Just a moment, Nurse Standing."

I followed her to the door, curiously. As soon as we reached it she stopped. "You haven't been to the theatre yet, have you?"

"No, Nurse."

She hesitated. "I suppose I must send you down. Roberts must leave in a couple of minutes. He's next on the list." She hesitated again. "I didn't want it to work out this way— Roberts is going to be a long case—and I should have preferred Nurse Forbes to carry straight on now she's used to it; but, as she didn't feel well during the last case, I can't send her back again, and you're my only spare junior." She looked me over doubtfully, then asked simply, "Do you faint easily?"

I said, "I've never fainted in my life, Nurse. But——"

"You've never been through with a theatre case?"

"No, Nurse."

She sighed. "This would be Erith's afternoon off. Well! There's nothing else to be done, so you'll just have to cope,

Nurse Standing." She told me in detail what I should be expected to do. "And, above all, remember—Roberts is scared stiff. So, no matter what you feel inside you, pretend to be quite confident. He's had his pre-med., and it'll take effect soon, but his morale needs boosting. You've got to do that for him while he's waiting. Understand?"

My mouth felt rather dry. "Yes, Nurse."

"Right. Then let's get back to him."

When we returned to Roberts in Bed 18 she gave him another of her rare and attractive smiles. "This is Nurse Standing, who is going to go down to the theatre with you, Roberts. Nurse will stay with you all the time, so you've got nothing to worry about. The doctor will give you another injection in your arm when you reach the theatre, and that will send you straight off to sleep. When you wake up it will be all over and you'll be back here. Nurse Standing will look after you while you are asleep, and come back here with you."

The theatre porter was waiting with the trolley. He was a tiny man with a wrinkled monkey face. Bennings had told me that the theatre porters were absolutely reliable. "They will know exactly what to do if anything goes wrong on the way down or back; do what they tell you and you'll be all right."

The porter patted Roberts' feet sympathetically as he tucked the top blanket over the stretcher. "You'll be fine, mate," he said cheerfully. "Me and the nurse'll be there to hold your hand."

When we reached the theatre the porter drew me momentarily aside. "Your first time down, Nurse?"

"Yes."

"Then just you hang on to his hand, Nurse, while he goes under. It'll help him, and it'll help you."

# 3

## *An Evening in the Operating Theatre*

THE general surgical theatre lay close to the main surgical wards. It was a large department, consisting of the theatre proper, with its encircling, but sealed-off, galleries; anæsthetic room; sterilizing room; duty-room; nurses' and surgeons' changing-rooms; glove-room; and instrument-room. The department was separated from the hospital by large, wide double doors; inside lay a broad white corridor, off which lay the various rooms; the theatre itself was at the end of the corridor. The patients and theatre staff were admitted to the theatre by means of another set of double doors; the galleries were reached by a staircase opening into the white corridor. When we had arrived at the outer doors a red warning notice glowed over the entrance, "Operation in Progress—Approach with Caution." There was another illuminated red notice over the theatre doors "Operation in Progress—No Admission under any Circumstances while this Notice is Red."

The porter guided Roberts' stretcher-trolley into the anæsthetic room. "You'll need a mask, Nurse," he whispered. "You dress up later when he's under."

"Thanks." I took a mask from the large glass jar by the door, tied it over my face, and went back to Roberts. He smiled dreamily. "You do look queer in that yashmak, Nurse." His hand reached for mine again. "I'm glad they send a nurse from your ward down with you here. It makes a difference, somehow. You don't feel so alone. I expect"—the expression in his eyes was anxious—"this kind of carry-on is all in the day's work for you? You bring a lot of chaps down?"

I swallowed. "Oh, yes. Yes, indeed. It's all in the day's work."

" And—you've seen lots of cases like mine? I mean, I'm not
what you might call out of the ordinary? "

" Of course not." I put all the confidence I could muster
into my voice. " Just routine."

The porter hitched the anæsthetic trolley closer with one
foot and tested the cylinders. " That's a fact, mate," he said
reassuringly. " Doing cases like yours all day long, we are.
Must do hundreds every year. That Mr Waring, he's a crack
hand at this business. At it all the time. Now, you take this
afternoon "—he leant a casual elbow on the cylinders—" just
one afternoon—and how many is it we're doing from Francis,
Nurse? Eleven, isn't it? "

" Yes, only eleven," I replied, copying his casualness.

Roberts relaxed. " Eleven. You don't say." He smiled at us.
" Well, I dunno, but it makes you think. And I dunno why it
should, but it makes me feel better."

" Feeling better, eh, laddie? " The anæsthetist had come
in. " Good show. Now just let me have your right arm, and I'll
give you something that'll make you feel even better." He
pulled down his mask. " You know me, laddie. I'm the chap
who looked at your chest in Albert last evening. Right? Good
show." He nodded at me.

" Just roll back his sleeve, Nurse. That's the form."

When Roberts was unconscious the anæsthetist told me to
go and dress up. " I'll be with him all the time he's under."

The porter caught my eye. " Nurses' changing-room. Door's
marked. Staff Nurse is in there. She'll show you what to put
on."

Without looking up, the anæsthetist asked, " First time
down, Nurse? "

" Yes, doctor."

" God help you," he murmured, " and you'll need it. It's
hellish hot in there."

In the changing-room the staff nurse was recognizable only
by her blue belt. She was hidden beneath a turban, mask, long
enveloping white gown and white rubber over-boots. She
looked first at my feet. " What size, Nurse? "

I closed the door behind me. " Four and a half, Nurse."

" Help yourself to a pair of fives. We've nothing smaller."

Then, noticing the uncertainty in my manner, she looked at me properly. "Don't tell me they've sent us another first-year! Are you the P.T.S. set too?"

"Yes, Nurse."

She groaned. "Not another green pro! What's going on in Francis Adams this afternoon? Who sent you down?"

"Nurse Bennings, Nurse."

She muttered something under her breath about staff nurses who thought other staff nurses had nothing to do but hold the heads of fainting pros. My heart sank. Poor Josephine. Poor me.

"Here." She handed me a gown. "Put that on over everything, and I'll show you how to fix your turban." She did so, efficiently. "That's it. Now tie your mask on again. Then find yourself some boots from that cupboard over there." When I had the boots on she studied my appearance. "You'll do." Then she dropped her brusque manner. "Feeling scared?" she asked kindly.

"A bit, Nurse."

Her eyes smiled over her mask. "Poor kid. I'll bet you are. But don't panic. You aren't going to see any awful sights, as your man will be completely covered by sterile towels, and you'll only see the operation site, which will look like nothing you've ever seen—and certainly nothing human. And don't feel that you'll be expected to do anything, as no one will expect you, a new pro., to do anything. You just have to be there, to keep an eye on what's going on, so as to be able to give a report to your ward sister when you get back to the ward. But at your present stage you needn't fret about missing some vital point, because, of course, you'll miss that point. Nothing you are going to see to-day will make any sense; but, as the surgeons write full notes on their ops., Sister Francis will only have to read their notes later, to know what went on. It is useful for the ward sister if she's got an experienced pro. on the spot in an op., which is one of the reasons why you ward pros. come down; to get experienced, you've got to start coming down some time, though maybe not as soon as you and that other kid. She went flat out. Did you know that?"

My stomach felt hollow. " No, Nurse."

" She did. So come over here." She opened the door of a small medicine cupboard. "Here's the glucose and there's the sal volatile. The dose is marked on both. Now, if the theatre starts revolving or you begin to sweat don't try to stick it out, as this is your first visit. You can be a Spartan later, not at first. Doesn't pay. So, if you do feel at all queer come out here quietly and help yourself to glucose and sal volatile. Then sit down and put your head between your knees." She smiled again. "Mind you, you may feel fine and not need a thing; but it saves every one's time if you know what to do, do it, and understand that we understand what you are doing. Don't ask permission to leave for that—just get out. We do try to avoid what happened with that other pro.; some one going out cold in the middle of a case is upsetting for the surgeons, and the person involved could fall across the table or hurt themselves badly going down. Luckily, I caught your colleague as she fell." She closed the cupboard door. "I'm afraid you haven't got an easy case to start off with, but that can't be helped."

" Is Roberts a difficult case, Nurse? "

She hesitated. "Not so much difficult as long. Mr Waring is a quick surgeon, but I doubt if even he will do your man in under an hour and a half. Maybe longer. And that's a long time," she added sympathetically, " in which to stand still in a hot theatre if you've never stood in one before. We have to keep the temperature up for the patient's sake and we are used to working in a heat-wave temperature; you aren't. But you will be. Very soon."

It was very hot in the theatre, and Roberts' operation did seem to take a very long time. So long that I half wondered if the hands of the theatre clock had stuck. My ankles ached; my back ached; my head felt hot; my hands cold; but otherwise I was all right. I was far too interested in what was going on on the table to have any thought of fainting.

I watched the steady, neat brown hands of the surgeons, and admired the telepathic partnership that existed between the S.S.O. and Sister Theatre. He never had to ask for anything. Sister anticipated his every need; each time he stretched out his hand in the direction of her trolley and her own gloved hand laid in his palm the right instrument he murmured, "Thank you, Sister," without once looking up from the wound. Once only he stopped momentarily, straightened his back, and flexed his shoulder muscles. He glanced at Sister. "Right?" he queried softly of no one in particular. Then he bent forward over the table again; the two house-surgeons assisting stood poised, their heads tilted slightly to one side; neither of them spoke a word. The anæsthetist looked up, "All right this end, sir." The S.S.O. nodded slightly without looking round; Sister Theatre shifted her position slightly and peered over his shoulder, while in the galleries the students came closer to the glass walls.

The bright white lights shone brilliantly on the white figures of the staff and the still, white-covered figure of the man on the table. There were only four colours in that theatre: white; silver; green; and scarlet. The gowns and caps were white, and so were the towels; the instruments and bowls were silvered; the oxygen cylinders green; and the rubber mackintosh on the floor was scarlet. There was no blood anywhere that I could see. I could not believe that that wound was on a man; I could see only instruments.

It was some time later that the S.S.O. said, "Right," again. This time there was no query in his tone. The atmosphere in the theatre changed, and in the galleries the students sat back and talked quietly to each other. Shortly after, the anæsthetist said, "Time to send for the next chap, Sister." I looked at the clock. It was an hour and three-quarters since the unconscious body of Roberts had been wheeled into the theatre.

The S.S.O. walked to one of the sinks and peeled off his gloves. "Where's the ward nurse?"

Sister Theatre nodded to me. "Behind you, Mr Waring," she told him.

He turned, untying his gown as he did so. "Nurse, this is what I want done for Roberts when you take him back to the ward." And he reeled off a long, detailed list of instructions. "Will you repeat all that to Sister Francis with my compliments, please."

Sister Theatre interposed quickly, " Mr Waring, Nurse is new to the theatre. Shall I send one of my nurses back with your instructions? "

He looked at her and then at me. Only my eyes were visible, so I doubted that he recognized me. I noticed his eyes for the first time. They were grey. Not steel grey, but the deep blue-grey of the English Channel on a winter's day. They looked as cold as the sea and as uncompromising as winter at that moment, and the whiteness of his mask accentuated their colour.

He asked briefly, " What have I said, Nurse? "

I hesitated. I did not understand quite what he meant. Was this his way of telling me to go back to Francis?

" Nurse," he said drily, " time may be immaterial to you, but I am afraid it is not so to this theatre. We have three more cases on the list. So would you be good enough to repeat what I have just told you? "

For the second time in my short nursing career I was grateful for my ability to ape a parrot. I did as he requested.

When I had finished he gave a slight nod, then turned his back on me, and began scrubbing his arms at the sink. " All right with you if Roberts goes back, Thomas? " he called over his shoulder to the anæsthetist.

" He can travel, sir. He's coming along nicely."

Sister Theatre told me to take Roberts back to Francis. As we left the theatre the S.S.O. asked, " Who's the next chap, Sister? Evans, isn't it? "

I went back to Francis Adams with Roberts, delivered the S.S.O.'s instructions to Sister Francis, took over from Josephine, who had escorted Evans as far as the anæsthetic room. Evans' operation was a short one; the two men following him were also minor cases. While the last man was being operated upon I took my first proper look round the theatre. I felt an old hand by then and very pleased with myself. I had had no lunch and no tea, but I felt splendid. I wondered if I would like to be a theatre nurse. Or even a Theatre Sister. Might be rather fun. Certainly be exciting. I closed my eyes at the thought of working smoothly with the S.S.O.—and there I made a mistake. A big mistake. I opened my eyes and blinked rapidly. The theatre started to revolve around me. I closed my eyes again; the darkness swam; I reopened them, and the theatre floor loomed upward, as though about to hit me in the face. I was standing only a few feet from the door; those feet lengthened into endless yards as I dragged myself to that door. Once outside, I leant momentarily against the wall. That did not improve matters. I knew I must sit down, and quickly. Now, where was that changing-room? Second door left—or right?

The theatre staff nurse put her head round the theatre door. "Bit too much, Nurse? Bad luck. Go down to the changing-room and do what I told you. Don't worry about your man. He's done now, and, as the list is over, I'm going to take him back to Francis for you. Wait in our room until I get back."

I said, "Thanks. Nurse—please—which way is——" But she had vanished.

I shook my head violently to see if that would clear it. It did, a little. The corridor was no longer spinning, merely revolving gently; I read some of the letters on the door opposite to where I was standing. The letters danced, but I read clearly "—NGING ROOM." There was something wrong about their being there; I had thought she meant go down the corridor—she must have meant across. Relieved, I stumbled over the corridor, reached the door, turned the handle, and then as I opened the door the floor really did come up and hit me in the face.

As it was coming up—or I was going down—I thought I heard some one say quickly, "Nurse! What are——?" But I did not hear any more.

There was a mist round me. A thick grey mist, and through the mist I could hear a drum beating. I could not understand why I should hear a drum, why I was in a mist, what I was doing.

A man's voice said quietly, "Take it easy, Nurse. Keep your head down a shade longer. You're coming round from a faint. Take it easy," and I felt a firm hand pressing not ungently on my head as the voice added, "Right. You'll do."

The mist began to clear and I recognized the drum-beat. It was the noise of my own arterial pulse in my temples. And then I recognized that "Right." I had heard it four times this afternoon. It was the S.S.O.'s way of saying he had things under control.

I opened my eyes properly, saw who was sitting on that bench beside me, and wished I could faint again. I closed my eyes, but it was not any good. I was finished with that faint. But why of all the men in this hospital did he have to be the one to act guardian angel?

He moved his hand from the back of my head and touched my wrist. "Better now. Good. Stay where you are and I'll get you some sal volatile."

I half rose. "I'm—fine—thanks."

He put his hand on my shoulder and pushed me down. "Sit, Nurse, and do what you're told."

I relaxed against the wall and watched him walk over to the cupboard. It seemed to me to be the wrong cupboard; the staff nurse had shown me a different one, but I did not like to say anything. I shut my eyes and left him to find it out for himself.

He pushed a medicine glass into one of my hands a minute or so later. "Knock that back, Nurse."

"Thank you." I sipped the liquid; it had a horrible taste, so I swallowed it quickly.

He smiled faintly at my involuntary grimace. "Revolting stuff, isn't it?" He took off his cap and pushed back his hair. "Your colour's back, so, if you feel up to it, I think I should suggest you go."

I jumped off the bench. "Of course. Thank you. I'll go back to Francis at once."

He said, "I think you would be better advised to go and wait in your changing-room, as the staff nurse suggested."

I stared at him and then at the room. And then I saw why the cupboard had been the wrong cupboard. It was in the wrong room.

"This," I licked my dry lips, "isn't the nurse's changing-room?"

He undid his mask with infuriating calm. "If it was I

should not be here. And, since this is the surgeons' room, I'm afraid, Nurse, you should not be in here. Which was the point of my suggesting that you left."

I did not know what my colour had been, but now it was puce. "I'm so sorry—I'm afraid I wasn't thinking—that is—I wasn't looking where I was going." My voice tailed away lamely as I made for the door.

He opened it for me with what I was certain was mock civility. "You appear to make a habit of the latter, Nurse. Possibly you should be more careful. If not, one of these days you may walk into something really serious." He looked me over as if I was an odd specimen under a microscope. "How do you feel?"

I felt as if I wanted to cry. I said, Thank you very much, I felt fine.

"Right." He nodded briefly, then closed the door between us. He had barely closed it when one of the theatre nurses bustled out of the theatre carrying a load of soiled linen. She stopped momentarily, "Hallo? You the pro. from Francis who was took queer? Lost your way?" She jerked her head across the corridor. "That door over there, Nurse! Not the one behind you. Can't you read, girl? If not, you'd better learn fast. No white woman is allowed to set foot in the surgeons' room—so watch out, as that's the door behind you!"

I said weakly, "Thank you, Nurse."

Her eyes smiled over her mask. "You're welcome. Glad I ran into you before you caused a riot. Most of the men are still nattering to Sister in the theatre; but the S.S.O.'s come out, and——" she glanced round, then lowered her voice—"if there's one thing that Jake Waring won't have, it's an infringement of his privacy. So just as well I caught you in time, eh?"

I said, "Yes, Nurse—just as well," and she trotted off towards the linen shute.

I went across the corridor into the right room, sat down on a chair, and pulled off my turban. Now, what, I thought, do I do now? Apologize to some one? And far more important—what's he going to do? Complain to Sister Theatre? Sister Francis? I thought of Bennings' comments in that eventuality and shuddered. Even Matron? I decided I would rather face Matron than Bennings; Matron had better manners.

The staff nurse burst into the room while I was still thinking this over. I noticed none of the theatre nurses walked anywhere. They seemed to explode into action as if as full of steam as their sterilizers.

"How are you feeling, Nurse? All right now? Good. I've told Sister Francis that you felt off-colour, but got yourself out of the theatre like a sensible child, and so didn't upset anyone. Now get changed and back to Francis, but don't fret about rushing as they aren't expecting you for a while. I've got to get back to my own clearing up, so I'll leave you to it. I just wanted to check up that you were all right."

I said, "Thanks awfully, Nurse—I'm quite all right, but I'm afraid——" then I had to stop as one of the theatre porters hammered on the door. "Casualty wanting to speak to you, Nurse Griffith."

The staff nurse groaned, "Oh, no! Not another case this evening, Jervis! I can't bear it. I'm coming." And she was gone again.

I removed my theatre clothes, combed my hair, fixed my cap, and returned to Francis with mixed feelings. If that pleasant staff nurse had not treated me as an angel child it would not have been so bad. I wondered what she would say when we next met—if the S.S.O. mentioned the subject. But wouldn't he have to mention it as he was S.S.O.? He was so keen on maintaining discipline and so on——I did not see how he could avoid complaining. I felt sick for the second time that afternoon; this time, unfortunately, there was no chance of my fainting away. I walked into Francis on legs in which the bones felt as if they had been turned to water.

Sister Francis was writing at her table. I stood in front of her with my hands correctly behind my back. "I've come back from the theatre, Sister."

She glanced up. "Feeling all right again, Nurse? Good." She consulted her work-list. "You have had no tea yet, Nurse Standing, so will you first go to the kitchen and ask Elsie to prepare you a tray? Eat your tea in the duty-room, then report to me again."

I said hastily, "I'm not at all hungry, Sister—honestly." I felt quite overwhelmed with guilt at the prospect of sitting down to tea in the duty-room on such a busy evening. "I would much rather not have tea, thank you."

Sister put down her pen. "Nurse Standing, I was not asking if you wished to have tea; I was merely telling you to go and have it." She took up her pen again and took no further notice of me. I murmured my thanks and shot down the ward to the kitchen, feeling very small and highly impertinent.

In the kitchen Josephine was laying the supper trolley. "So you're back! How are you, Rose? We heard you fainted too."

Elsie propped her fists on her broad hips and glowered. "And I suppose you've come to tell me as Sister wants me to make you tea, Nurse?"

"I'm afraid she did say that, Elsie. I'm awfully sorry. I hope you don't mind. I don't really want it, but Sister says I must." Elsie frowned horribly and said what things were coming to she wouldn't like to say, she was sure. "What with suppers at six-thirty instead of six, and tea for Sister"—she stormed round the kitchen—"and tea for Nurse Standing and a cup of coffee with no sugar for old Sir Henry!" She slapped a cloth on a tray. "Well, really, I don't know, Nurse! What am I running, that's what I'd like to ask? A kitchen or a café?" She thrust some cut bread under the grill and lit a match. "Hard or soft, duck?"

"Hard or soft what, Elsie?"

"Eggs, duck," she said patiently. "Do you like 'em hard or soft?"

"But I don't want an egg," I protested; "Sister just said tea."

Elsie called on the ceiling to witness the goings-on from which she, a hard-working ward-maid, was forced to suffer. "When I makes you tea," she announced, filling a small saucepan with hot water, "you eat what I gives you and no nonsense or I go straight to Sister and ask for me cards. Sister knows as I'm going to give you an egg. I always gives an egg when I makes tea for a nurse what's missed it; so you eat what you're given, duck, and no more saying you can't eat this

and that!" She lit another gas burner. " You young nurses!
All alike! Think you can keep going on nothing! " She turned
on me. "And you, Nurse Standing, standing there looking like
a ghost with a waist like a match-stick and saying as you
don't want an egg! Never heard anything like it! Never!
And, what's more, I won't have it! Not in my kitchen! So
what's it to be? Hard or soft? "

I smiled at her. " I give in. Middling, please, Elsie."

She shook her head at Josephine. " No pleasing some people,
eh, Nurse Forbes? "

In a few minutes' time I ate a peaceful and enormous tea
in the duty-room. When I returned the tray with thanks Elsie
scrutinized the remains. "Don't know where you put it all,
Nurse Standing, I'm sure! Now you get out of my kitchen
and perhaps I can get on with my work! "

Sister was half-way up the ward, making beds with another
of the nurses. She told me to help her with the rest of the
beds. "Nurse Blake, go and help Nurse Bennings with the
operation cases."

Bennings was hidden behind one of the eleven sets of
drawn curtains that hid the operation cases, and I had not set
eyes on her since my return from the theatre. I was glad not
to see her; I did not expect her to be as tolerant about my
faint as Sister. Josephine had told me how scathing Bennings
had been on her own return. "Honestly, Rose—you'd think I
passed out on purpose, just to make a scene!"

To my surprise, Bennings said not one word to me either
that night or later. Not one word about my faint, that is; she
said a good deal about my inefficiency as a junior pro. in the
ward.

"All the same, I don't get it," I told Josephine as we sat
drinking coffee in the canteen after lunch next day; " I should
have expected Bennings to make hay out of my passing out
too. But not one harsh word about it have I had. Maybe we've
misjudged her." I stirred my coffee, thoughtfully. "Maybe
she's got a heart of gold beneath her young battle-axe exterior.
After all, think how wrong we all were about old Sister
P.T.S."

Josephine hooted with laughter. Being Josephine, she

managed to do this discreetly. "Rose, you can't truly believe that? My dear, she's just biding her time for reasons of her own. Bennings hasn't got a heart of gold—she hasn't got a heart at all. She's just a highly efficient nursing automaton. I'll bet she runs on oil." She looked round the canteen. "She's just like her beloved young man. I noticed in the theatre yesterday—he's got about as much sensitivity as a machine. Really, we, at least, don't have to worry about the effect of automation on the hospital world; we've got it already." She remained staring across the canteen. "But how I wish I could have seen his face when he picked you off the floor of his private room, Rose! I'd give a lot to have seen that! I have to hand it to you, Rose. I'd never have had the nerve to pass out in there."

"But I didn't pass out in there on purpose," I protested, "and I don't think he actually had to pick me off the floor. I'm quite hazy about it all, but I do remember coming to on that bench, so maybe he just gave me a shove on to it. Be honest—can you see any pro. choosing that spot for a laugh? I may be daft, Josephine—but I'm not as daft as all that."

A voice over our head inquired, "Is that for the record, Nurse?"

We both looked up. The large, dark-haired student who had been in the basement that evening when I upset Mrs Clark was standing by our table. He beamed at us, then gave an affected bow. "Afternoon, all! Is this a private session, ladies, or may a lowly student man join in?" Without waiting for a reply he pulled a chair from the next table and sat down between us. "I'll shove off if you have strong views on drinking with the Medical School, but if you can stand the strain may I introduce myself? Name of Martin—William Davis Martin." He half rose, bowed as before, then subsided and nodded affably at me. "I had the pleasure of meeting you before, Nurse."

I said, "Oh, yes. You did." I caught Josephine's eye. "I met Mr Martin one evening when we were still in the P.T.S."

The student nodded again. "We ran into each other, as you might say. Tell me, Nurse, how's that wax character getting along? Lost any more legs recently? And do tell me something else, about which I am agog. I have no shame and I could not help overhearing what you were saying to each other just now. So do, I beg, tell Uncle all! What's all this about the surgeons' room?" He lowered his voice to a conspiratorial whisper. "Don't tell me that our golden-haired boy has taken to luring young blondes in there between cases? Or, rather, do tell me that he has! Because that would be one bit of gossip, ladies, that would rock Uncle and my namesake of a hospital to its aged foundations."

"For heaven's sake! It was nothing like that! Anything but —so please, Mr Martin, just forget what you heard. There's no gossip value in it at all—I just made the heck of a mistake! And, to be honest, the S.S.O. was pretty decent about it, and the least said the better—for me. This," I told him sternly, " is right off the record. Please."

He laughed, "Relax, love—my lips are sealed. No cause to panic—but do tell me all, nevertheless."

There seemed no alternative; so I did as he asked. When I finished he laughed again. "I must admit I'm disappointed. I was hoping that I had stumbled on the finest bit of gossip I had heard in years."

Josephine spoke to him for the first time. "Are you so fascinated by gossip, Mr Martin?" Her tone was cool.

He looked at her, then grinned. "But fascinated, Nurse. What else can a character be when his finals are looming on him? Must have something to keep the mind otherwise occupied or one goes right up the wall." He sat back. " Some characters heave rugger balls about; others hit the bottle; others chase the girls; a few neuros flog the books non-stop and get nervous breakdowns. All a question of temperament. Now me—I natter. Gossip. I get around, keep my ear to the ground and my fingers in every pie. It amuses me, serves as a high-powered counter-irritant. But I can take a hint, girls— particularly when it's handed me straight in the teeth. Gossip's out. So let's get down to facts and be matey. I've told you my name. Care to tell me either of yours?"

Josephine's prim expression faded with a speed that surprised me. She smiled charmingly. "Why not? I'm Josephine Forbes, and this is Rose Standing."

He shook hands with each of us in turn. While he was still shaking my hand he glanced up, then stood up. "Afternoon, sir. Something I can do for you?"

The S.S.O. was standing behind Josephine's chair. "Yes, if you would, Martin. Forgive my interrupting your coffee, but, seeing you here, I thought I might as well get those tickets you mentioned from you now. I'd like a couple, please."

Bill Martin said he would be delighted to oblige. "I have 'em here, sir." He produced a book of tickets from his breast-pocket, tore off two at the perforated edge, and handed them to the S.S.O. "Glad you've decided to come, after all. Should be a good show. We've got hold of a decent band for a change."

The S.S.O. said he was glad to hear it and produced some money. "I hope the Rugger Club becomes solvent again after this. Thanks, Martin." He had been regarding Josephine and me with the complete lack of recognition that we now expected from every man in a white coat. Consequently I was genuinely shocked when he wished the top of my cap a "Good afternoon, Nurse Standing," and walked on, pocketing his tickets.

Bill Martin sat down and scratched his head. "Well, well, well. So Jake Waring's coming to the Rugger Ball. What do you know about that, girls?"

Josephine asked what there was to know. "Don't the resident staff traditionally go gay at these affairs?"

"Traditionally," agreed Bill, "they do. But Jake has long been the exception proving every rule in this dive. Most of the chaps here work hard when they can't get out of it, and play hard whenever they can. Jake goes along on the work angle; but so far no one as yet has seen him play. History, although you two don't realize it, has just been made. Fact. I've been Hon. Sec. of the Rugger Club for the past two years, and this is the first time I've sold him a brace of tickets for anything or heard of anyone else doing the same. And if anyone else had done it I should have heard because I hear everything." His black hair was now standing on end. "Now, of course, the next thing I want to hear is who's the lucky woman?"

Josephine said brightly, " Our staff nurse in Francis? "

He raised his eyebrows. " You got your money on Jenny Bennings? " He looked at me. " How about you, Nurse Standing? Did you get an insight into any of this in your sojourn in the surgeons' room? "

" All I got out of the surgeons' room was a dose of sal volatile and a stern warning that if I didn't keep my eyes open one of these fine days I'd walk into real trouble."

He considered this in silence for several seconds. " You know, love," he said mildly, " he could be right there."

A friend hailed him from the other side of the canteen. " Bill, got any more of those tickets with you? I've made a sale for you over here. What's my cut? "

" You buy me a beer you mean, Nigel! " Bill stood up. " Nice to have met you, girls. See you around." He moved over to the other table.

Josephine watched him go. " I wish we weren't in our first year." She sighed. " I wish we could go to these dances."

" Can't we? As first-years? I didn't know that."

She said it was out of the question. " There are dozens of unwritten laws that say so. Erith told me."

I smiled. " Well, I can't truly say that that is one set of laws that will bother us. We don't know anyone here to ask us to dances."

" Rose, we know this man Bill Martin now."

" And so, I'm dead sure, does every nurse in the hospital. He's the matey type. But, personally, I don't much mind if we have to be Cinderellas for one year; my feet couldn't take a dance. Can you imagine facing Bennings the morning after a jolly night out with the Rugger fifteen? " I shook my head and stood up. " No. Not for me. I need early nights and two good feet to stand the pace of Francis Adams."

Josephine pushed back her chair. " I'm sure they wouldn't let us really go to town, here," she said thoughtfully, as if it was really important to her.

" Then stick to strict tempo, Josephine—or olde-time dancing—or even the minuet. You still have to be on your feet, and mine aren't the feet they once were. But, now I come to think of it, I'd like to be a wallflower at that ball for a spell.

I'd adore to see Jake Waring jiving with Bennings. If I could sit down and watch . . ."

Josephine had an inspiration. "Maybe that's why Bennings hasn't beaten you up about fainting as she did me. Maybe he told her all about it, and asked her to the ball—and, consequently, filled her with the milk of human kindness."

"It's rather a long shot—but perhaps you are right. It is peculiar that she shouldn't have mentioned it. As he and she are pals, she may know all by now."

Josephine had quite convinced herself now. "And he has to take either a staff nurse or a sister, and she's the best-looking staff nurse, so—obviously, Rose—that's it! "

"Why does he have to limit his choice? Can't he take anyone out of their first year?"

"Goodness, no! Not possibly." She was so definite that I laughed. "No, seriously, Rose. I'm right. Erith told me. Nurses in training and the senior residents live in different worlds. Every one insists on that. Tradition, etiquette—the lot."

"Suits me," I said cheerfully, "very nicely." And the funny thing was that then I honestly believed that statement.

# 4

## *Hunches can be Right*

B Y the end of that week even Josephine had changed her mind. "She couldn't be so foul if her love-life was under control, Rose. I obviously jumped to the wrong conclusion. Whoever the S.S.O. has asked to that dance, it can't be Bennings. She gets worse by the day."

"You mean she gets worse by the hour!" I hung my corridor cloak on my peg in our changing-room in Francis. "Oh, Lord! That's her calling me now. What didn't I finish before that lecture?"

I soon discovered. Bennings was waiting for me in the ward doorway. "Nurse Standing, the sluice-room was a disgrace when I went in just now. Did you not dust the high shelves? You did? Well, you did not do it properly. Go and do them all again."

A few minutes later she came into the sluice. "Nurse Standing, the top of the acid cupboard is dusty. You must polish it again before you start your routine work."

I said, "Yes, Nurse; sorry, Nurse."

Half an hour later she came into the kitchen. "Nurse Standing, are you going to take all morning to give out those drinks? Your routine is all behind! When will you learn to move quickly?"

That night even Erith admitted that Bennings was out-Bennings-ing herself these days. "I know she's always had a thing about junior pros., Standing, but I've never known her have such a thing as now. You seem to get in her hair, so do try and keep out of her way as much as possible. That's the only technique left to a pro. when some one like Bennings gets cracking on her. And console yourself; you do get on all right with Sister Francis, and it's the sister who writes your ward report—not the staff nurse."

" Thank the Lord for that! But just tell me, Nurse—how do I keep out of her way? She is my little shadow; she sticks closer than a brother. So—how? "

Erith grinned sympathetically. "I know. I've seen that. Still, perhaps you can fade into the background tactfully; worth a try. By the way, is she getting you down? "

" She doesn't reduce me to tears of sorrow," I replied, "just blind rage."

Erith said that was the way to take the Benningses in the nursing profession. " No point in letting them get under your skin. And they don't last for ever. Sooner or later you move on to another ward and don't see them again."

I agreed that that was a great consolation—in theory. " Snag is, I love Francis. I like Sister, and the men are angels."

They were. They seemed to grow nicer every day and they helped me in every possible fashion. " Nurse Standing, you'll not mind my mentioning it, but it's ten minutes to eight and you've not collected the newspapers yet."

" Nurse Standing—pardon the liberty, miss—but you left your dusting-tray on that wheel-chair over by Eighteen. Better fetch it away afore she sees it."

" You like to fetch me over all your ashtrays, duck, an' I'll give 'em a proper shine for you? Reckon you can do with a hand this morning, like."

Roberts, the man who had been the first patient I had taken to the theatre, was now my greatest friend and ally. The short journey to and from the theatre had joined us in a friendship that was clearly going to last for life. If I forgot anything Roberts was the first person to notice and tactfully draw my attention to the omission; I grew to rely so much on his whispered, " Nurse Standing, half a tick," that I never left the ward without asking him quietly, " Roberts, have I finished properly or left something out? "

He had done very well since his operation. He had had to have that operation as the delayed result of an old war injury. The theatre porter had been quite right when he said that Roberts' operation was one regularly performed by the S.S.O.;

there were several similar operative cases in Francis while I was there, but none of those other men had Roberts' past medical history.

Roberts was a Londoner. He was small, thin, prematurely grey, and in his mid-thirties. He had a typical Londoner's quick sense of humour, unbeatable courage, and stoicism. He never complained at any time, was always cheerful, and never stopped talking unless asleep. Consequently, when, one evening about two weeks after his operation, he sat watching me in silence as I dusted his locker I looked at him curiously. As I did so I saw him give a slight wince.

I put down my duster. "Is your wound bothering you, Roberts? Or have you a headache?"

He smiled with his lips. "I'm all right, duck. Just a mite under the weather to-night, I reckon."

I did not believe him and said so. "Quite sure you haven't a pain anywhere? You had your stitches out this morning, didn't you?"

He nodded. "That's right. Come out lovely, they did. No trouble at all."

I said slowly, "Then—what's up, Roberts?"

He hesitated. "Well—to tell you the truth, Nurse—it's hard to say, like. I feel quite all right in meself, but——"

"Nurse Standing!" Bennings stood at the foot of his bed. "You are supposed to be dusting the lockers! Not gossiping with the patients! Will you kindly get on! Sister will be back from supper and ready for Prayers in five minutes, and you have yet to do all the ashtrays."

I turned to face her. "I'm sorry, Nurse. I was just asking Roberts how he felt."

She looked me over coldly. "Nurse Standing, Sister and I are here to attend to the patients. You are far too inexperienced to trouble our men with foolish questions that can only fatigue sick patients. Will you be good enough to do your own job in future and leave Sister and me to do ours? If you will only do that perhaps one day you may finish your own work on time." She dismissed me with a curt nod, then walked to the head of the bed. Her manner changed instantly. "Now, how are you, Roberts?" she asked in the gentle tone she reserved for men. " Do you feel better now you have your stitches out? Or is anything worrying you?"

Roberts assumed a blank expression. " I'm doing nicely, Nurse Bennings. Ta very much."

She took his pulse, looked at his face, then nodded to herself and walked away. I had no further opportunity to question Roberts. I finished my dusting and the ashtrays, feeling decidedly unhappy. I did realize that I was quite inexperienced, but I had a nasty, niggling little feeling that Roberts was keeping something to himself. The short time I had spent in the ward had shown me how incredibly patient and brave the average patient can be. At the same time I knew that Bennings was an excellent nurse; she had taken his pulse, and I noticed she was keeping an eye on him from her seat at the centre table. She would surely discover if anything was going wrong with him. Yet I could not get rid of the feeling that something was wrong, that he was about to tell me it was more than feeling under the weather; only I did not know what it was, and, above all, I did not know what to do about it.

I thought about it as we waited in the darkened ward for Sister to come in and read the Evening Prayers. Should I mention anything to Sister when she dismissed us for the night? Would she think me foolish or presumptuous? In view of what Bennings had just said in the hearing of the whole ward it was hard to believe that Sister would not think me both of those—but could I let it go? I decided I could not. What if she did think me absurd and impertinent? I felt much better as I got up from my knees, having reached a decision.

The decision did me no good. Sister vanished to Matron's Office directly after Prayers, leaving Bennings to dismiss the juniors. I did some more worrying over supper. There were several of my set at the table with me, but for once I was in no mood to chat. Some one asked, " Going into a decline, Rose? You've only had two helpings of stew. Got to keep your strength up, ducks! "

" I'll do that," I promised absently, and reached another decision. Directly supper was over I hurried back to Francis

Adams without giving myself time to consider what I was going to do or say when I got there.

The ward was very quiet and in semi-darkness. Sister sat at her table, giving the day report to the night nurses. I hesitated in the doorway for a second to see where Bennings was; she was at the far end of the ward. I pulled off my cloak, deposited it on one of the fire-buckets, and walked into the ward. It is not etiquette to wear a corridor cape inside a ward.

Sister Francis glanced up from her report. "Who's that?" I heard her ask her senior night nurse.

The nurse peered down the ward. "One of your juniors, Sister. Nurse Standing."

I had arrived at the desk. Sister looked at me with a faint frown of displeasure at having her report interrupted. "Why are you back, Nurse Standing? I thought Nurse Bennings had taken your report and told you to go to supper."

I said, "Yes, Sister, she did, but——" Then I did not know how to go on, and the curious stares of the night nurses only increased my nervousness.

Sister asked, "Was there something you forgot to mention in your report to Nurse Bennings?"

"Yes, Sister. That is—well—no, Sister. It's about Roberts," I added rather desperately.

"What about Roberts, Nurse?" Sister's tone was scarcely inviting.

I hesitated again. "Well—when I was dusting his locker to-night, Sister, I—er— didn't think he looked very well." My words sounded so stupid under the circumstances that, having said them, I fully expected Sister to dismiss me with a stern warning about wasting her time.

Instead she asked, "Why did you think he looked unwell, Nurse?"

"Because he was very quiet—and he winced, Sister."

"Did he complain of any pain?"

To make this more difficult, just as she said that, Bennings appeared out of the darkness and stood watching me from the other end of the table. Sister glanced up at Bennings, then back to me. "Did he complain, Nurse Standing?"

I said, "No, Sister."

She looked hard at me, then back to Bennings. "You settled Roberts just now, Nurse Bennings. How was he? Comfortable?"

"Quite comfortable, Sister," answered Bennings calmly. "His temperature, pulse, and respirations are normal; his wound has healed; he says he has no pain or discomfort of any sort. I have just asked him again."

"Thank you." Sister looked down at the table and then up to me. Her expression was thoughtful. "I am sure you feel much happier now, Nurse Standing."

I said mechanically, "Yes, Sister. Thank you, Sister."

Sister folded her hands and smoothed her cuffs. "I appreciate the fact that your anxiety for a patient should bring you back to my ward, Nurse Standing, and I hope you will always tell me if you feel worried about one of our patients. I am glad we are able to reassure you. Now, hurry off or you will be late for Chapel. Good night, Nurse." She turned to her night senior. "Now, Nurse MacGill, I was discussing Evans. He has had a fair day and——"

I did not hear any more as after one glance at Bennings, who looked back and straight through me, I tiptoed out of the ward. "She looked at me," I told the girls after Chapel, "as if I simply wasn't there. But I'll bet she remembers in the morning."

Josephine said I ought to have my head examined. "You know that for all her narking Bennings is a jolly good nurse. As if she'd let anything serious slip past her! You are a goon, Rose!"

"But she wouldn't know there was anything to slip," I protested. "Roberts is so tough. He never complains, so if he says he's feeling under the weather something must be going wrong."

In a tone that would have done Bennings credit Josephine told me to remember I was only a junior pro. "Juniors don't know a thing about illness. So how on earth can you tell that something must be wrong?"

"I can't. But I've just got a hunch."

She roared with laughter. "Rose, here I draw the line! I really do! You can't start having hunches! You can drop plates and chuck vases about, fall asleep in lectures, faint in odd corners, day-dream all round Francis Adams; but if you are going to start having hunches you'd better retire here and now, because that sort of nonsense really will get you thrown out of Martin's!"

The other girls agreed with her. A good nurse, they lectured me, had to stick to common sense and base her judgments on facts.

"And the fact you've now got to face, Rose," added Josephine, "is that you have deliberately disobeyed Bennings. And that fact is going to cause you a packet of trouble and strife in Francis Adams. You must be punch-drunk, my dear. Haven't you had enough from Bennings already?"

I felt very dispirited when I went on duty next morning. In the cold light of 7.30 A.M. my last night's behaviour seemed quite daft. Josephine had the day off, and for once I was early on duty. I left my cape in the changing-room and went to report on duty to the senior night nurse. I found her in the sluice. "Good morning, Nurse MacGill."

She gazed at me wearily. "Don't tell me it's seven-thirty already? Where has the night gone?" She dried her hands, then produced the work-list from the bib of her apron. "Let's see—Standing—where are you? Oh, yes. Will you make beds with Erith when she gets here, and then help my junior get the ward straight before you start your own routine? Right?" She tucked the list away. "And, incidentally," she added conversationally, "the next time you get a feeling in your bones about one of the patients, do me a favour. If I'm not with Sister be sure you let me know too."

I guessed she was being sarcastic. "I'm sorry about that, Nurse. It was stupid of me to flap."

"It was not stupid at all. It was possibly the most intelligent thing you ever did."

My jaw dropped. "Intelligent? Me, Nurse?"

She cleared a dressing-trolley as she replied. "Yes—you. One does get these quaint notions at times. I've had 'em often at night, and I've never been wrong yet. It's odd, because when one has them one has nothing to go on. The chart and the general appearance of the patient is all according to the book; but one just feels in one's bones that the chart, the given facts, and all the books are wrong." She yawned. She looked very tired this morning. " I trust my bones, Standing. I back them against anything, and they've never let me down yet. After last night I trust your bones too. So, as I said, next time you get worked up will you make sure that I know about it? You helped me a lot last night. You really did."

" Roberts? "

She gave a grim little nod, and I added anxiously, " What's happened, Nurse? How is he? "

" Not very well." That, being translated from hospital terminology, meant very ill indeed. " But he's better than he was at three o'clock this morning. He was down in the theatre again by half-past three." She explained in detail why that had been necessary. " The S.S.O. said last night that it's a complication that crops up in roughly one in ten thousand cases. He's only met it three times." She yawned again. " He and I went into every possible complication when he did his night round at eleven. Roberts was sleeping quite well then and not showing anything. He didn't shoot that sudden pulse until the small dark hours, and then it went up and up. We got the S.S.O. up; he came and took one good look at Roberts, and said, ' Well, Nurse MacGill, I can't say you didn't warn me. Only one thing to do—theatre, stat.' "

" Did you warn him, Nurse? "

She nodded. " I told you. We went into every conceivable complication during his night round." She washed the top of her trolley and kicked it against the wall. " When you've done as much night duty as I have, Standing, you'll find you develop an extra sense about possible complications. I could tell last night that you were genuinely upset about Roberts. So could Sister. That's why she let you off lightly. She loathes having her report interrupted. Of course, I realized you might have been flapping, but I wouldn't say you were the flapping type. So I told the H.S. and the S.S.O. about it. The house-man, being newly qualified, obviously thought I was a little odd myself to take any notice of anything a pro. said; the S.S.O., being a very old hand, took it as seriously as I did. Pros. often know more about the patients than anyone else, as the patients always talk to pros. when they may shut up like clams to higher authority. Which was why he and I went through Roberts' notes with a mental tooth-comb; the S.S.O. listed all possible snags that might be lying dormant, and what actually happened was on his list.

"Between him and you we night girls were well and truly prepared. We even had a theatre pack and a transfusion setting ready—just in case. If it hadn't been needed it would have been good practice for my junior, and, as it was, it saved a lot of time. Mind you, I would naturally have spotted what had happened and got up the S.S.O. in any event; but it makes life so much easier if one's not caught absolutely by surprise."

The other day nurses joined us in the sluice then, and she gave them their early-morning work. As I followed Erith to the door MacGill called after me, "Might interest you to hear the S.S.O.'s comment at three-five A.M. 'Out of the mouths of babes—and so on, eh, Nurse MacGill?' With which I much agree."

Erith nudged me as we walked into the ward. "What was all that about you and the S.S.O., Standing?"

"Just a joke of MacGill's." For some reason I did not want to discuss it. I changed the subject by asking how senior was MacGill. "She wears a fourth-year belt, I can see. But she's so—normal."

Erith pulled a chair to the foot of one bed, smiled a good-morning at the man in it, and began stripping the bed neatly. "Not every one alters as they sail up the hospital ladder," she murmured as we met at the foot of the bed. "She —the person you mentioned—has always been the same. I can remember her as a second-year when I first started. She was normal then. It is possible to remain so and be good at the job." She smiled once more at our patient. "Do forgive our chatting over your feet, Davis. It's shocking bad manners, so we'll stop. Tell me, how are you this morning? Did you sleep well?"

"Mustn't grumble, Nurse. But I'm sorry to hear poor old Bobs got took queer in the night. Ever so quiet they must have been down the other end. I didn't hear the trolley at all, and they say he went down to the theatre. Course, I did see that tall fair chap in here early when we was drinking our tea. On the go most of the night he was, so they tell me. I don't know"—he shook his head solemnly. "I don't know how these chaps can stand this doctoring racket. They never seem to get no sleep at all."

Erith fluffed his pillows. "If the S.S.O. gets a whole night in bed, Davis, it makes history."

I asked, "Does he get called up every night?"

She picked up the chair, and we moved on to the next bed. "You've got the wrong word there, Standing. The word is calls." She put down the chair. "Morning, Bowen. How are you this morning? Sleep well?"

I glanced momentarily down the length of Francis Adams. Every one of the forty beds was occupied, and Francis was merely one of the many surgical wards. It was certainly one of the S.S.O.'s own wards, but he was also responsible for every other surgical ward and every surgical patient coming to this hospital. No, I thought as I nipped round the bed, clicked the castors straight, moved the chair on to the foot of the next bed, and began to strip it with Erith, I could hardly blame Jake Waring for being slightly impatient with my daft behaviour, and I was not at all surprised that he found no time in which to lead a gay life. Tradition might bar us first-year nurses from joining in the social side of the hospital; solid hard work must bar the senior residents. Yet he must relax some time; every one had to do that or crack. I thought of his thin, intelligent face, his cool grey eyes; he certainly did not look like a man about to crack or a man who needed to relax. He looked as if he was doing what he wanted to do with his life—and did not suffer fools gladly. I closed my eyes involuntarily and clutched the blankets I was holding; why should the poor man suffer fools gladly?

"Standing!" Erith leaned over the bed and tugged at a corner of the blanket. "What are you doing? You can't fall asleep here! Wake up, girl! We've seven more beds to make and twelve minutes in which to make them! Get moving!"

"I'm so sorry!" I rushed back into action with too much zeal and knocked over the chairload of bedclothes. Bennings, who was taking temperatures at the next bed, leapt forward and caught the chair and the clothes before they touched the floor.

"Nurse Standing! When will you learn not to be so clumsy?" She straightened the chair and the clothes. "Really, you beat the proverbial bull in the china shop! Please try to be more careful in future."

Erith and the patient smiled at me sympathetically as I apologized to Bennings. When she returned to her temperature-taking the man said, "We all got to make mistakes, Nurse—that's what I say."

"But the trouble with you, Standing," said Erith softly, as we moved on to the next bed, "is that you never stop. Makes one wonder what you'll do next."

For once I did not have to wonder. I simply looked at Erith and knew the answer to her question and one it had never occurred to me to ask myself. And then I thought: I can't do that. I'm going to be working here for the next four years and, anyway, he's much too old.

"Standing!" Poor Erith was really annoyed. "You've tucked the quilt in as if it's a sheet. Pull it out quick—or it'll get creased. And mind that tooth-mug—oh!" But she was too late. My elbow had caught the edge of the tooth-mug on the locker and jerked the mug and its contents into the air. The pink disinfectant fell clear of the bed, luckily; the set of false teeth shot up over my head. My hand went up of its own accord, and I caught the teeth, which by some miracle were clamped together. The toothless owner beamed at me. "Nice bit of fielding that, Nurse," he remarked appreciatively; "you ought to have been a lad, seemly. Might have done something good in the cricket field."

I gave him his teeth, many apologies, and the promise to refill his tooth-mug for him directly I had finished making beds. I should have liked to talk cricket with him; having only brothers, I had grown fond of cricket in self-defence, but Erith's expression decided me against small talk. We finished the rest of the beds in a heavy silence. I was quite glad to be silent. I wanted to think out the extraordinary notion that had come into my head.

What in the world had made me suddenly decide that the next thing I was to do was to fall in love with Jake Waring? It was absolute rubbish. I hardly knew the man—and I had not liked what I had seen of him. So why? I broke two flower-vases and one clinical jar, but I still could not find an answer to that. Nor could I blame Bennings at all for what she said to me when I told her of my accidents. She was perfectly right. I had not been thinking what I was doing; it was extremely careless of me; I ought to be ashamed of myself —and I certainly would be when I got time to think about it. Just now I had to think about the S.S.O.; I had to work out why he had suddenly become so important to me. It was not as if he was the first thrill of my life. I had been mildly in and out of love with my brothers' friends half a dozen times; I had not taken them seriously, because none of them ever took me seriously. This was different, very different. It was strange and exciting and sad at the same time. I knocked over the dispensary basket as I came to that mixed conclusion; fortunately, the bottles were waiting to be refilled, and no one saw me; so I picked it up and replaced all the bottles quickly.

I was off duty that morning at ten, which was a good thing, as by the time I went back at one o'clock I hoped I should have my brain and my limbs under some sort of control. I strolled along to Matron's Office for the post, giving myself a sharp lecture every foot of the way. I found three letters for Josephine, two for myself. I recognized my mother's handwriting on one of them; the other was in unknown writing and unstamped. I turned it over, incuriously, slit the envelope with my scissors, and read it as I wandered back into the main corridor on my way to the Home.

It was from Bill Martin.

" The chaps and I," he wrote,

think it's time we broke with the glorious past and moved forward to a newer and fuller life. Why, we demand, should we not ask a first-year pro. to our dance? So how about it, Nurse Standing? Or can I be matey and call you Rose? Will you do me the honour of accompanying me to the Rugger Ball? Might be fun, and I should like it very much if you would. So will you come dance with me, and if you're good, who knows, you may even get asked to dance by old Jake himself! Only that'll have to be in a Paul Jones, seeing as he's what you might call a conservative character. I hope you decide to come.

Yours,<br>BILL MARTIN

I stopped in the middle of the corridor and read the letter twice. It was nice of him to ask me—but I was not going to accept. No point in deliberately flouting convention, unless you really cared about the convention; this one did not bother me at all. And the prospect of snatching a couple of minutes in a Paul Jones with Jake Waring did not attract me. That was not how I wanted to dance with him. Also, I was perfectly certain that if Jake Waring and I did come face to face in a Paul Jones he would suppress an obvious shudder, and step smartly to one side to avoid the degradation of having to dance with a junior pro.

As if to underline this thought, at that moment I looked up and saw a line of white coats walking towards me down the corridor. The S.S.O. walked in the centre; all the men walked with their heads bent, their shoulders hunched, and their hands in their trouser-pockets. They did not look up from the floor as they came towards me, and, although they may not have seen my face, they must certainly have seen my feet. Not one of them altered his pace or the direction in which he walked, and if I did not want to be mown down by the oncoming surgical firm I should have to make a quick leap to one side. I leapt accordingly. As they went by, still oblivious of my presence, I looked after them. My eyes rested on the S.S.O.'s silver-fair head. How in the world could I imagine myself so suddenly attracted to him? I might as well fall passionately in love with one of the many stone busts of long-dead physicians and surgeons who lined that corridor; they could scarcely be less responsive or more above my present lowly status than Jake Waring. And then I could not avoid thinking what heaven it would be if by some miracle I was suddenly transformed into a staff nurse, and the note in my hand had come from the S.S.O. and not Bill Martin. Then I recollected something my eldest brother, Hector, once said: " Never any good beating about the bush, Rose. It's always the wrong girl who's free when you want to make a date. And you'll find it's always the wrong chap who wants to date you. A dead bore—but yet another fact of life."

I walked back across the park to our Home and wished that Hector had not got his horrible habit of being right.

# 5

## *An Invitation refused*

I WENT straight to Josephine's room. The room was empty, the bed made, the dressing-table tidy, and Josephine obviously out. I was surprised; I knew she loved staying in bed until midday on her days off. I went next door to see Angela, who was also off for the day. " Angie, where's Josephine? "

She was enjoying a late breakfast in bed. " Hi, Rose! Come and have some tea, you poor, hard-working creature. Josephine? She's gone out on a date. Sit down" —she moved her feet to one side of her bed—" and take the weight off your two feet."

I sat down and took off my shoes. " Josephine out on a date? At this hour of the morning? Who ever with? And why didn't she even stop to collect her post? I've just brought it over with me."

She grinned. "Dearie, if you could have seen the speed at which our graceful Josephine threw herself into her clothes half an hour ago you wouldn't wonder. She was gone with the wind—aided and abetted by a natty line in Yank cars. I watched it all from my window."

I was so intrigued that I forgot my own affairs. " A Yank car? Angie, what are you talking about? "

She hopped out of bed, rinsed her tooth-glass, filled it with tea, handed it to me, and said, Well might I ask. " I was sleeping peacefully about an hour ago, when Josephine suddenly bursts into my room and says can I lend her my wedding hat? Naturally I ask who's getting married, and she says no one, but she wants to lay on the glamour because some wonderful man with a peculiar name like Gus has rung her to ask if she could fix to have to-day as a day off. All this at the crack of dawn, mark you, Rose! So———" she took a much-needed deep breath—"I did not ask any more questions, just chucked her my hat, and she vanished in a cloud of dust towards the Old Kent Road—plus Gus."

I rubbed my ankles. "Josephine? Our Josephine? Miss Nightingale Forbes herself? Angie, I can't believe it. She's just not the type."

"Not the type for what?"

"Gallivanting with the boys. Even if the boy is a wonderful man called Gus. She's so terribly serious about work— etiquette, doing the discreet thing at the discreet time— everything. It's just not like her."

Angela said reasonably, "She's got the day off, Rose. She's not a pro. to-day. She's Josephine Forbes, twenty-one and single. So why shouldn't she gallivant?"

"No reason at all when you put it like that." I drank some tea that tasted of tooth-paste. "It's only that I never thought of her as interested in anything but nursing."

She looked at me as she lit a cigarette. "Rose, you are green. You really must not go round taking people at their face value. It's a fatal mistake. Do you honestly believe that Josephine is only interested in nursing? You who are about her closest friend here? Don't you know why she came to Martin's?"

"Because she wanted to be a nurse?"

"Because she had broken off her engagement to some man —might be this Gus—and thought to bury herself in a hospital was the best solution. She's not the first girl to have taken up nursing—and made quite a success of it—for that reason. But Josephine's loaded with sex appeal; you've only got to look at her figure—and to look at the boys looking at her figure— to see that. Think how she walks—and that sway is natural. Also," she added firmly, "think of her face. She's a pretty girl. Pretty girls with glorious figures are seldom unaware of the fact, and seldom have one-track minds about careers. Why should they have when every time they look in a mirror they see a very pleasing obstacle to their turning into career girls staring back at them from the glass? If Josephine survives six months in Martin's unmarried, then all Martin's men must be queers. Ever heard of a queer playing rugger?"

"Hector says ballet's more in their line," I said absently, and spilt some tea over my apron. I mopped it with Angela's face flannel, my mind on Josephine. "I never thought about Josephine's looks. I know she's got a smashing figure, but it didn't strike me that she knew it. And I never knew about her engagement. Poor Josephine! She never mentioned it to me. I wonder why not?"

She said that if I would forgive her she didn't. "You're a nice kid, Rose; but you're still an absolute infant. You haven't yet discovered what time it is or that two and two make four. She probably never mentioned it to you because she realized it would be clean over your head. You've clearly got a natural talent for exams., Rose, and I shouldn't be surprised if you've got a natural talent for nursing; but, apart from that, you're quite crazy, and we like having you that way. You are our light relief, dearie; you cheer us when we get too serious and are always good for a laugh and a party if it's only illicit cocoa in tooth-mugs after lights out. Straight out of the Upper-Fourth-dormitory life!"

She smiled not unkindly. "You keep us young, Rose—but don't be hurt if we don't run to you with tales of our broken hearts, because broken hearts are not up your street. You haven't yet learnt that hearts can do anything but go *lub-dupp* and beat at a normal seventy-two per minute. And as for your being able to run a Lonely Hearts' Club and advise us on our love-life"—she lay back and laughed—"my dear Rose, have you heard of love away from the movies? I'll bet you haven't! And I'll bet that the day you fall in love, Rose, will be the day! That I must see! Because, what with your normal absent-mindedness, that day Martin's really will rock!"

I concentrated on my ruined apron. "I expect so." I held up my apron. "Think this is going to stain?"

She told me to take it off and soak it in hot water at once.

"That should shift it—I think. How's the ward, incidentally? Been having any more hunches?"

" Hunches! Huh! You can take that smile off your face, Angie! " And I told her why.

She stared at me. " It's not true! "

" It is," I replied soberly. " It certainly is. He was back in the theatre at three-thirty this morning."

" How's he doing? "

" ' As well as can be expected.' But Sir Henry was in to see him twice before I came off this morning—and, although I did not see him, Erith told me the S.S.O. was in and out non-stop."

She grimaced. " The night nurses must have had a picnic. And heaven help poor Waring. He's had a run of dawn ops. this week. I know that, because Toms, our staff nurse in Martha, is engaged to Waring's senior H.S. Man called Smith. Gervase Smith. Know him? "

" Short and fair, or tallish and reddish? I know one is Smith and the other Heller, but haven't yet sorted out which is which."

" Gervase Smith's got red hair, and he always assists the S.S.O., which is how I'm so up to date on the surgical side."

I soaked my apron in her hand-basin. " You aren't telling me your staff nurse chats with pros? "

" No. But she's a nice soul, for all that. I got it from our senior pro. Which reminds me, Rose, have you heard the latest from the grapevine? " And she went on to tell me about the S.S.O. buying tickets for the Rugger Ball.

I said I not only heard it—I was in on it. " A student called Bill Martin was having coffee with Josephine and me, when the S.S.O. came up and bought them." I broke off suddenly as inspiration dawned. " Josephine! of course! That explains it! "

Angela demanded to know what explained what. " You're not suggesting the S.S.O. is asking her? Come, come, Rose. She may walk with a wiggle, but even Helen of Troy could walk unnoticed in a first-year uniform. Unnoticed by the senior residents, that is. They "—she waved her hands expressively —" do not see us."

" You," I said meaningly, " are telling me. I've just escaped being trampled into the corridor by the surgical firm this very moment. If I hadn't got my back to the wall smartly I'd have been ground into the floor-boards. But I wasn't talking about the S.S.O.; I was talking about Bill—that student. I've been wondering why he suddenly bulldozed his way to our table —and now I come to think of it—I did sort of notice Josephine getting matey. Now I get it." Then I recollected the note I had just had. "No, I don't. I don't get it at all. Why doesn't he ask her? "

" Rose," she wailed, " will you please take a deep breath and start at the beginning again! What is all this about a student asking Josephine something? And since when have she and you been on coffee-drinking terms with bulldozing students? "

I sat down on her bed again. "Listen." I explained all that had happened. "And now I get this note." I gave it to her. " It's very civil, but obviously I can't go. Only, now I've seen the light I can't follow why he bothered to ask me. Why doesn't he just ask her? "

She read the note, then looked up. " There is the thought that maybe he doesn't want to ask her. He wants you."

At least I did not have to pretend to be obsessed with my apron over Bill Martin. I smiled at her. " Angie, remember me? Rose? As you've just so rightly said, I'm not that sort of girl. I've had dates—yes, scores of them, with my brothers' friends, who all wanted me to be a sister to them. I'm the kind of girl that gets taken to rugger matches or to swing the boom on a boat. That suits me. I like being a sister to my brothers and I like doing the sort of thing they like doing. I do far better on the back of a horse or in a small boat than when trying to behave like a little lady at home. My mother long ago said she had given up treating me as a daughter, and just lumped me in with the boys. So, even if I'm a bit adolescent about mending broken hearts and such, I do know quite a lot about young men like this Bill Martin."

I waved her down when I saw she was about to interrupt. " Hang on, Angie—I'll explain some more. It's this way. Ninety-nine per cent. of the boys' friends behave and talk exactly as Bill Martin does. I recognize his type at first sight. I've known dozens of Bill Martins, And, as far as any girl can

know how any man's mind works——All right! Laugh your
head off, but I do roughly know how his mind works—or, at
least, how it doesn't work! So just let me tell you, Angie, that
he hasn't asked me to this dance because I'm me, but because
he's got some other motive up his sleeve. I couldn't work out
what that was when I first read his invitation; I only reacted
instantly to the fact that it wasn't genuine. Oh, yes, the invitation's genuine enough—it's just that he doesn't want me to
go with him because of my lovely blonde hair. It's no good
trying to save your face now, Angie," I ended sternly. " I know
dead well I'm under-sexed. Can you imagine anyone asking
Josephine to be their sister? "

She stopped laughing with difficulty. "Am I being hoist
with my own petard! And there was I saying you took every
one at their face value! Really, Rose, you shake me as much
as Josephine has shaken you. This seems to be a shaking kind
of morning. But tell me something else. What happened with
the 1 per cent. who weren't like Bill Martin? "

" I used to fall in love with them—every time. But it was
never any good; they patted me on the head—until I grew
too tall—and told me to run away and play trains or dolls or
something." I helped myself to one of her cigarettes. " Then
they went off and got themselves engaged to my various girl-
friends. The plump ones." I stood up and looked at my shape
in her mirror. " You know, Angie—I think women are daft to
bother to slim. You noticed something? Ever seen a chubby
girl who wasn't engaged? And, as for fat women—they're
always married. Hector says that's because men like to feel
the difference when they feel a woman."

Angie said if I told her much more I'd shock her. " Rose, I
had no conception that you even knew the facts of life."

I hooted with laughter. " With three brothers? "

She picked up Bill's note again. " I suppose they do make a
difference. But if you hadn't told me all this I'd never have
believed it. It's your wide-eyed stare and lack of war-paint
that foxed me. All the same, I still don't see why you should
think this is a line! What's he got to have a line about? From
what you've just said I'd say this was exactly the sort of
maniacal suggestion he would make."

I read the note over her shoulder. " It's maniacal all right; but it's still a line. Of that I'm sure."

" Another hunch? "

I thought it over. I had not wasted any thought on Bill at all yet; now I considered him and his note. " Yes. Call it that."

" What are you going to do? Don't you want to go? "

" Not particularly. Even if we were allowed to."

She agreed that it would be unwise to accept. " The men can break with precedent and get away with it. We certainly can't. What are you going to say to him? "

I rinsed my tooth-mug, collected my wet apron, and picked up my cloak. " I'll tell him the truth. I'm growing wise at last. So wise that I'm going to get my last lecture written up before Sister Tutor has to chase me again. Have a nice day-off."

She called me back. " You've forgotten your shoes." As I pushed my feet into them she asked, " Don't you feel rather hard done by, not being able to accept? A ball's always fun —and you'd have a front seat at all the gossip. You'd see who the S.S.O.'s asked. That should be amusing."

" I doubt it," I replied casually. " It'll probably be Bennings in the end. I see quite enough of her on duty. I'd rather go to bed early."

When I got out into the corridor I discovered I was breathing carefully. This was going to be difficult, very difficult. This was the one time when the girls would have to do without their good laugh. I had never minded being laughed at before; but never before had I felt about any man as I now so suddenly and irrationally felt about Jake Waring. Josephine returned from her day-off looking radiant. I was in bed when she came in and switched on the light in my room. " Hallo, Rose! How's Francis? " Then, without waiting for an answer, she hastened to tell me she had had the most glorious day. " Rose, I'm too happy to talk about it, but I'll tell you everything some other time. Now I'd better go and make up a clean cap. See you in the morning."

For once I did not feel like talking either. " You do that. So glad you had a good day. Give me a shout if you don't hear me getting up after the bell."

She promised to bang on the wall and added that she didn't

think she would sleep a wink. She went out humming to herself.

I was pleased she had had a happy day; we had not had a happy afternoon in Francis, and to-morrow looked like being equally hectic. Roberts' condition was quite satisfactory, but we had had another heavy operation list that afternoon; Erith had spent four hours in the theatre, and Bennings had been tireless in her work and her lectures to myself. The only good thing about that long afternoon and evening had been that the pressure of work had entirely prevented me from having any private thoughts. Now that I had time to think I was far too sleepy. I seemed only to close my eyes and then I heard Josephine thumping on the wall that divided her room from mine. " Rose, the first breakfast bell's gone! Are you up? "

I told Josephine about Roberts as I gulped my breakfast. I was half-way through when Night Sister rose to say grace. We jumped up, swallowed what we could surreptitiously as we stood with bent heads behind our chairs; then, still chewing, we raced off towards Francis. " MacGill," I continued breathlessly, " says she often has hunches. She says you can't always go by the book."

She blinked and managed to look dreamy with her mouth full. " I take it all back, Rose. I thought I could run my private life according to the book too. It seems I can't; and I can't tell you how wonderful it is to find I'm wrong."

" All well between you and Gus? "

" His name's Guthrie! I suppose Angie told you? Yes, all's superbly well—but here we are back in dear old Francis, and I mustn't start thinking of Guthrie or I'll take to dropping things, like you. I say! " She gazed at me. " I suppose you aren't in love, Rose? Is that what ails you? "

I hung up my cape. " But of course! How did you guess? " I beamed like the Cheshire Cat. " Taking to having hunches too? "

She smiled back. " Rose, you're bats! "

I had no opportunity to reply to Bill's invitation that day; next afternoon in my off-duty I wrote a brief—and, I hoped, civil—reply thanking him for his invitation but saying that I did not consider myself sufficiently strong-minded to face the break with tradition, much as I loved dancing. And if he wants Josephine now, I added mentally, he can try asking her. He's too late, but I doubt that that will worry him. Probably competition'll spur him on. Then I got to wondering if that was not one of the fundamental differences between the male and female angle on such affairs. If a man belonged to some one else, I automatically lost interest in him; but I had frequently heard my brothers saying that so long as the bar was not an actual wedding-ring the presence of another man in the picture only added spice to the situation. Or was that simply the attitude of mind of the very young male? Possibly, I decided, licking the envelope. Well, Bill Martin was very young, a mental eleven—if you were being kind—was the conclusion I reached.

I left the note in the porters' lodge on my way back on duty just before five. The lodge stood at the entrance to Casualty Hall; the Hall was a short-cut to all the wards and officially not allowed to be used as such. Unofficially it was used as such constantly. I looked round for a dark blue dress. Sister Casualty was not in sight. I did not know anything about her or had even set eyes on her, but I had been long enough in the hospital to retire at once at the sight of a dark-blue dress. The Hall was sprinkled with patients and a staff nurse was standing in the doorway of one of the dressing-rooms, looking away from me. I crossed the Hall quickly, turned right by the Eye Department, and was half-way down the little corridor that joined Eyes with the main corridor when I met Angela.

She said she was in a frantic hurry to get some wet plates from X-ray. Her hurry did not prevent her stopping to chat with me. "Rose, have you seen that poster?" She gestured towards Eyes. "There's another in the main corridor. I've just been admiring it. It's a smashing poster—makes the Ball sound fascinating. Aren't you wishing you had the nerve to go? They've booked a splendid band."

I said I had not noticed the poster and was not going to change my mind. "I'll come back with you and have a look at it. It's only ten to five—so I've got the time."

We walked back through the Eyes corridor and stopped at

the poster. It was very attractive. Angela murmured something I did not catch as we stood admiring it. I guessed she was repeating herself. When Angela had a point to make she had a habit of doing that. " It does look fun," I agreed, " and if I wasn't a first-year I'd leap at the invite. I adore dances, but I don't want to break any more unwritten laws. I've done quite enough breaking already without going out of my way to do it with my eyes open. And what in the world," I added intentionally, " do I care whom the S.S.O. takes! The man couldn't interest me less."

She did not answer, so I glanced round. Then I saw she was not there. I turned right round, wondering what had happened to her. She was standing about ten feet away, looking very pink in the face and listening to Sister Martha, who was looking very displeased. Angela was pink-faced; I think my own must have changed to scarlet as I saw who was standing directly behind me reading the poster over my head.

As I could not ignore him . . . I said rather nervously, " Good evening, Mr Waring," and then wished my mother's training in good manners had not sunk so deeply under my thick skin. Good manners as ordained in the outside world do not apply in a hospital. This was no case of a lady recognizing a gentleman but of a sub-human junior daring to address one of the two most senior residents in the hospital. By the expression on the S.S.O.'s face it was clear that he had not forgotten that we were standing in Martin's.

"Evening, Nurse Standing." He withdrew his gaze from the poster momentarily, then studied it again without another word.

I hesitated. He must obviously have overheard the words I had thought I was saying to Angela. I wondered if I ought to apologize. I looked up at him and decided against it. Only make matters worse. I walked away and back to Francis as quickly as if Bennings were on my track.

Bennings certainly spent most of that evening on my track, but her scolding rolled over my head. I had too many other things on my mind to bother with her. Roberts cheered me a lot that evening. He was now free of his enclosing curtains and well enough to tell me how he felt. " Proper poorly I've been, Nurse Standing, an' no mistake. But that Mr Warin's done another good job on me, I reckon. He says as I'll be a new man once I get rid of this new packet and won't have no more trouble not ever. And you know, Nurse, I feel that in meself, I do. Sort of stronger, even though I'm what you might call weak as a kitten still."

I had just finished my evening tidying in the sluice when Bennings returned from her supper and came to inspect my work. "Nurse Standing, those bowls are still dirty! Wash them again at once." She ran her fingers along the top shelf. Her fingers remained clean, but she said the paintwork was stained. "You must get it and keep it white." Then she walked over to the sink. "If you allow your draining-board to get as wet as this the bottoms of your detergent packets will get soggy "— she picked up one vast packet to prove her point—"and give—— "

But she did not have to say any more, as what she was about to forecast happened. The sluice was deluged in white powder.

I was holding an armful of stacked enamel washing-bowls. I said apologetically, "I'm awfully sorry, Nurse—it's all over your feet and legs. I'll just get a cloth and then I'll mop the rest." I dumped the washing-bowls on the draining-board; I was not looking at the bowls but at the mess, so I did not dump them carefully. They promptly rocked, then over-balanced into the sink. The sink was full of hot water, which naturally overflowed to the floor. The water and the detergent powder mixed as magnificently as on the pictures on the packets, and in a couple of seconds the sluice floor and Ben-nings' feet were hidden in a bubble bath. I stood stock still, uncertain whether to laugh or cry. Bennings, not surprisingly, was furious. She was also practically speechless. She only gasped, "Nurse Standing! Really! " And with a flick of her apron skirts swept herself and a large number of bubbles from the sluice.

I leant against the sink and began to laugh weakly. Then I took a string-cloth, the floor-mop, and a bucket, and cleared up the mess. I had just finished when Sister Francis returned from her own supper. She glanced in at the open doorway, then stopped. "That does look very nice and clean, Nurse Standing," she said with an approving smile. "I am glad to see you take such pains with your sluice, but you have no need to wash the floor. The floors are not your work. But I have to admit a newly washed floor does finish off your cleaning very nicely."

I told the girls about it at supper. "Just imagine, I was doing the right thing at the right time! You can't imagine how this has helped my morale! None of you are going to know me in future. I'm going to turn over a new leaf. I'm going to listen with both ears, keep my eyes open, walk quietly, say nothing. Discretion will be my middle name. After another four weeks in Francis even Bennings will be eating out of my hand!"

Angela said, "But you aren't going to have Bennings for another four weeks. The change-list has just gone up outside Matron's Office. Sister Martha told us; so I tore down before coming to supper. You're leaving Francis at the end of this week, Rose."

I knew they expected me to be delighted, so I beamed. "Goody!" I thumped the table. "I'll hate leaving the men, but, apart from that, it's the best news I've had in years. Where am I going? Not that it matters. Anywhere will be a sinecure after Bennings."

Home Sister called sternly down the table. "Less noise, Nurse Standing—if you please. And unless, perhaps, you wish us all to join in your conversation it might be advisable to lower your voice."

I said, "Yes, Sister. I'm sorry, Sister."

"A new leaf," murmured Angela, "isn't that what you said, Rose? Quiet, discreet, tactful. That's you, dearie."

Bill Martin rang me at the Home that night. "What's all this about having cold feet?"

"Sorry," I said, "but that's what I've got. I'm no pioneer; not even an instinct for a revolution—and I do like a quiet life."

He laughed. "You do, eh? Well, not to worry, love. Uncle understands. And if you look like having a quiet life let me know. I'd like to be in on it."

" I'll do that." I thanked him again for asking me. " I hope it's a good party."

" It'll be that all right. Too bad you're going to miss it. Some other time perhaps. See you around in Francis, Rose."

" Not much longer you won't. I'm moving to Casualty at the end of the week."

He whistled down the receiver. " Are you, indeed! There's a thing, now."

" Why? Something unusual about a first-year in Casualty? "

" How you do harp on about your first year, love! "

" Difficult not to. It gets dinned into us all the time."

He laughed again. " You take Uncle's tip and don't take it too seriously. Never take anything too seriously—although I doubt that I have to tell you that. You aren't the serious character some of your colleagues become."

I made a face at the receiver. So much for taking people at their face value. I promised Bill not to become serious.

" That's the form, Rose. Cheers for now. See you around Cas., then. That should be interesting."

" Why? "

" Cas. is an interesting place," was all he said as he rang off.

# 6

## A Pro.'s Eye-view of Midwifery

I N the middle of the next morning Erith was sent off-duty
with a suspected attack of appendicitis. Sister Francis had
to rearrange the pros. off-duty, and I found myself with another free 2 to 5 P.M. I went for a walk in the nearest park,
fed the ducks, and thought about leaving my nice men in
Francis. I did not think about Jake Waring. I did not think
about him on purpose. I was now getting very good at
lecturing myself *à la Bennings* about having ideas above my
station. I gave myself a really high-powered talk on thinking
only of my job, Casualty, the future, and not reaching for the
moon or believing in fairy-stories. Cinderella was a good story,
but she did at least have one chance to meet her prince on
equal terms; it needed no imagination to realize how impossible that was ever going to be for me. It would be roughly
three years before I approached the strata of nurses in training who mixed socially with even the registrars; the S.S.O.'s
appointment lasts two years. I did not know how long Jake
had been S.S.O.; I only knew it would never be long enough.

When I returned to Francis, Josephine was looking harassed and weary. "Rose, it's been ghastly. Every one has
been on the warpath! The S.S.O. has shot between us and
the theatre like a jet; Sister's spent half the afternoon
in Matron's Office; and that poor wretched Bennings—hell
though she had been—has carried the ward, Sir Henry's
round, chaperoned for Dr Gretton, who would choose to-day
to look at Simmond's heart, done all Erith's work, and organized the theatre men! She has blown me through the roof a
couple of times for form's sake, but, Rose—can that girl work!
She staggers me! No wonder she got a gold medal."

I reached the same conclusion for the hundredth time myself before another hour had passed. At six I came to a far more novel and surprising conclusion. I discovered Bennings was human.

She glided into the clinical room, where I was stacking the flower-vases for the night. "Nurse Standing, those flowers," she pointed to a vase on the floor, " are dead."

I apologized and said I would throw them out instantly.

" Not to-night," she replied calmly; "there's no time. Have you got a cold? "

I stared at her. " No, Nurse."

" Sore throat? Sore finger? "

" No, Nurse."

" And what, apart from your routine, haven't you done? "

I thought a moment. "Seven's back, Eleven's dressing, Fourteen's poultice, Thirty-four's mouth, and the extra fluids."

She nodded. " Right. I'll do them. And the drinks. Elsie can cope with suppers alone for once, then Sister and I will do the routine between us. Sister wants you to go to Mary now."

" To—Mary, Nurse? To-night? "

" Yes. For the evening. They are having a crisis and must borrow a pro."

I thought, And what are we having here? My expression must have shown my thoughts, because Bennings laughed— she actually laughed—not at me, but with me. " In Mary, Standing, a crisis is a crisis. We may be hectic here, but no general ward can touch Mary when it comes to a real crisis, and they simply have to have an extra pair of hands to-night. We are the one ward with a Sister and Staff Nurse both on duty this evening, so we can lend a pro. most easily. Take your cloak and go there now; then when you finish don't come back here to report—go straight to supper and then Chapel. All right? "

I said, " Yes, Nurse."

She seemed very amused about something. "Sister and I can manage the pros.' routine, Standing," she said drily. " We —er—were once pros. ourselves, although I doubt if you'll believe me when I say that." She disappeared then, leaving me to collect my cape, scurry off to Mary, and think what a pity it was that poor Sister Francis could not be struck down with something too, as then obviously Bennings would soften into a truly pleasant person.

The maternity block lay at the opposite end of the hospital. I took a short-cut across the park and walked as quickly as I could, but I was not quick enough for Sister Mary. She stood, a short, well-corseted, red-faced woman, waiting impatiently for me in Mary corridor. "Are you the junior from Francis Adams, Nurse?" she demanded as soon as I appeared at the head of the stairs.

"Yes, Sister." I pulled off my cape. "I'm Nurse Standing."

She told me to bustle to, immediately. "I haven't got all evening to waste here in the corridor. Come with me." She marched into the kitchen and thrust a diet-sheet into my hand. "First I want you to see to the suppers. My mothers are sensible and co-operative women; they can all eat what they choose; that list is to help you get your numbers straight. I have no time to take you round, so you'll have to find out for yourself who is who. If you want anything I'll be in the large nursery"—she opened the kitchen door and pointed out a door—"that door there. Remember, you must not enter either nursery without a mask. Now, to return to the suppers, you will need"—she had closed the kitchen door and now opened the 'fridge' door—"milk." She took out a vast jug, closed the 'fridge,' and opened a cupboard. "Here you will find cocoa, meat extract, tea. Do the food first—Kate, my ward-maid, will be up with it directly; then take round the drinks. When you have done that come into the nursery and help me with the babies. It is all quite straightforward routine. Do you understand what you have to do?"

I said a little breathlessly, "Yes, Sister."

She looked at her watch. "You have fifteen minutes to get suppers and drinks round—and here is Kate! Look sharp, Nurse Standing!"

Kate pushed the electric food-trolley into the ward, and we certainly looked sharp. I had thought the speed at which we worked in Francis Adams could not be improved upon. I discovered I was wrong. The rate at which Kate and I served those suppers made my pace in Francis seem like slow-motion. Kate was a tower of strength and far better-humoured than Elsie. The women were helpful and considerate. " You new, dear? " they asked, as I handed round plate after plate. "There now. It must make ever such a nice change for you to come up here after working in the busy wards with all the sick people. Mary's ever such a restful ward, what with no one being what you could call properly ill."

I had no breath to spare for conversation; so I grinned at each in turn to show I agreed that I was having a pleasantly restful evening, and rushed on with my plates. Every few minutes Sister Mary's head popped like a masked Jack-in-the-box round the nursery door. " Not done yet, Nurse Standing? Get on, child! You haven't all evening to dawdle round with those hot milks! My babies are getting impatient."

When I had delivered the last cup of hot milk Kate told me to leave the clearing up to her. " Sister'll create if you aren't along in the nursery soon—and don't forget your mask! "

" Thanks, Kate, for everything," I said gratefully. I took a mask from the ward jar, tied it round my face, and knocked at the door of the large nursery. Sister bellowed from within. " Come in, child. Don't bother to knock. My babies aren't fussy about such formalities."

I went in and closed the nursery door behind me. Then I had to stand quite still, momentarily transfixed by the sight of all those babies—and the noise. There were only thirty babies in that nursery, but they looked to be more like three hundred, and every baby was lying on his or her back, flaying the air with furious little white woollen-clad limbs, and demanding food at the top of his or her infantile but extremely powerful lungs.

Sister Mary roared above the uproar. "Don't stand and stare, child! Get on! Here." She offered me a baby. " Take this little fellow to Mrs Hilden, No. 23." But before she let go of the baby she inquired briskly. " I suppose you've held a young baby before? "

"Yes, Sister. One of my cousins had twins last year. She lives near us at home, and I've seen quite a lot of her babies."

" That's a mercy," she said frankly " This boy is quite an old man; it's his tenth day." She touched his head gently. "But I am relieved that your experience of babies is not solely based on your training with Janet. Take him to his mother."

Master Hilden felt soft and he smelt sweet. I held him against my right shoulder; his ear was close to my mouth. "You're much nicer to hold than Janet, duckie," I murmured, as I took him to his mother, "and I must say I like a lad to have three chins."

Having delivered him to Mrs Hilden, I returned to Sister. She said she would finish changing the babies, and wanted me to take the others round. "Begin with that line of cots on the left. Their cots are marked, and they have their name-tapes tied round their right wrists, so you cannot make a mistake. Go into the ward, call out the names, and the mothers will direct you."

I did as she said, and the mothers told me where to go. "Who you got there, dear? Young Sims? Mrs Sims—she's No. 12."

"Baby Black? Over to 15, Nurse."

"Gillings? That's mine, Nurse, dear. That's my Mabel!"

"You got my Charlie this time, love. I can see by the colour of his hair above the shawl. Bring him over to Mum. Hallo, lovey! And how's my boy to-night?"

Sister Mary came in, a baby tucked under each arm. "Here you are, ladies. They're all yours." She walked round the ward, supervising the mothers, babies, and myself. When all the infants were distributed she told me to go back to the nursery. "Make the cots up with fresh sheets as you were taught by Sister P.T.S. The linen is waiting on the radiators." After a few minutes she came into the nursery to see how I was managing. "Hand me that pile of clean sheets, child, and I'll do this side." As she stripped the small cots she asked after Francis. "I understand your ward is quite busy to-night? It was good of Sister to spare you under those circumstances. Of course, Sister Francis," she went on as she tucked under the clean sheets at double the speed I was tucking, "was once one of my staff midwives. She appreciates the fact that I never ask for help unless driven to do so. I had to have help this evening. All my pupil-midwives are held up in the Labour

Wards this evening. We expect six new babies to-night."

"Six? To-night, Sister?"

"Get on, child," she replied mechanically, but her eyes smiled at me. "Yes. Six. Possibly seven. We've had one woman in as an emergency, and there is some question of her carrying twins, but we are not certain yet. My pupils are all very thrilled, and so is the mother; so we can but hope they will be twins. Now"—she straightened her back and rubbed it as if it ached—"take all that soiled linen to the laundry shute, then wash your hands, and start re-collecting the babies. I'll show you how to tuck them down for the night." She looked at the nursery clock. "I may get called away. If I do when all the babies are in go back to the ward and settle the mothers. They like to have a little sleep before the ten-o'clock feed."

She was tucking down the last baby when a pupil-midwife came into the nursery. "Sister, please? Nurse Ellis says could you come?"

The nursery was wonderfully quiet when she had gone. Most of the babies were already asleep; the few awake made soft, contented little chewing noises; no one cried. There was an air of peace in the nursery, and it smelt of baby-powder and clean linen and the faint, sweet scent of clean babies. I walked round all the cots to see if they were all all right, and wondered if any corner of Martin's to-night was as pleasant as this silent nursery. I stopped by one cot, leant down, and touched the sleeping baby's petal-soft cheek with one finger. The baby did not stir; he slept on with one hand that had escaped his shawl pressed against his cheek like a fat little starfish. The baby had flaming red hair, and I recognized him as Charlie. As I looked at him I thought of the expression on his mother's face when she had taken him from me; and then I remembered how all those other women had looked—they had looked as if some one had switched on a light inside them.

I knew I ought to get back to the ward and the routine, but I stayed where I was a couple of minutes. Then the door opened slowly, and Kate peered cautiously round. "You in there, Nurse? I don't want to push you, dear; but you did ought to be getting on with the final drinks. Sister Mary won't half create if you don't carry on with your routine."

I stifled a sigh. "Thanks, Kate. I'm coming." I took a last look round the nursery, then followed her departing head reluctantly. Some one was always only too ready to create to me if I didn't get on with my routine. But perhaps that was not such a bad thing. Routine has to be done—and in doing it you do not have time to think. I had been so busy in Mary that not only had I been unable to think—I had not even had time to make a mistake.

The thought made me smile. I was still smiling when I joined Kate in the kitchen, and she asked what the joke was. "Or are you just happy in your work, Nurse?"

I set a tray with cups. "Expect that's it, Kate."

She opened a fresh quart-bottle of milk. "From Francis, aren't you, dear?" I nodded and she smiled. "I mind about you, dear! You must be Nurse Standing."

"Kate," I protested, "don't believe a word of it."

Her smile widened. "Elsie told me of you, dear. 'Talk about clumsy,' says Elsie, 'I tell you, Kate, you've not seen the like! That Nurse Standing, she'll break a pile of plates as soon as look at 'em! And our Staff Nurse—she tells her off all day! But it don't worry young Nurse Standing.'" Kate shook her head over the milk saucepan. "I mind that Staff Nurse Bennings when she was a pupil-midwife up here. A proper little madam, she was! But it's easy to see she don't put you out, dear. You just take things as they come. And that's the way to get on in a hospital. Just do your work and don't take too much notice of them as tells you off. It don't do to fret and wear a long face. Because what I says is, why worry? It may never happen."

I said, "You're right there, Kate," and set another tray. I wondered casually what her reaction would be if I told her that what was secretly worrying me was the thought that something I wanted was never going to happen.

The Rugger Club Ball was held two weeks after that evening in Mary. I moved to Casualty during the first of those two weeks and promptly became so engrossed in that department that the ball, Bill's invitation, Francis Adams, and even Bennings slipped from memory. The only person I could not have forgotten was Jake Waring, even had I wanted to forget him. He was constantly in Casualty, as he had personally to see every surgical patient admitted to the hospital; his opposite number, Dr Spence, the Senior Medical Officer, saw all the medical admissions, and the two men, of necessity, haunted Casualty Hall.

Sister Casualty was on holiday during my first few days; the Senior Staff Nurse, Nurse Davis, ran the department in her absence. As Casualty at Martin's was so large, two staff nurses worked there on day-duty and not only one, as in the wards. Nurse Davis was a tall young woman, who looked amiable and wore a sister's belt. None of my set had yet worked in Cas., and Nurse Davis was an unknown quantity; so the girls advised me to walk warily with nurses wearing sisters' belts. "And call her Sister, Rose," added Angela; "it'll pay. Can't go wrong if you use a little tact."

With this advice in mind, I said, "Good morning, Sister," when I first reported to Nurse Davis for duty.

"Goodness me, Nurse!" Nurse Davis blinked through her spectacles. "You must not call me that. Sister Casualty is the only sister in this department. I am Nurse Davis, and this "— she nodded at her colleague—"is Nurse Blake."

I sighed inwardly and apologized aloud.

Nurse Davis remarked pleasantly that I must be Nurse Standing. Then she noticed my white belt. "Oh, no!" She exchanged glances with Nurse Blake. "You aren't as junior as all that! You are surely not the P.T.S. set?"

"P.T.S. but one, Nurse. I've come from Francis Adams."

She said that Sister Casualty had mentioned before going on holiday that a new pro. was coming from Francis Adams. "But I understood from Sister that it would be a second-year."

"Perhaps Matron is short of second-years now Nurse Erith is warded," I suggested, then wished I had kept quiet, remembering how much Bennings had disliked any suggestions from juniors. And Bennings did not even wear a sister's belt.

Nurse Davis only smiled. She had a charming smile. "It may well be that. And I believe the second-year exams. come up again shortly. I suppose Matron did not want to move anyone else from a ward at this juncture. Well!" She looked again at Nurse Blake, then back to me. "I hope you will be able to manage the work here, Nurse Standing. We do not have much time to spare for teaching, which is why Sister Casualty prefers not to have very junior nurses in her department. So you will just have to do your best to pick up the work as quickly as you can, and we will all do our best to help you. But I am afraid Sister Casualty is not going to be very happy about the situation. Still"—she gave me another of her attractive smiles—"I expect you will manage quite nicely."

"I hope so, Nurse. Thank you." And most sincerely did I hope I would be able to manage, too; but I also felt very gloomy at the prospect of my immediate future.

As the day progressed I grew even gloomier. It was Monday; Casualty Hall was full most of the day. The crowd terrified me, but Nurse Astor, the Casualty Senior, who was in her third year and had been detailed to show me my work for this one day, surveyed the packed Hall coolly. "Slack for a Monday," she murmured. "I wonder why. It isn't Bank Holiday or anything, is it?"

I said I did not believe there were any Bank Holidays in November.

"Most extraordinary." She gazed round and appeared really hurt that London could muster no more than a couple of thousand patients for our Casualty on a Monday morning. "Perhaps," she brightened, "we'll get busy as the day goes on. I hope so. I do so dislike being slack."

I said I disliked being slack too, then saved my breath, as I needed it to keep up with the swift canter at which she was showing me round the place.

Casualty had thirty dressing-rooms. Nurse Astor ran through them verbally. "They are all divided into main groups: male; female; children. Then split into the different firms: medical; surgical; gynæcological; orthopædic; and so on. Then subdivided again: acute medical; chronic medical; straight acute surgical; dirty surgical; old wounds; etc., etc. You haven't a hope," she added reassuringly, "of taking all this in to-day;

but don't let that upset you. No one remembers what's what and who goes where at first; but you get it straight in time. In any case, delegating the patients doesn't ever concern you. Sister Cas. or one of the S.N.'s is always on duty in the hall to direct the patients as they come in. The only problems about the rooms you may meet at your present stage are Doctors' Letters, and they are a law unto themselves. So, whatever you do, Standing, don't make a mistake over a Doctor's Letter, or all hell is let loose."

I had no notion of what she meant, but promised to be very careful with Doctors' Letters. Did I have to deliver the medical staff's mail or something, I wondered.

"Until six o'clock," she went on, "all Doctors' Letters are seen by the S.S.O., the S.M.O., or their registrars. No one else. Got that?" I nodded dumbly. "Remember—never a C.O."

I had to stop her. I was now utterly lost in all these letters. "What are—or rather is—a C.O., Nurse?"

She smiled. "Sorry. I forgot how junior you are. As you were. The C.O.'s are what the housemen are called when they work down here. Casualty Officers. But the S.C.O.—the Senior Casualty Officer—isn't a houseman at all. He's a senior registrar, and up in the senior-resident bracket. Now, the C.O.'s see the people who wander in here from the streets—and most of our patients do that. In this part of London people use Martin's as their G.P. They've done it for centuries and no newfangled Health Service machinery is going to make them change their habit. They don't call in a family doctor if the old man or the kids feel queer; they just potter into Cas., sit down on one of the benches, and leave it to us. It's rather a nice habit, we think, and it makes Cas. a very homely spot. They know us; we know them." She looked round the Hall thoughtfully. "This place may be the size of Waterloo Station, but you'll be surprised at how matey it can be. You'll find you'll see the same faces over and over again, and very soon most of the patients will know you by name. And after a couple of months in Cas., whenever you set foot outside Martin's, you'll run into old patients who will shake you warmly by the hand and ask after the ' old 'orspital.' But don't forget —the exceptions to all this are the Doctors' Letters. So whenever a patient flaps an envelope at you and says, ' I got a letter from me doctor, Nurse,' take the patient and letter straight to Sister."

I asked how the patients evaded Sister in the first place.

" They get muddled—not surprisingly—because most G.P.'s will address their envelopes to ' The Out-Patients Department, St Martin's Hospital.' It applies to some hospitals; not this one. Our Out-Patients only take clinics, and we get all the new patients here in Cas. Every single patient coming into Martin's with anything from a cut finger to a bad road accident comes through Cas. Which can make it confusing when you are new, as we can be madly hectic. But the scheme really works pretty well, and Sister Cas. is a magnificent organizer." She led the way into a dressing-room. " We'll check the stock in here."

I watched what she did. " Has Sister Cas. been here a very long time? "

" She's been Sister here just over three years." She shut the drawer and opened another. " Pass me that basket over there." She refilled the second drawer with clean rolls of cotton wool. " That's done. Let's do the bottles." She crossed quickly to a china shelf on which stood a long row of lotion bottles, and held each up to the light to see how much fluid it contained. " Sister Cas. staffed here for four years under old Sister Cas., then took over when the old girl retired." She handed me two bottles. " Ether and flavine. We'll take them to the stock-room and refill 'em. I should have remembered to bring the stock ether and flavine with me, as those two we always need, but I haven't stocked and tested for quite a spell, and I forgot that point." She straightened the bottles on the shelf and returned to her former subject. " Sister Cas. is pretty young to be the sister of such an important department, but Matron's keen on young sisters. When they are as nice as Sister Cas. I'm with Matron every time. Sometimes I'm not so keen." She glanced over her shoulder. " Worked in Agatha? "

" Only Francis."

" Then you've got it coming to you! You've met Bennings— well, Sister Agatha is Bennings in a blue dress and frilly cap without Sister Francis to keep her slightly under control."

I could not worry about Sister Agatha and the possibilities of the future. The present in Casualty was more than enough for me. "But Sister Cas. is different?"

"Sister Cas. is a dear," she said warmly, "and an angel to work for, I think. Consequently, although I'm thrilled for her sake about the latest bit of news that's buzzing round Martin's, I can't help being sorry for future Cas. nurses. There'll never be another Sister Cas. like Margaret Mercer."

"Is Sister leaving, Nurse? Has she got a new job?"

She glanced at me. "You are junior! You aren't even in on the grapevine. Never mind, Standing. You'll hear it all in time. I can't go into it now, as we've finished our stocking and testing and it's time we reported to Davis."

'Stocking and testing' was the name given to the thrice-daily check and refilling and replacing of all the equipment used in the dressing-rooms. It became my official job, and in doing it I learnt which room was which in the shortest possible time. By my second evening in Cas., having visited every room six times, I had a very good idea of the geography of the place, and was able to talk quite intelligently about minor-sepsis, acute-surgical, or straight-medical rooms. I enjoyed sailing round the hall on my own, feeling like a hospital version of a cross between a cigarette girl and a milkmaid, on account of the large basket of clean dressings which was held against my middle by a strap going round my neck, and the large stock bottles of ether and acriflavine I carried in each hand. It did not take me more than a couple of rounds to discover that Astor was right; I saved yards of walking and many precious minutes of time by carrying those two lotions with me, since more ether and acriflavine was used in the dressing-rooms than any other liquid. I had little to do with the patients during that first week; when I was not stocking and testing I was running errands and taking messages all over the hospital for Nurse Davis. On the rare occasions when I was not needed as a stocker or errand boy Davis told me to stand by her in the hall and watch how she sorted out the non-stop stream of incoming and outgoing patients.

The place fascinated me; it was exciting and interesting, and I learnt more of the running of a large teaching hospital in one week in Casualty than I would have learned in a year in the wards. I also learnt a lot about the medical staff.

On my first evening Davis warned me, "You must know the name of every doctor on the staff, Nurse; and you must know what they look like. The patients often ask for, or about, a specific man, and you must know of whom they are talking. You must also keep a special eye on the S.M.O. and S.S.O. Those two men are in constant demand from the porters, as the wards ring down here whenever they want them. You can save every one a lot of time if you can say, 'Dr Spence is in Room 12,' or 'Mr Waring has just gone to Eyes.' And time is all-important down here. Tell me—where's Mr Waring?" She shot the last question at me.

I answered without thinking, "Just gone into fourteen, Nurse."

"Good girl." She nodded approvingly. "I saw him, but didn't think you had noticed him. Where's Dr Spence?"

I hesitated. "I think he's just gone by, Nurse—but I didn't notice where."

She said, "Of course, as you've only been on the surgical side you'll know the surgeons better than the physicians. But you must keep your eyes open. Dr Spence has gone to the lodge. Next time watch where he goes too."

"Yes, Nurse."

At the end of my first week I was enthusiastic about Casualty. "It's terrific," I told the girls over cocoa, "and the staff are much more matey than in a ward. I forget I'm a first-year frequently. Even the staff nurses break down and call me Standing, and not just Nurse."

Josephine had not heard from Gus and she was in a bad mood. "I'd much rather be called 'Nurse.' I detest being a surname."

Angela said that was not what I had meant. "No one seriously likes being called by their surname, but it's the thought behind that counts. I wish they'd send Bennings to Cas." She was now in Francis. "Might humanize her. I don't know how you girls survived her! How I wish I was back in Martha."

Josephine said tartly she preferred Francis, even with Bennings. "Martha's so quiet, and I can never get those ghastly, complicated medical diets right. I don't know what you'll do when you get to a women's medical ward, Rose. The silence is unnerving. Wouldn't suit you at all."

I was feeling happy that night. I had seen Jake in Cas. most of the evening, and just seeing him about at present made my day. And once he had said, "Thank you, Nurse Standing," when I handed him something. It had been a golden evening. I beamed at poor Josephine. "Then isn't it splendid that I'm in Cas.? There is so much noise going on in the Hall all day that if I dropped every tin tray in the place I doubt that anyone'd notice it. What with ambulances driving up to the door all day, stretchers being shoved about, plus wheelchairs, portable X-ray machines, students, patients, relatives, stray coppers, and heaven knows whatnot else, the place is about as quiet as—Angie's favourite rush-hour in Piccadilly. And I love it!"

Josephine said she wished Matron had sent her to Cas. "Anywhere but that morgue of a Martha."

Angela defended her beloved Martha. "It's a lovely ward, and it has to be quiet. Those women are ill; not fine, healthy surgical men."

Josephine refused to be impressed. "And that Dr Spence! He's such an insignificant little man. I never know if he's in the ward or not. He doesn't seem to bother about etiquette. He just drifts in at all hours and wanders round alone."

Angela laughed. "Poor little Dr Spence. He isn't insignificant! He's just unassuming and frightfully clever, Sister Martha said. I know he isn't a smashing type like Mr Waring, but on the law of averages you can't have an S.M.O. and an S.S.O. both looking like Greek gods."

Josephine said she disagreed. "Mr Waring isn't at all like a Greek god. He's got the wrong nose and too much jaw. I think he just looks like a statue—non-Greek. He never shows any feeling at all. Unless," she yawned, "he's looking at Rose."

I said nothing.

Angela took that up at once. "How does he look at Rose?"

Josephine said, "He frowns at Rose."

I still said nothing.

Angela was intrigued. " Why? Because you're always bashing into him with something, Rose? "

I shrugged. " Don't ask me. This is news to me too."

Josephine began to cheer up. " I thought you knew, Rose. I meant to tell you. I noticed it first that day I spilled your cocoa, and again in the canteen when you were nattering to Bill Martin. He looked quite peeved that morning. I suppose he thought you were behaving in an unseemly way again."

" I suppose so." I pretended to be bored with the subject. " By the way "—this was another line, as I was longing to ask this question—" have either of you gathered who it is he's taking to that dance? To-morrow, isn't it? "

They exploded into gales of laughter. When I could make myself heard I asked if I could share the joke.

" Dear Rose," spluttered Angela, " dear, dear Rose! You still haven't a clue! Here you are telling us how much you know about the hospital and all that's going on and, sink me, you haven't heard what's going on in your own backyard!"

" In my backyard? In Cas.? What's going on? "

" Angie means," explained Josephine, " that that dance is not to-morrow, but to-night. And your Sister Cas. has come back from her holiday one day early and set all Martin's alight with expectation. The reason why she's back—as every nurse in the place, bar you, has heard—is to go to the dance to-night. And three guesses—who do you think has asked her? "

" The S.S.O.? And it's to-night? I thought it was to-morrow."

They started laughing again. " Good old Rose," said Angela, " the bright girl of the set! On the ball every time! No flies on our Rose! Yes, dearie, Sister Cas. has a heavy date with Jake Waring, and we are all thrilled! Such a smack in the eye for Bennings! Sister Cas. has got every pro. in the place rooting for her! So listen, my pet—the next time you want to know anything about Cas. just come to Josephine and me. We'll tell you all." She stopped for breath. " That's a promise, Rose."

" Thanks, girls," I said, " that's big of you." I stood up and said I was going to make more cocoa. " Both want more? "

" Please." Angela smiled up at me. " And we'll toast Sister Cas. and drink damnation to Bennings. I haven't been so pleased since I don't know when."

I smiled back at her. " Nor me. It's splendid news." It was a relief to get out of the room and be able to stop smiling.

# 7

## *Casualty allows no Time for Tears*

I THOUGHT a lot about the dance that night—about Sister Casualty, whom I had never seen, whom Nurse Astor described as a dear; whom Nurse Davis said was not going to be happy about finding me in her department. If it was any consolation to Sister I was not at all happy about being found there. Then the absurdity of that thought struck me, and I smiled at the darkness in my room. What did a first-year matter to a sister? Having dealt with that, I had to consider the prospect of her dancing at this moment with Jake Waring. I wondered what she looked like, how long they had been friends, and why I had not taken a chance and accepted that invitation. Perhaps if he had seen me out of uniform—but that was no good, and I could not pretend that it was. In or out of uniform he simply did not see me, and the sooner I accepted that fact the better. I did manage to accept it, but in the accepting I found I grew more miserable that night than I could ever remember being before. If this was falling in love I could do without it. But I knew I could not do without it, and no amount of self-mockery about girlish passions and hopeless schoolgirl crushes could persuade me that what I felt was under my own control. It was not; and, as there was nothing I could do about it, I would have to put up with it —and hide it from the girls.

I was determined to show Sister Casualty that a first-year could make an efficient Cas. junior; so I took double care with my stocking and testing that morning. I also took double time. When I realized this I speeded up accordingly, congratulating myself as I did so on noticing a mistake before some one else pointed it out to me. My lectures to myself must be showing results. I felt very smug as I raced round the remaining rooms, and returned my empty basket and stock-bottles to the stock-room a few minutes before nine.

Astor was waiting for me. " Ready? Good. Sister's waiting for our first report."

I changed into a clean apron quickly. " Coming, Nurse."

Sister Casualty was a slight young woman with dark-brown hair which she wore in a neat bun low on her neck. Her hair-style was old-fashioned, but it suited her regular features and generally unruffled appearance. She told us she was pleased to be back from her holiday, gave each of us our morning's list of work, then turned to me.

" I do not, as a rule, care to have nurses as junior as yourself here, Nurse Standing, but Matron has told me that she is very short of second-year nurses and was consequently forced to draw on the first-year. Nurse Davis tells me you have settled down quite nicely." She glanced at Davis, who earned my undying love by nodding amicably as Sister continued. " So, apparently, it is all working out satisfactorily. Certainly, from your point of view, this experience received so early in your training will prove invaluable in the future." And she went on to explain, what I had already discovered, about the insight working in Casualty could give into the administration of a teaching hospital.

She was still speaking when a shirt-sleeved student knocked at the half-open door. " Frightfully sorry to interrupt, Sister; but I think there's been a little mistake somewhere." He held up a bottle marked " Ether." The bottle—like all our lotion bottles—was made of dark-green glass. " Of course, I could be wrong; but, as I've never come across yellow ether before, I thought I had better mention it." As he spoke a second youth appeared at his elbow.

" Excuse me, Sister—but are we using colourless flavine? And surely, even if we are, this isn't the proper strength? And why is it so volatile? And "—he offered his bottle—" why should it smell of ether? "

My heart lurched against my ribs, then felt as if it had stopped beating, as Sister took both bottles in silence, smelt them, held them up to the light, poured a little from each into the palm of her hand. "Who," she asked very quietly, "did the stocking and testing this morning?"

I said hollowly, "I did, Sister."

She handed me the bottles. "You realize what you have done, Nurse Standing?"

"Yes, Sister. I have put the flavine in the ether and the ether in the flavine."

She looked at me. "Which rooms are those bottles from?"

I read the labels on the bottles. "Nineteen and twenty-two, Sister."

"I see." She turned to the students. "I am very sorry; there has been a mistake. Will you go back to your rooms and apologize for me to the Casualty Officers? I will see you have the right bottles very shortly." She looked at me. "Get your stock-tray, Nurse Standing, and go and collect all the ether and flavine bottles in use and bring them to me. And you, Nurse Astor, will you go round and stock and test in every room and make sure that there have been no more of these disgracefully careless mistakes."

As we crossed the Hall to the stock-room Astor whispered, "Why on earth did you have to pick on this morning, Standing? You've done all right so far, but think of the first impression you've made on Sister. She doesn't often get cross, but she is now, and, honestly, I can't blame her."

I could not blame Sister either. I was red-faced with embarrassment and fury with myself. Whatever had made me think I could work quickly and well? It would have been better to be late and have done the job properly. And what would the C.O.'s and the students say?

They said a good deal, and none of it was complimentary.

In the first few rooms I visited, as there had been no mistake, they were reasonably polite. "I say, Nurse, you can't run off with my ether. It's the only bottle I've got and I need it—stat." Which in hospital jargon means "at once."

"Nurse—damn it—I'm using that flavine. Give a chap a chance. If you swipe the stuff I'll never get my dressings done."

Mercifully the medical rooms held neither ether nor flavine;

but the last few surgical rooms I visited were in a state of minor riot.

"What the devil have the dispensary dished up for ether? Think they've dropped a couple of egg-yolks in by mistake?"

"Look here, Nurse—this flavine's positively alcoholic! I can't use it. What am I supposed to do? Has some lunatic been having a practical joke?"

"Nurse, I've just ruined a set of needles. I poured out this stuff that's supposed to be ether and it's come out yellow. Some maniac's bunged in the wrong fluid by mistake. I thought Martin's nurses were meant to be efficient!"

I apologized to the patients, C.O.'s, dressers. "I am very sorry. It was my fault. I mixed the bottles. The new ones are just coming. I am very sorry to cause you all this delay."

I chanted this miserably in and out of the surgical rooms, and continued to chant it to the irate dressers who stopped me in the Hall. "Nurse, why have you swiped my ether? I've got to get half a dozen bits of strapping off. What am I supposed to use? My teeth?"

The waiting patients once again amazed me by their patience. "That's all right, duck. Don't take it to heart. We all make mistakes. Nurses are only human."

I doubted that anyone on the staff of St Martin's Hospital, London, would subscribe to that outrageous suggestion, but felt decidedly cheered by it and their consideration. With the protests and demands still following me, I returned to the duty-room with my basket loaded with bottles. When I reached that room had I not had the basket strapped round my neck I should probably have dropped the lot. The nurses had all gone, but Sister was not alone. She was talking to the S.S.O.

He looked round as I knocked. Sister said, "Bring them in, Nurse Standing, and I will check over them with you."

I hoped that meant Jake was on his way out, but he did not move. "Having a bottle muster, Sister?" he asked curiously.

Sister looked down her nose. "There has been a slight mishap. The ether and flavine have, unfortunately, become mixed."

"Ether and flavine? But—how? They are totally different in colour and smell."

"So," replied Sister icily, "one would have thought. I must tell you that I am very upset about this occurrence, Mr Waring. I do not like, and will not tolerate, carelessness in my department." She told me to put all the bottles on her table.

Jake lost interest in the bottles. He said he could see Sister was busy and had better be getting on.

"But you said you wanted to tell me about that man Gibbs," she reminded him.

"Gibbs, yes." He looked at his feet. "I think Gibbs is going to have to wait, Sister. I've just realized that it's after nine and I was supposed to make a phone call at nine sharp. With your permission, I'll go and make it and we'll go into Gibbs later." He smiled at her. "That suit you?"

"Very well, indeed," she returned his smile. "I shall be on all day." But before she could say any more Nurse Davis came to summon Sister to take a personal telephone call. Sister told me to wait for her. "I'll be back directly, Nurse."

I expected Jake to go with her to his own telephoning, but he lingered for a moment in the duty-room doorway looking out at the Hall. Then he turned back, walked to the table, and picked up one bottle. He uncorked it and sniffed the contents. "This one's all right." He put the bottle to one side. "Don't blacken things unnecessarily for yourself, Nurse. Why don't you sort them while you are waiting for Sister? It's always a good idea to get things organized, and—er—a little method is generally much appreciated in hospital."

I was too upset even to marvel at the wonder of his speaking to me. "Yes, yes, I'll do that."

He smiled; he really smiled at me and no one else. "Don't look so distressed, Nurse. I realize you have been lamentably careless, but—this has happened before."

"It has?"

His mouth twitched slightly. "Last time I believe it was the ether and gentian violet; it might have been the vermilion red. I'm a little hazy. But I do distinctly recollect a row of students with stained hands scrubbing themselves and complaining bitterly at the sinks." Then he seemed to remember he was the S.S.O., because he suddenly looked over the top of my head and told the wall that young nurses would try to work too quickly.

I said meekly, "Yes, Mr Waring," and when he walked out of the room I nearly hugged the row of bottles I had been hating passionately a couple of minutes before. I had expected him to be scathing, superior. His unmistakably kind words acted as a barrier between me and the world. I heard all Sister Casualty had to say to me—and she said a good deal—but it did not register at all. And when she had finished with me and sent me to wash all the bottles and return them to the dispensary I sailed across the Hall to my task, feeling that life had little more to offer.

It took me an hour to deal with the bottles and then a long time to remove the flavine stains from the stock-room sink. The yellow liquid had stained everything, including my clean apron. Astor came in to find me. "Standing, Sister wants you." She noticed my apron. "You can't go like that. Here." She pulled a clean one from her case. "Put that on, quick. It'll swamp you, but better be swamped and clean than look as if some one's been throwing eggs at you."

I changed aprons, tidied my hair, straightened my cap, and went into the Hall. Sister was standing by the closed door of one of the smaller dressing-rooms. "You've been a very long time washing those bottles, Nurse Standing." She glanced at my apron and frowned. "Why have you not altered the hem of that apron? It's three inches longer than your dress skirt."

I explained that it was not my apron.

"And why did you not bring a spare apron on duty, Nurse?"

I explained that also.

"I see. Well, Nurse Standing, I am very displeased with you. I want you to go"—and I thought wildly, she's going to send me to Matron, and closed my eyes.

"Nurse Standing!" she snapped. "Have you fallen asleep?"

I opened my eyes instantly. "Oh, no, Sister."

She said drily, she was glad to hear I was awake. "That was not the impression I received. In future will you please pay attention when I am speaking to you? Thank you. Now,

I want you to go into Room Four and apply a dry dressing to the neck of the small boy you will find in there with a policeman. Just a straightforward dry dressing and a bit of strapping; he has only grazed his neck, but do not minimize the importance of his wound to him. His name is Trevor Brown and he takes his health seriously." She smiled slightly. "So be tactful with him, and when you have dressed his neck the policeman is going to take him home."

Trevor Brown was six. He had black hair, a very dirty face, and he was in a very bad temper. "I told 'im," he jerked an irate thumb at the paternal young policeman, "as I didn't need 'im to 'ang around. But you know what them coppers are, Nurse—they will fuss a bloke."

The policeman said mildly, "I only want to take you back to your mum, Trevor. She may be worrying over you."

Trevor snorted. "Me mum won't worry. She knows I can take care of meself."

The policeman looked at me. "You weren't exactly taking care of yourself, son, when you got your head stuck in those railings on the bridge."

Trevor fingered his neck. "I'd 'ave got meself out if you'd let me be! I was just 'aving a look at them barges. I likes to see 'em lay their funnels down. Nurse, see—and then along 'e comes "—another thumb jerk—" an' wants to know what I'm a-doing of. What's 'e think I was a-doing of? 'Aving a look at them barges, see!"

I said I saw, and dressed his neck.

He was delighted with the strapping. "Expect I nearly broke me neck, eh, Nurse?" he asked with simple pride.

"You might have done, Trevor."

He said he reckoned as I mended broken necks daily. "You ever 'ad a bloke come in what's pulled 'is 'ead right off, Nurse?"

The policeman coughed faintly as I apologized for my lack of experience. "I haven't been nursing long, Trevor."

He assured me kindly that there was plenty of time. "I could tell you was new by your belt." He tapped it with a grubby forefinger. "They gives you a black belt when you've done a year, doesn't they?"

"They does—do." I smiled at him. "You seem to know a lot about this hospital."

"Cor, I do an' all. I been coming up to old Martin's since I were a nipper, see."

I said, "I see. That explains it."

The policeman looked meaningly at the door, then walked out of the room. I offered Trevor one of the children's papers from the small pile on the couch. "I've just got to go outside a moment, Trevor. Shan't be long."

He climbed on to the couch with an experienced air. "I know you got to see about me cards, Nurse. The Lady Almoner—she 'as 'em. You don't need to 'urry for me. I likes looking at these 'ere space pictures. Smashing pictures they 'as in this 'orspital."

Outside the door the policeman said he was sorry to bother me, but he wondered if the Sister had got the lad's home address from the Lady Almoner yet. "We ought to be getting on now he's done. I wouldn't have troubled you with the lad at all if I could have got his home address out of him, but he flatly refused to give it. He said he always came up to St Martin's by himself when he cut himself, and he wasn't having no cop messing with his cut neck. He wanted a real hospital, he said. So I had to bring him here to find out his address. The Sister said she knew the lad and would get it for me." He smiled apologetically. "I don't like worrying you here when you are so busy; but I did not want to take him in as lost when he wasn't doing any harm and isn't lost, as he says he knows his way home. I'd say he was capable of getting there, too; but you can't leave a little lad of six to wander round London with a cut neck. If you can find out if the Sister has that address yet, Nurse, I'll see him safely home. And I reckon his mum will have something to say to him, for all that he says she's not the worrying sort."

Sister had just received Trevor's address from the Out-Patient Almoner, and I met her on her way to give it to the policeman. When Trevor and escort had gone Sister sent me on a row of errands, then told me to help Nurse Davis in one of the female surgical rooms. I had been in there about an hour, when Sister beckoned to me from the door. She looked very grave. "Nurse, will you go quickly to the canteen and buy tea for two." She gave me some money. "Take the tray to Room Two. You will find a young couple waiting there— relatives. They are very distressed and shocked, and I expect may refuse the tea; but try to get them to drink it. Then stay with them until I return to them. I must go back to their child first, but I will be with them as soon as I am able. If they ask you about the child, simply say that you are very sorry but unable to answer, as you have only just been called to fetch them tea."

The canteen was crowded. I ignored the black looks I received from the queue at the counter and pushed my way to the head. "Please"—I flapped my money at the voluntary worker behind the tea-urn—" I'm from Casualty."

"From Sister Casualty——?" She leaned forward and listened to my message. "I'll get you a tray, Nurse. Wait there." She made a small pot of tea and set a tray, then handed it across to me. She refused to take any money. "Tell Sister we wouldn't think of charging for this, Nurse."

When I returned to Casualty Nurse Blake was directing traffic in the Hall. Sister was nowhere to be seen. I took the tray to Room 2, hoping to find her in there. But the young man and woman standing by the window in that room were alone. I explained that Sister had sent me. "Sister thought you might care for a cup of tea."

The woman turned to me. She was crying. "Nurse—how is she?"

Her husband put an arm round her shoulders. "Don't take on so, love," he said unhappily; "they'll tell us as soon as they know. The Sister promised."

I longed to be able to say something comforting and kind; but I did not know what to say, not only because I knew so little about the cause of their anxiety, but because I had never seen real grief before. Then I remembered that Sister had told me to do something for them, so I poured out some tea. "Do have a little. It's such a cold day. It will do you good. It really will."

The woman dried her eyes. "Ta, duck. Ta, ever so. But I don't think I can swallow anything. I couldn't touch it." Then as I held out a cup to her dumbly she took it from me. " All right—if you think it best—I'll try." Her hand shook and the cup rattled against the saucer, so I took the saucer and she cradled the cup in both hands, sipping the scalding hot tea between her words. " You see—I thought she was playing with the other kids. . . . I couldn't see them—mind—but I could hear them calling to each other outside my kitchen window all morning. She's always been so good—she's not a one to go off by herself, like. So I didn't think to see where she was when I went round the corner to the shops. I told me neighbour I was going and she said she'd keep an eye, like. I went off quite happy, never thinking she'd—— " the poor girl shuddered uncontrollably—" she'd gone near the river. But when I got back the police were there and they were asking for me—— " Her face crumpled and she began to cry again. The tears poured down her cheeks, and she made no effort to dry them.

I took the cup from her hands and suddenly her head was on my shoulder. I said, " There, there," because it seemed the only thing to say, and because that was what my mother had said when she comforted the boys and me as children. I wanted to weep with her, but I could not, as her husband was looking to me for support too. He said heavily, " I'm glad as you've come, Nurse. It helps the wife—having another woman here. The Sister said as she would send some one." He drank his tea absently. Then, " You see, Nurse—she can't swim. She's a clever little thing, but she's only little—and she can't swim. But—they got her out in time? They did," he insisted, " get her out in time? She is going to be all right "— his voice cracked—" isn't she? "

Sister had come in as he was speaking, but I noticed that she did not answer his question. She looked concerned and compassionate. " You've had some tea. I am so glad."

" Sister? " The mother raised her head and moved from me. " How is she? "

Sister put her arm round the mother's waist. " Sit down, my dear. Please sit down, both of you. I want to talk to you." But before she said more she told me to go to Room 12. " Nurse Davis may need you. I shall be in here for a while."

The door of Room 12 was open, but the interior of the room was hidden by the red screen placed across the door. It was the first occasion upon which I had seen one of those screens in Casualty. A red screen in our hospital stood for danger. I walked quietly round the screen, then stood quite still. None of the occupants of Room 12 heard me come in. I was glad of that. I needed that brief, private moment.

On the floor in the middle of the room was a stretcher. Grouped round the stretcher stood two ambulance men in shirt-sleeves, a policeman with his jacket slung over his shoulder, Dr Spence, and one of his housemen, both unrecognizable without their white coats, both with their shirt-sleeves rolled above their elbows, and with their stethoscopes dangling loosely round their necks. The houseman was breathing hard, as if he had been running. Nurse Davis stood beside him. They were all watching the man kneeling on the floor at their feet. The kneeling man swayed rhythmically forward and backward, as if he was rowing; as he moved he spread and closed the arms of what looked like a tiny white limp doll. A doll with a mop of wet flaxen hair.

Dr Spence bent down and raised one of the child's eyelids. " No good, Joe. Go back to the thoracic method. And you had best change over. You've done long enough." He pulled off his stethoscope and gave it to the houseman. " Hold that for me, Bryan. I'll take the next shift, then I had better go and see her parents." As he went down on his knees he glanced at Davis. " Where did Sister put them, Nurse? Room Two? Right you are."

I recognized the man he had called Joe as Dr Ross, the senior medical registrar. The S.M.O. said, " Ready, Joe? " And Dr Ross grunted to save breath. He was red with effort, and his forehead was damp. Dr Spence slipped his hands over the registrar's and for a few seconds they swayed together, then Dr Ross moved his hands away and sagged sideways and forward to get out of the way and recover his breath.

Nurse Davis noticed me and beckoned. " Is Sister staying with her parents? "

" Yes, Nurse." I could not take my eyes off that pathetic little figure. " Is she going to come round, Nurse? "

Dr Ross overheard me as he stood up. " I wish we could answer that, Nurse." He was looking at Davis. " How are her parents taking this? "

Davis turned to me. " You've just seen them, Standing. I haven't. How are they? "And all but Dr Spence looked my way.

I said, " They seem—very upset."

No one made any comment. They merely looked back at the child on the floor.

A few minutes later Dr Spence asked breathlessly, " What time is it, Nurse Davis? "

" Ten minutes to one, Doctor."

He sighed. " I promised the S.S.O. I'd look at a case of his in his room at a quarter to one. Could you send some one to explain I'm held up? I must see these parents first."

Davis told me to go across. " Then go back to the canteen and get tea and sandwiches for these men," she added quietly. " They've been at this for a long time and it's exhausting work."

" Yes, Nurse."

The S.S.O.'s room was across the hall. When I reached it I thought it was empty. Then Jake's voice called me from the small office at the far end of the room. " Did you want me, Nurse? "

" Yes, please." I went into his office and explained my message. He did not seem surprised to get it.

" I asked the chap to come back this afternoon when I heard about that child. How is she? Round yet? "

" Not yet." Then I had to get an answer from some one, so I asked, " Mr Waring, did Sister tell you about her? Is there any hope? "

He stood up, moved round the desk, and leant against it. " Yes, Sister did tell me. She also told me the infant is five. So she's got a five-year-old heart." He put his hands in his pockets, looked down at his feet, then up at my face again. " Sister said she was in the river for some time before anyone noticed she was missing. It's a—cold day. But I expect you've heard the history? "

" Not all. Her mother told me a little. She was too upset to say much."

He said, " I can believe that. Well, they think her teddy fell in to the water and she jumped in to pick it out. It wasn't an intelligent thing to do; but who expects a kid of five to act with intelligence? " He was silent for a couple of seconds, then he went on, " And who with any intelligence would allow a kid of five to stroll alone along the Embankment? " He jiggled something in one of his pockets. " You haven't been in Casualty long, Nurse, so you may not yet be aware of the number of children we get in every week with the same tale. You've seen her parents; I haven't. But didn't her mother say, ' I thought she was all right, Nurse; I thought she was with Mary, or Tommy, or Jane? ' Right? "

I said, " Yes, she did."

He moved to the door with me. " When you are looking after infants you oughtn't to think they are all right. You ought to know. And if we could only get the very kind and loving mamas, in this area alone, to realize that we should probably save the lives of five kids every week." We crossed the larger room slowly. " I'll go over and see the S.M.O. I've finished early for once. You going back there? "

I explained that I had to go to the canteen.

He gave me a shrewd glance. " You don't appear to approve of your errand, Nurse? "

He was obviously so concerned about these children and the river, and somehow so much more approachable in his concern, that, momentarily, I forgot he was the S.S.O., and felt only that he was an older and more experienced human being than myself. I said impulsively, " It's not that I don't approve, but it seems too dreadful to think of things like tea and sandwiches when they still don't know if that child is going to live or die—if there's any hope."

He stood still. " Now, just you listen to me, Nurse," he said very seriously. " I've told you this poor brat is no isolated case. Another may have come in already—or be on the way. And if not a similar case, one thing is certain—and that is that something equally acute is on its way in. You can lose your heart over a patient; but don't ever lose your sense of proportion. We may all feel like standing about and wringing our hands at times; but can you tell me what good that's going to do? "

I shook my head dumbly.

He gave a brisk little nod and continued, "Life, meals, routine, have to go on like clockwork. It may seem all very cold-blooded to you at your present stage, so I'll put it to you another way. How would you feel"—he looked hard at me—"if you were the mother of a very sick child to-night, and you brought her in here to be seen by Dr Spence and then heard that Dr Spence had collapsed from exhaustion because he had been on his feet for eighteen hours and had had no time to get to a meal all day? And, I assure you, Dr Spence frequently works those hours, and if Sister Casualty—or the ward sisters—did not produce sandwiches and hot drinks for the medical staff at odd times that kind of thing would very likely occur. Regular meals at regular hours are not the general rule for residents in a large hospital."

I said, "I never thought of it like that."

"I don't suppose you did," he said kindly. "It's not normally something one discusses. It's just something one takes for granted. Now, you had better get along to the canteen."

"Yes, I must." But I hesitated. "Thank you for explaining this to me."

He inclined his head in a small movement that was more than a nod and less than a bow. "Perhaps I should just explain something else while I'm about it. You mentioned just now something about the physicians not knowing if there was any hope in what they are doing?"

"Yes, I did." I had not dared press that question. I could not now face the thought of that child dying. Death I had never seen; but death surely must be old and weary, and not young and small and limp as a doll thrown down by a bored child.

He said gently, "You know, hope doesn't come into it. We've just got a job to do and we do it, and often go on doing it long after there is any conceivable ground for hope. That's where routine comes in. You don't stop to ask yourself questions; you just do all you can while you can, until you are forced to accept that it's too late for anyone to do anything. And what do you do then?" He gave a slight shrug. "You drink a cup of cold tea, smoke a cigarette—and start all over

again. And again. And again. That's all there is to it. No time
for drama—or tears. Just time for tea and a smoke, and then
the bell or the phone or the walkie-talkie calls you up to the
next on the list. And if you care to look in the fire-buckets
outside Casualty or the wards you'll see how seldom it is that
anyone ever gets the time to finish their cigarettes." And,
with that, he walked out of the room and across the Hall
towards Room 12.

# 8

## *Working with Jake*

I was late for lunch that day, and Home Sister was annoyed. "Nurse Standing, will you please come to meals on time? And what are you doing in that ill-fitting apron? Go and change it directly you finish your meal. You cannot return to duty so incorrectly dressed."

I met Bill Martin as I hurried across the park, having changed into one of my own aprons. "Hello, Rose. Where's the fire?"

"I'll be late back on duty if I don't rush. Sorry, Bill. Can't stop now."

He fell into step beside me. "What have you been doing to yourself? Casualty wearing you down? You look very white."

"Must be Cas.," I said, and left it at that. I could not tell him of the picture that was sitting in my mind and refusing to fade. Even if I had not been on duty I think I should have gone back to Cas. with some excuse. I had to find out what had happened to that small girl whose name I did not know.

I did not find out what had happened until half-way through the afternoon. As soon as I reported for duty Nurse Blake, who was still in charge in the Hall, sent me to chaperon Dr Linton, the junior medical registrar. "He's in Thirty-two seeing the medical women. The room is still full, as he's the only physician free to take it. It's going to run late to-day."

The patients who should have been seen in the morning were still there in the early afternoon. When Dr Ross came into 32 at half-past two three women remained to be seen. One of them, an elderly lady with tight lips, had been complaining of the delay for the past hour. She pounced on

Dr Ross. "So there you are, Dr Ross! At last! I have been waiting to see you since half-past twelve! It's too bad of you to keep me hanging about in this manner! That nurse there" —she gave me an old-fashioned look—"said you were *busy*. Too busy to see your patients! Is that it?"

Dr Ross said he was very sorry about the delay, but it had been unavoidable. "And, as Dr Linton has been seeing my patients as well as his own, I am afraid it's taken him double time to get done."

The lady said it was all very disgraceful. "I've my shopping to do, my son's tea to cook when I get back; and I'm sure I don't know how I'm going to manage! I went down to the canteen for a snack, like the nurse outside said; but it was only a snack, I can tell you, doctor." She added peevishly, "I'm getting quite peckish."

Dr Ross and Dr Linton exchanged glances. Dr Linton had not attempted to go to lunch; a cup of cold tea standing on his desk was scarcely touched. That tea reminded me of what Jake had said this morning. I thought, I'll never see another cup of tea on a desk without remembering this morning—and I never have.

Dr Ross was a calm young man. He soothed his irate patient by sympathizing with her peckishness and saying he would see her right away.

She was only partially soothed. She picked up her shopping-bag with a belligerent expression and stalked into one of the examination rooms. "You'd think," she remarked, as I helped her off with her coat, "that there'd be some proper organization in a hospital of this size. First you get one doctor, then you get another"—she glared at us—"and you really don't know where you are! And what I'd like to know is, where do you all get to while we're kept waiting about? But then, we are only patients! We can wait! We don't count! Anyone can see that!"

Dr Ross caught my eye. All he said was, "Very trying for you, Mrs Evans." And he managed to produce a professional smile. "Now, how have you been getting on? Those powders suiting you?"

When the last patient had gone Dr Linton came into that

examination room. "How did you get on with that child, Joe?"

Dr Ross was sitting at the small table by the couch. He sat back in his chair, and his professional manner fell from his shoulders like an old discarded coat.

"We didn't," he said flatly, avoiding our eyes. "We've had to admit the mother. Shock."

I said, "Oh, no."

They looked at me. Dr Ross said, "Oh, yes, Nurse. I'm afraid so."

"But—why, doctor? Did she suddenly collapse?"

He hung his arms over the back of his chair. "Why? Because she didn't get to us in time; because she didn't get out of the water in time; because they didn't discover she was missing in time. Certainly she collapsed. But that was before the cops or the ambulance chaps got working on her. Those chaps are hot stuff at this sort of thing; they did what they could and brought her in, but they knew the score when they arrived. We all did; but we went on in case we were wrong. We weren't." He looked down at the table. "Wish to God we had been. She was a pretty little kid. Just like Spence's youngest."

Dr Linton asked, "Spence very cut up?"

Dr Ross looked up at him. "Yep." He gave a small grimace. "It wouldn't have been so bad if the poor kid had been ill, but she was a fine little thing—just playing a game." He stood up stiffly. "I must be getting old, Tom. God knows I'm used to seeing stiffs—but not a kid like that."

The telephone jangled in the room beyond. I answered it. "Casualty, Room Thirty-two."

"This is Sister Out-Patients, Nurse!" snapped a voice. "Have you Doctors Ross and Linton with you?"

"Yes, Sister. They've just finished in here."

"At this hour? It's three, Nurse!"

Automatically I replied, "Yes, Sister. I'm sorry, Sister."

"Would you please," she continued impatiently, "remind Dr Ross that he is supposed to be taking Dr Archibald's rheumatic clinic in my department at this hour? And would you also remind Dr Linton that the skin-clinic is scheduled to start at two-thirty, and Dr Mackenzie-Brown would be glad of his assistance—at once!"

"Yes, Sister."

I heard her say to some one, "I cannot imagine what those physicians think they are doing in Casualty at this hour of the afternoon." Then she replaced her receiver.

I went back to the men. "What now, Nurse?" asked Dr Ross wearily.

I gave my message, softening it slightly.

Dr Linton said, "I'll bet that wasn't what Sister O.P.'s said. Thanks for muffling the blow, Nurse."

Dr Ross said, "And thanks for seeing my women, Tom. Sorry to pile them on you."

Dr Linton looked at his colleague; his expression showed they were old friends. He did not answer directly. Instead he picked up Dr Ross's stethoscope off the desk and held it out. "Come on, Joe. Let's get moving before Sister O.P.'s blasts Nurse Standing again."

Dr Ross fixed his stethoscope round his neck. "May as well." As they went out he said to me, "I'm sorry, Nurse." And we all knew that he was not apologizing for Sister O.P.'s telephone call.

A few minutes later Nurse Blake bustled into the room and found me tidying the chairs. "Finished at last? Good. Will you go to the orthopædic room and clear in there? I'm afraid it's in a shocking mess, as they've been taking off and putting on plasters all morning; but no one has had a chance to get to it yet. Then, when that's done, will you go to Seventeen and help Nurse Astor with her dressings?"

"Yes, Nurse. Thank you."

I was glad to be so busy. I wanted no time on my hands that afternoon. I did not get any time on my hands. Casualty was packed for most of the afternoon, and when I went off duty at six it was only half empty.

It was very dark outside in the park, very dark and very cold. I walked slowly because my feet hurt; I shivered and drew my cape more tightly round my shoulders. Now I was alone and free I could no longer postpone the thoughts that were so much blacker than the low London sky. Why had it to happen? Why had it to be too late? Why, why, why? Here we had everything that modern medicine could provide; we had the equipment, skilled staff—and none of it had been of any use. I thought about that policeman, the two ambulance men, and the three physicians in Room 12. I remembered their expressions. I thought, that's how men must look when they are facing defeat and refuse to admit it.

Angela had an extra free evening that week. She was waiting for me when I reached my room. "Rose, you are late. And you look whacked. Take off your shoes, dearie, and change quickly. I've got tickets for a concert, and we're going out."

I sat down on my bed. "Angie, I can't. Not to-night."

"Why not to-night?"

I explained.

She sat down on the bed beside me. "I know how you feel," she said quietly; "we lost a child with a rheumatic heart when I was in Martha. I know exactly." She was silent for a little while. Then, "But it's no good, Rose. You can't just sit here all evening and think about her. You've got to take a grip. I'm not suggesting you go out on the town and go gay, but a concert'll do you a power of good. So get your uniform off, and tell me what you want to wear, and I'll get it out for you."

I pulled off my shoes and rubbed my sore ankles. "You never mentioned anything about that when you were in Martha, Angie." I glanced at her cheerful, ordinary face. "I didn't know you had been upset."

"Does one ever talk about the things that really shake one? I don't think so. I think one waffles on and on about unimportant little details like what Bennings said and whether Gus is going to ring Josephine. But the big things you keep to yourself. You must know that, Rose. Or haven't you got around to knowing it yet?"

I took off my cap. "Yes, I have. So—right. Let's go and listen to some music."

On the return from the concert she asked if I had heard how the dance had gone. "No one in Francis went. Any Cas. girls besides Sister go?"

"I don't know. Hasn't been time to ask."

"That reminds me—what's she like? I remember seeing her occasionally when I was part-timing. She looked quite nice. Does she still do her hair in that Jane Eyre-ish fashion?"

"Yes. It suits her. But—oh, Angie—— " I suddenly remembered those bottles. Was that really only this morning? "I made a ghastly mistake!" And I told her what I had done.

She did not laugh as I expected. "Rose, you must take a grip. You can't go on putting up blacks like that—and, above all, not in Cas. Cas. is the nerve-centre of Martin's. You mustn't play the fool there. Do try and keep your mind on your job from now on."

"I'll try; I really will. And I have tried, honestly, Angie. Then I get in a state because I'm late, and forget."

She said the only thing to do was not to get in a state. "They won't stand for it in Cas., Rose. And if you carry on like this I'll end up the first year on my own. And, fond as I am of Martin's, that would make life too grim and earnest."

"You'll have Josephine."

"Think so?" She shook her head. "I don't. In fact, I'll be very surprised if she reaches the nine-month mark. I think she's due to quit any moment now."

"Gus? Have they made up their last row?"

She said she had not had a verdict for twenty-four hours, so she could not say about Gus. "That engagement reaches the all-time high in instability. I can't keep up with it. One minute life is a song *tra-la*, and the next it's over for good and no one is allowed to mention his name to Josephine. Goodness alone knows what'll happen if those two marry, but that's their affair. They must enjoy fighting or they wouldn't do it."

"Then why do you think she'll quit?"

"Because she can't take the work."

"Rubbish, Angie! Sheer rubbish! I've worked with her. I know. She's good—calm, quiet, all the things I'm not. Of course her work's all right!"

"I didn't say her work wasn't all right," she replied mildly. "I only said she couldn't take it—and she can't. It's not her fault; she's just not made to take it. And don't beat me down

again, saying you've worked with her and I haven't—I know
that. But I've talked to her a lot and she's talked to me. You
knew Francis and Bennings got her down; you know she had
to say she could not take the theatre; and now you've heard
her about Martha. Martha's a heavenly ward. I'd say Matron
sent her there on purpose. Authority is pretty good at spotting
what's going on and whose morale is flagging; Matron probably sent her to Martha to let her see what a good, peaceful
medical ward under a genuinely reasonable sister and S.N.
is like. Well, you know what Josephine says. She's miserable
in Martha. Personally, I think that at the next change-over
Josephine will pack it in."

I said slowly, " I never guessed any of this. I know she
grumbles, but we all grumble. It's just something to do.
Angie, are you sure you're right? Remember how keen to
nurse Josephine was in the P.T.S. She really came to Martin's
with her lamp alight."

Angela's tone was dry. " You mean she was keen to do what
she thought nursing entailed? To drift around with a gentle
smile and lay a cool hand on a fevered brow? About which
—who blames her? Didn't we all have some sort of vague
idea that we'd be doing that kind of thing until we got into
the wards and down to earth? "

I had to smile. " You mean, down to cleaning at the double,
to bustling to, looking sharp—and avoiding S.N.'s. But it
wasn't really so bad, Angie! Even at the worst moments it
was exciting; and, honestly, mostly Bennings' narking made
me laugh! Although there were odd times when, if I'm being
honest, I have to say I could have cried as easily."

She said, " But you laughed. And so do I—and all the other
girls, bar Josephine. We don't love being pushed around in
our first year, but we don't mind it; we realize there's nothing
personal in the pushing around, that it's just all part of the
job. Who knows? Three years from now you and I may be
the toughest of fourth-years and the poor juniors will quake
at the grim prospect of working with Nurse Standing or
Nurse Black."

I laughed. " Can't you just see us! "

She said thoughtfully, " Oddly enough, I can't, Rose. Not

you. That's what worries me. I can—vaguely—see myself and the others all dressed up as fourth-years, but I can't see either Josephine or you. That worries me a lot," she repeated. " Not for Josephine; I do think she made a mistake in trying to nurse and would be much happier in another job; but I don't think you'd be. I know you like the work and I'm sure you could make the grade easily if you kept your mind on it. Look how well you did in the P.T.S. exam. You've got brains, Rose "— and she sighed as if my brains saddened her—" so why not try using them? If you don't you'll find yourself being thrown out. Remember that clause in our contracts that says if we fail to maintain the necessary standards—and so on? "

I remembered very well. Her advice made a great impression on me. I had never admired Angela as I admired Josephine, but I liked her very much. I liked her kindness and the common sense she pumped into all of us and the way she was as happy to laugh at herself as at life in general. The more I watched Josephine in our off-duty during the next few weeks the more I now admired Angela's insight. I should have guessed how nursing was affecting Josephine, but until Angela pointed it out to me I had not guessed, just as I had been unaware of Gus's existence. And, as Angela was right about Josephine, I felt she could be right about myself. I knew that my position in Casualty had been precarious since Sister Cas. returned from holiday; I was not at all sanguine about the report Sister Francis had made on me to Matron, as Bennings must have had some say in that report; and I knew very well that the only time I had pleased Sister P.T.S. had been during the final examinations. If I got three bad reports in a row Matron might well suggest I resign. The standard required of Martin's nurses was known to be the highest in the nursing profession; nurses were not infrequently advised to resign during their training. That was not an unused threat, but something that happened four or five times every year. I could not contemplate that happening to me, not only because it would mean my not seeing Jake Waring again, but because I genuinely wanted to stay and finish my four years and then face the world with a Martin's certificate. I decided I really must do something about all this. I stopped trying to be careful and instead was careful. This effort and the continual pressure of work in Cas. so engrossed me that I was taken quite by surprise when, one morning a few weeks later, Sister Casualty called me into her office and asked me whether I wanted my extra half-day during Christmas week or the week after.

"Christmas, Sister? It's not Christmas yet?"

Sister smiled. Her manner had mellowed with me lately. "Nurse, Christmas Day is next Tuesday. Have you forgotten?"

"I had, Sister. I thought we had just begun December. I'm so sorry. But I really don't mind about my half-day. Any day will do."

"Is your home too far off for you to reach it in a half-day? Bad luck, Nurse, but thank you for being so accommodating. This means I can let the nurses who live near London have priority. Now, about your work this morning. You have been in the medical room for a long time, and I consider you are now capable of running it alone for one morning. If you get into any difficulty come to me. But I expect you will be all right." She explained that she was one staff nurse short. "Nurse Blake is doing her Christmas shopping, and I cannot spare Nurse Astor, as the dressers are changing over to-day, and I must have my experienced nurses in the surgical rooms to show the new men what to do."

The morning passed quietly for me, as I chaperoned alternatively for Doctors Ross and Linton. The two men always worked well together and never wanted me at the same time. They and I had now become old professional friends, and they always greeted me with an amicable, "Well, Nurse Standing—how's trade?" and wished me, "Good morning" or "Afternoon" when we met in the medical room. When we met in other parts of the hospital they looked correctly through me. Their varying attitude to myself made it far more easy for me to accept that fact that once again Jake Waring was ignoring me. Naturally, being so junior, I never even chaperoned for the S.M.O. or S.S.O., and when I worked with the surgeons it was only with the house-surgeons in the dressing-rooms. I often wished that this rule did not hold, but knew there was no sense in wishing for the impossible.

The years dividing us stretched blackly between us; even blacker was the thought of Sister Casualty. I had seen her stern and pleasant; in either mood she was an attractive young woman with an original personality. It used to fascinate me to watch her almost as much as I watched him. There was something about Sister that I had not met before and could not place; she was no ruthless Bennings, efficient but cold-blooded; nor a gentle figure-head like Sister Francis; and she was like no woman I had ever met outside a hospital. She seemed utterly absorbed by her work, seldom took her full off-duty, and yet managed to remain composed and even-tempered, despite the incredibly long hours she worked. I watched her with Jake whenever I had the opportunity. I knew what the hospital was saying, and that knowledge was what seemed so black; but when I saw them together, again and again, it seemed to me that they behaved as very old and good friends and nothing more. My brother Hector once said, " If a man and woman don't light a spark in each other at sight, Rose, they never light it. All this rubbish about love growing gradually is—— " Hector used a word my mother would not allow in the house. With Hector it was a term of endearment, and I could never think of him without that word. I kept all this to myself; I knew none of the Cas. girls would agree with me. Each one of them was convinced a romance was blossoming in our midst.

Astor had been at the Rugger Ball. " You wouldn't have recognized Sister, Standing. She had her hair on top of her head and long ear-rings, and she looked out of this world! I'm sure that's why she's leaving. Positive."

" Is she really leaving? " I remembered what she had said on my first morning and reminded her of it. " When? "

" Can't say for sure, as she hasn't said anything to me, of course. But Davis has been tackled by Matron about staying on as Sister Casualty when her time is up in—two months, I think. I expect they'll work together for a while, then Davis will take over. We won't want two Sister Cas.'s."

" No, of course not. Then "—I concentrated on the gauze I

was packing into a dressing-tin—"I suppose Sister'll retire to become Mrs S.S.O.?"

Astor laughed. "High time. They've been going steady for years. But Jake Waring's obviously no ardent, high-speed lover. He reserves his speed for the theatre. Still, they are both old enough to know what they are doing, and if they're taking it slowly it must be because they like it that way. But it's a pity."

"Because Cas.'ll lose Sister?"

She nodded. "Cas. and Martin's. She's so—I hate using the corny expression, but I must—absolutely born for the job. You can train most normally intelligent girls into good nurses, but you can't train anyone to be what Margaret Mercer is. It's—her whole life. I'm not really surprised she's taken so long to accept poor old Jake. He's a nice man, but she's more than half in love with her job. Must be the hell of a wrench."

I asked, "But you think she'll make it?"

"My dear—of course. She's a woman. What woman doesn't fundamentally want marriage and a family above all else?"

I very nearly said, "But she isn't an ordinary woman." Only I did not like to, in case she might wonder why I was so anxious for Sister Cas. to remain an active member of the nursing profession.

I thought over what Astor said, and decided she must be right. I was rotten at judging people, and Hector must be wrong for once; or else this long-standing affair was the exception to prove his rule.

At lunch that day I asked Angela if she knew Christmas was so close, and was delighted to find she too had forgotten the date.

"Rose, who wouldn't? One day is just like another here. I never even know if it's the week-end or a weekday; I lost track of the calendar when we left the P.T.S. Christmas!" She gazed gloomily round the large, bare dining-room. "I can't visualize Christmas here. Wonder what it'll be like?"

"Didn't you work over Christmas when you were part-timing?"

"No. They gave us all a week's holiday, and we started

again a couple of days after Boxing Day. Certainly, I've always heard that hospital Christmases are a riot; but between you and me I can't see how. Patients go on being ill, Christmas or no Christmas."

" I suppose so." And, for the first time in hospital, I was homesick. I thought of my parents and the boys and friends dropping in, and parties and fun. But here we were within a week of Christmas and I had forgotten the date. I agreed with Angela. I too had heard all the legends; like her, I did not see how there could be any truth in them. " I'm off from two to five," I told her, " and I must do my shopping for the parents and the boys then. When are you off? "

" Been. This morning. I'll do mine to-morrow."

When I reported off duty at two Sister asked me if I would mind returning to duty an hour early. " I'll make the hour up to you some other day, Nurse."

I was so thrilled at being asked to work overtime that I would gladly have missed all my off-duty. When we were unusually pressed in Cas. Sister had occasionally asked the other girls to do this, but had never bothered to request my help before. I said I should be very happy to return at four. " I'm only going shopping, Sister."

She replied amicably, " Do not worry if you get delayed by the traffic; but if you can manage it I shall be glad to use you."

I promptly decided to avoid the West End and the worst traffic. I could buy my parents' presents locally, and the boys could have gift-tokens and so save the inevitable, " Dear sister, I love you more than life itself, but can you see me in this tie? " or, " Rosie, let's face it, if I start using scented shaving-lotion I'll be only one step removed from a Teddy boy."

When I got back to Casualty at four Sister was standing in the Hall talking to Jake. She did not notice me until he said, " Sister, does Nurse want a word with you? "

She turned and smiled at me. " Shopping all finished, Nurse? Splendid! Will you go and take over in Room Nine? Ask the nurse in there to go to tea. They are still fairly full, but I think you will be able to manage. Do exactly as you

have done in the medical rooms; that is, supervise and or-
ganize the patients; wait on the Casualty Officer, but leave
the dressings and treatments to the dressers. And if you get
any problem you do not understand come out here to me."

"Yes, Sister, thank you." I glanced at Jake, but as usual he
was regarding the top of my cap. As I left he said something
to Sister. I looked round and saw they were both smiling.

Room 9 was not fairly full; it was packed with minor
surgical patients. The room-nurse looked pleased to see me.
"It's all yours, Standing," she said, quietly handing me a stack
of history cards, "and I wish you joy. It's been a grim afternoon. Not only new dressers but the new C.O., who came on
at two. Have I to go to tea?"

"Yes. Anything special about anyone?"

"If there was you and I wouldn't be in here. No. All
straightforward—and all yours."

I looked rapidly through the cards I held, then round the
room. A row of men were sitting patiently on the bench
against the wall; several more were in wheel-chairs by the
sinks; three in hard chairs by the dressing trolleys. The four
shirt-sleeved dressers were working on the men by the sinks;
the C.O., who stood with his back to me, was writing in the
room log-book at the high desk.

I went up to him. "Good afternoon, doctor." I hoped 'I
sounded professional.

He glanced over his shoulder. "What's so good about it?"
Then he grinned. "Well, well, well," said Bill Martin softly,
"so it's you. I thought you had taken up residence among—
the physicians?"

I nodded at his short white coat. "When did you put
that on?"

"Hush," he murmured; "keep it dark, love. It's so new it
squeaks. Lunch-time to-day. Let's get cracking. Who's
next?"

I read the name on the top card. "Smithers, H. J."

"Right you are." He strolled forward confidently, looking
unrecognizably spruce in his spotless white coat. His black
hair was smooth and neat, his grey trousers beautifully
creased, his shoes shining with polish. It was the first time I

had seen the transformation that takes place when a medical student qualifies. It was hard to conceive that this tidy young doctor was the tousled student I had known previously.

"Mr Smithers?" Bill asked.

A man raised a hand. "Coming, sir."

"And what can I do for you?"

A few seconds later he called me. "X-ray here, please. Then the wet plates to the S.C.O. Next?"

"Green, M. R."

Mr M. R. Green had already removed the bandage from his foot. He dropped it into my hand. "Got a shocking cut here, I have, doctor," he announced proudly, "regular deep."

Bill examined it. "You certainly have. You'll need some stitches in this, chum. Do you mind stitches? Good man. Stitches here, please, Nurse. Let's have his card, and I'll write 'em up."

I moved the men forward; distributed bowls, footstools, slings, wheel-chairs. Bill examined, ordered treatment, wrote notes, signed certificates; the dressers dressed wounds endlessly; the men waiting moved their feet and told each other that you couldn't expect them to go no faster, you couldn't, and that young dark chap was an old hand at the game, you can see. "No hesitation; on the job every time! Experience what counts, it is, every time!"

"Nurse Standing," a porter called me from the doorway, "I got a chair. Who was the man for X-ray?"

"Nurse," requested a student, "lend me your scissors. Some one's swiped mine."

"Next, please, Nurse Standing," said Bill.

"Nurse." A second dresser was beside me offering me a broken hypodermic syringe. "What do I do with this? And can I have a new one?"

"Miss!" It was a patient this time. "Can I have a drop of water? I feel ever so dry."

As I handed him the glass I saw he was very pale. "Do you feel all right? Why not sit outside? I'll keep your place for you."

He said he didn't want to give no trouble. "I'll be O.K., miss. I'm just a bit hot, like. It's the smell of that ether what always turns me up." He drank the water thirstily. "Reckon I'll be fine now. Ta."

I took the glass away, then returned to him. He did not look any better—he looked greyish. "I think you had better come out into the Hall with me."

He stood up. "Maybe you're right, miss. I——" He suddenly pitched forward on top of me. I grabbed at him and did break his fall, but he was too heavy for me to do more than that. The other men called, "Here—doctor . . ." But as they called some one came quickly into the room and took the man's weight from me.

"Get a chair, Nurse," said Jake calmly. "I'll hold him on the bench until you do."

Bill pushed a wheel-chair forward. "Want a hand, sir?"

"You hold the chair, Martin; I'll shift him in." The patient was a heavy man, but Jake lifted him off the bench as easily as I might have lifted a child. "I'll take him out to Sister," he told us. "You carry on here, Martin."

Bill moved to the desk. "What was that chap's name? I ought to make a note of this and the time."

"Ellis, D. S."

As he wrote Bill asked, "What was the boss doing in here? Did he want anything? Or was he just having another check-up?"

"No idea. Does he check up?"

"When we're new boys? All the time. He's been hanging round Cas. like a broody hen all afternoon." He put down the pen. "I've lost the thread—who's next?"

"The injured right foot—chair by the sink."

Sister came in. "Will you tell Mr Martin that the S.S.O. has seen that man Ellis and I'm sending him home in a car? All right, Nurse?"

"Yes, thank you, Sister."

She said she was going to tea. "Nurse Blake is in the Hall if you need her."

"Tea," murmured Bill when she left, "what is that quaint old-fashioned custom? Surely no one in Cas. knocks off for tea? Or do they?" he added hopefully.

"Not when they are C.O.'s running a room. Will you see

that Priority slashed wrist next? He's soaking it in peroxide at the end sink."

"Anything you say." He washed his hands, then did as I asked. A couple of seconds later he called me. " Is the S.S.O. still outside? I'd like him to have a look at this wrist if he is; I think there's a damaged tendon or two here. If the S.S.O.'s gone this chap must go to the S.C.O."

" I'll go and see."

Jake was talking to the porters outside the lodge. He turned as I approached. " Wanting me, Nurse? "

" Please, Mr Waring." I explained why, and he went back to the room with me.

When he had looked at that slashed wrist he said slowly, " I think you had better come straight in, laddie. We'll need to do a proper job on that wrist."

" Oh, no, I can't come in, doctor," protested the young man. " I can't, honest. I've got to get back on the job. I'm working now, you see. That's why the Nurse outside gave me one of those Priority cards. I brought a letter from the firm."

Jake touched the wrist gently with his neat hands. He had very small hands, as good surgeons always do. " Listen, laddie," he said, " I know you're a Priority worker, but this is your right hand. That's a priority if anything is."

The young artisan agreed reluctantly that it certainly was.

" And if we just patch you up now, you may get some stiffening. What's your job? "

" Fitter, sir."

Jake smiled at him. " You need two good hands for that, don't you? And you must know the difference in your line between doing a quick bit of patching and a proper job. This doctor and I "—he nodded towards Bill— " think you need a proper job. We'd like you to come in and let us do it. What do you say? "

The man hesitated, then grinned. " I'll come in, sir. No good moaning. I know you can't hurry when you want to get a machine right—you can't do a real job in a few minutes; reckon it must be the same with your job. If you say you

have to have time you have to have time. As you said, sir,
I've got to have two good hands in my job."

"Sensible man. Right. Ask Nurse Blake to admit to Henry,
please. I'll sign the admission form now."

When this was done and the fitter had gone with the porter
up to Henry Jake told Bill to go and get some tea. "We'll do
that hand in the theatre at six-thirty, Martin. Will you let
Sister Theatre know?"

Bill looked round the still half-filled room. "Now, sir?"

"Yes. I'll finish off in here. Who's next, Nurse?"

Bill said quickly, "I don't mind carrying on, sir."

"I'm sure you don't," replied Jake; "but go and have some
tea. I'll see you in the theatre. And now, Nurse Standing?"

I beckoned the next patient forward to a dressing-chair,
and Jake went over to him. "What's the trouble?"

Bill washed his hands again. As he went out he murmured
to me, "What's got into old Jake? Is he in the habit of
standing in as acting-unpaid C.O.?"

I shrugged. "Never worked with him before. Don't know."

Bill turned and looked at the S.S.O.'s bent back. "This
needs looking into. Curious. Well, thanks for the moral
support, Rose. See you around."

I nodded in answer. There was nothing for me to do at
that exact second, but I did not want to seem to be standing
chatting. I did not think there was anything odd in Jake's
behaviour; Sister Cas. often did the same thing for us. I only
thought that they had much in common in their attitude to
juniors.

Bill vanished, and the room settled down again; but,
although the work I did was what I had been doing all
afternoon, I was now nervous. I dropped all my history cards,
forgot three men's names, and twice gave Jake the wrong
form to sign.

On the second occasion he remarked mildly, "Nurse, I've
already signed this. It might be a sound scheme if you read
each form before handing it to me."

Like a simpleton, I blushed. "I'm so sorry."

Only this morning, I remembered gloomily, I had longed
to work with him; and now that opportunity had arrived

I was longing for him to go. In a very short time he did go. He was, naturally, far quicker than Bill, and he dealt with the remaining patients in a third of the time it would have taken a C.O. When the room was cleared he wished me a formal, "Good evening, Nurse; thank you," and went across the Hall to Sister's office. Sister had returned from tea, and I was convinced he was going to tell her I was hopelessly incapable of running a room. Filled with acute despondency, I tidied Room 9, and when Sister told me to stock and test I wandered round Casualty with the absolute conviction that I was stocking and testing for the last time.

As I was finishing Astor came to find me. "Standing, Sister wants to see you in her office."

My heart could not sink any further, so I did not trouble to ask Astor what I had done now. I knew only too well.

Sister was writing at her desk. "All done, Nurse? Then, will you please come in and close the door? Thank you."

I obeyed in a trance of misery. Incompetent, chatty with housemen, not mindful of the patients. It could be any of those or all. I waited in front of the desk with my hands behind me.

Sister began, "Nurse, I was talking to Sister Tutor at supper." And I thought—this is the end. I knew what Sister Tutor thought of me; she told me each time we met at a lecture—absent-minded, careless, and unpunctual. But Sister Cas. was continuing calmly, "And Sister Tutor tells me you illustrate your notes very nicely. Does that mean you can draw, Nurse Standing?"

I said, "Draw, Sister?"

She smiled. "Yes. Draw. Paint. Can you?"

I said weakly, "Yes, Sister. I can, sort of."

Her smile broadened. "Then do you think, Nurse Standing, you could sort of draw me one vast Donald Duck?"

# 9

## *Operation Children's Party*

ONE of us, I thought, must be mad. "Donald Duck, Sister?" I echoed.

"Yes, please. A big Donald and about half a dozen nephews. And I must have penguins; rows and rows of penguins. I want a frieze of penguins all round the Hall. Can you do them for me, Nurse? I'll provide the cardboard, paper, and poster-paints, naturally."

I beamed with relief. "For your Christmas decorations, Sister? Yes, I think I can."

"Splendid." She looked amused. "We always decorate the Hall, as we have our annual children's party here on Christmas Eve. All the local children who have come to us as patients during the year come, and they bring their brothers and sisters. We get somewhere around two hundred children attending. We make the decorations ourselves; the students help by putting them up, and the medical staff do the amusements. You'll hear about them later. The important thing now is to get the decorations made. I was discussing this at supper when Sister Tutor mentioned your anatomical drawings, so I instantly thought you might be the very person I am most needing."

I was enchanted by the prospect of the party and the thought that some one thought I could do something well. I said I should love to draw penguins, Donald Ducks, and hosts of nephews.

"Come with me, Nurse." Sister left her desk and led me to the plaster-room. She looked suddenly years younger. "I hoped you would be able to help, so I got everything ready for you. We always use this room on these occasions. Now "—

she placed a chair at the table for me—"settle down and see what you can produce. Don't trouble to be too precise; draw everything much larger than life, as it will all have to hang up. I want large cartoon drawings and strong colouring. All right, Nurse?"

"I think so, Sister. Thank you."

When I was alone I sat for several seconds staring at the clean sheets of cardboard. Now, I thought, I've heard everything. I'm past surprise. No matter what anyone tells me to do in future I shall be bland and calm. First I find myself running a surgical room with Bill Martin; then I find myself running it with the S.S.O. and making an utter mess of it; and then, when I think I'm being sent to Matron, I'm sent to the plaster-room to draw Donald Duck. And his nephews.

I closed my eyes. How many nephews had Donald? And what did they—he—look like? I opened my eyes and reached for a pencil. Did he look like this—or this? I scribbled a couple of tiny figures, and then I remembered him. I caught his furiously good-intentioned expression, his neat jacket, and irate stance. I finished Donald and began a rough sketch of one nephew; he turned into triplets. Then I recollected Sister saying she wanted at least half a dozen nephews; so I drew seven more. I was concentrating so much on the absurd little figures that I did not hear the door open or notice that anyone had come in until Sister appeared at my elbow.

"Nurse, they're perfect! You clever child."

She was not alone. Jake stood behind her.

"Sister," he remarked, surveying my drawing, "I'm loath to say this, but Nurse is cheating horribly."

"Cheating, Mr Waring?" She looked up at him and smiled. "Tell me how, please?"

"Donald has only three nephews. You can't possibly saddle the poor chap with ten."

Sister said, Not at all, of course she could! "We are going to have nearly as many nephews as penguins. I told you I wanted a frieze of penguins. And then I thought we might have a cottage—Snow-white's house or something like that—by the entrance. If we moved one of our portable lights into the cottage the children could look through the window and see, well "—she gestured widely—" Nurse Standing can draw some dwarfs or pixies for us to illuminate."

Jake said he considered that would be most effective. " How are you going to build your cottage, Sister? Blankets? Or something more permanent? "

Sister said smoothly, " I am hoping that the surgical side will solve that problem for me."

He looked at me. " I walked into that one, didn't I, Nurse? The general surgeons are in for a merry week-end as brick-layers. Oh, well. Makes a change. But tell me something else, Sister. How are you introducing Father Christmas this year? "

Sister said that was quite simple. " Dr Spence says as all modern children are so air-minded he has no option but to arrive in a jet."

A muscle twitched in his cheek. " That, no doubt, makes it all so simple. Are you considering borrowing a jet from the Air Ministry? "

He turned to me again. " I must tell you, Nurse, that Sister Casualty is not only capable of asking the Air Ministry for a jet aircraft for her children—she is also more than capable of getting one."

Sister studied my ducks. " That's all settled," she replied calmly. " The physicians have promised to make me a jet this week-end. We're going to try it out with Dr Spence inside on Sunday night if all's quiet."

Jake said he would look forward to the rehearsal. " It's my week-end off, so I should be free to come and watch. And now how about the orthopædic department? And the gynæcologists? You're not letting them off? "

" Good gracious, no! They'd be so hurt if I did! The ortho-pædic department have been building me a miniature merry-go-round for some weeks. It's nearly ready. It works by hand and will do for the very small children who aren't interested in organized games. They are going to put it up outside the Almoners' room. The gynæcologists are coping with the chil-dren at the other end of the scale; those too old for round games. We are going to have—— "

" The Big Dipper? " suggested Jake.

" No—not this year." Her eyes laughed at him. " No. We are

sealing off the area outside Eyes and building a small-size moon."

He said he was glad the moon was going to be on the small size. "But how about Mars, Sister? The Red Planet is an absolute must. Wouldn't you like my house-surgeons to knock you up a replica instead of a cottage? We could shove it in the main corridor."

She said seriously, "Do we really want Mars as well as the moon? Won't it be rather overdoing——" Then she noticed his expression. "Mr Waring, you mustn't mock me. If you do I'll demand a Mars as well as a cottage from you and your young men!"

He laughed with her. "And we'd make them for you, Sister. You know that."

"I do, indeed. And I can't tell, you how grateful I am to you all." She drew me back into the conversation. "You see, Nurse, for so many of our children this is the big party of the year. They look forward to it so much, and as a good many of them come year after year until they reach the age-limit of eleven, we do try to have a host of fresh surprises every year. It makes a wonderful afternoon for all of us—if a shade exhausting. But I'm sure you'll enjoy it."

Jake added, "And I'm sure that never in Nurse's life will she have heard anything to beat the noise that comes from this Hall on Christmas Eve afternoon. But we do have a good party. A very good party." He picked up one of my drawings. "And, as this is going to be the last Martin's Casualty party for so many of us, we had better make this one worth remembering."

I felt suddenly cold as he said that. I looked at his face. His expression gave nothing away. Then I looked at Sister. She was glancing over his shoulder at the drawing he held. There was a faint colour in her normally pale cheeks, and the corners of her mouth were turned upward as if she was smiling to herself.

Astor talked to me about the party as we went off duty that night. "S.M.O. is the traditional Father Christmas. Dr Spence looks gloriously right; as round and benign as a chubby little figure off a Christmas cake."

I asked the question that had occurred to me directly I heard of the party. "What happens to the patients on Christmas Eve?"

"O.P.'s take over for the afternoon. Their clinics stop at lunch-time. It's the only time in the year that Cas. closes, and then it's only for four hours—from two till six."

"How do we get it ready if we are open for patients until two?"

"At the last moment. That's why everything has to be taped beforehand. The decorations go up—generally the evening before; but the side-shows, food, etc., is all set and waiting. Then Sister gives the word and wow! Operation Children's Party starts and Cas. is transformed. You won't recognize the place, Standing. It all looks quite fantastic, but it's a lot of fun. You'll love it."

During the next few days Cas. and the hospital appeared superficially indifferent to Christmas. The stream of non-stop patients came into Cas., the dressing-rooms were as crowded as ever; the steady trickle of wheel-chairs and stretchers carrying new patients up to the wards never halted. But when the late evening came the atmosphere in Cas. altered, and anxious-faced young men in shirt-sleeves carrying strange lengths of wood and cardboard arrived in the office to ask Sister's advice.

"Should the merry-go-round be red, Sister? We feel it should, but wondered if you had any strong views on pastel colouring for infants?"

"Red," said Sister firmly, "is essential, Mr Menzies. Children detest innovations. All the best merry-go-rounds are red."

Doctors Ross and Linton came in furtively, bearing between them what looked like a vast, hollow, silver-paper fish. "Sister, we're worrying about our wing-span. Will this get through the front door? We've had to widen the body; it wouldn't accommodate S.M.O., plus sack, as we first made it; but now we have reached the unpleasant conclusion that it'll jam in the front door."

Sister admired the unfinished jet. "It's going to look wonderful, doctors. And I'm sure it'll pass through the door if we open both parts and tie them back. But how are you going to manage about smoke? It must smoke. Or can't it?"

They grinned and said the jet effect was on the Top Secret List. "We've roped in the senior dispenser, Sister. He's got the answer."

The gynæcological registrar staggered in with a pile of space helmets. He slipped one over his head. "How's this, Sister?"

Sister summoned me from my painting. "You are the nearest to the present younger generation, Nurse Standing. What do you think of it? Will this satisfy an expert young space-man?"

I had difficulty in not laughing outright at the superb spectacle of the solemn face of the registrar peering at me through the clear plastic helmet that contrasted so gloriously with his clean white coat, neat collar, and sober tie, and above all with the inevitable stethoscope that dangled from his neck. I said I thought the helmet was exactly right.

Sister agreed. "How did you make it, Dr Evans?"

He removed it gingerly. "Soaked old X-ray plates clean, then set them on the heads of the busts on our landing. Just the job for size and shape." He stacked it with the other helmets. "The moon's taking shape nicely above stairs. Perhaps you'd care to step across and take a look at it to-morrow evening when you come up for the senior residents' sherry party, Sister?"

She thanked him warmly and said she would be delighted to inspect the moon. When he had gone Davis came in to admire the helmets. "I do think the men have excelled themselves this year, Sister. Really, if they gave up medicine I'm sure they'd all get work as stage decorators."

Sister looked up from the report she was now writing. "I've reached that conclusion every year I've been in the hospital. And down here I certainly do not know what we would do without them. I remember old Sister Casualty telling me when I took over that I could always rely on the men to make my party for me, no matter how busy they might be. They make the time—if only in the middle of the night. And I'm afraid my cottage has been built in the small hours this time. The theatre has been unusually busy these last two days." She blotted her page. " Nurse Standing, it's past nine, and time you were off. I don't know what Home Sister will say to me if I let you stay any longer at my decorations. Pack up now and leave the rest for to-morrow evening. You should be able to finish them all then. Saturday evening is generally quiet; the rush does not start until Saturday night."

I went to see if there had been another post before going back to the Home. I found four cards for myself, looked in the ' B ' and ' F ' pigeon-holes for Angela and Josephine; they had two and five respectively. I stacked the lot under my apron bib and strolled out into the corridor. For once the main corridor was empty; all the juniors at this time of the night were either off duty or in Chapel. I had been excused Chapel when I asked permission to return to Cas. and paint after supper, which was why I was in no hurry. The senior nurses remained in the wards and Casualty until half-past nine every night, overlapping with the night nurses for half an hour at the end of the day, just as we all overlapped with the night staff for half an hour in the morning. The students had vanished to their lodgings and homes; the Consultants and lay-workers had all gone too; and the hospital now belonged to the resident staff and the nurses.

As I walked down the corridor I thought, the hospital belongs to me. This is my home; this is where I belong. And then I began to think of the other nurses in other uniforms who had walked down that corridor. Martin's had been standing for several centuries; and, although parts of the hospital had been added as time went by, the main block through which this corridor ran was part of the original building. I thought about those nuns who were the first women to nurse here. Why had they in time been replaced by the gin-swigging Sarah Gamps? I wondered what the Sarah Gamps thought of Miss Nightingale when, with ruthless courage, soap and water, a scrubbing-brush, and fresh air as her allies, she swept them from the wards. I thought of the three lines of tucks in the hem of my dress skirt, of my cape, and small muslin cap which I now found quite manageable. Miss Nightingale had designed the blue print of my uniform, and now every nurse in every training-school in the world wore some variation of her original design.

As I walked on I passed her large stone statue. It was roughly ten feet tall and very imposing. I looked at it and smiled. Some student had decorated the statue for Christmas. A long spray of greenery was wound round the neck and over one shoulder like a scarf; a small bunch of mistletoe was fixed to one of the stone pleats of the cap; and the lamp was hidden by a vast bunch of holly. I thought Miss Nightingale would smile too if she was with me. I had read her *Notes on Nursing*. Those notes are full of common sense and humour.

"Now, if you would only sit at her feet, Nurse Standing," called Bill Martin's voice from behind me, "that mistletoe might serve some purpose. As it is, it's no good to man or beast. Shockingly thoughtless lot of characters our student men must be. If I'd done her up I'd have put the holly in her cap and mistletoe in her lamp. You're right under her lamp now."

I turned and smiled at him as he caught me up. "Hallo. You're working late to-night."

He fell into step beside me. "What do you mean—to-night? Night hasn't started yet. This was this afternoon's session. And talking of late, love, what are you doing in the hospital after nine p.m. what time all good little pros. should be tucked up in bed swigging gallons of cocoa?"

I said I was on my way to swig cocoa. "I've been making decorations in Cas. and got permission to stay on. It's given me a whale of an appetite. Can't think why, as I only had supper an hour and a half ago."

"Nervous strain, that's what. Play's havoc with the blood-sugar—and my blood-sugar is down to nil. We didn't have time for tea—the characters are taking it in the surgeons' room now. Remember the surgeons' room, love?"

"Don't remind me of it. Let's just draw a decent veil."

He smiled. "The memory of old Jake tearing you off a strip too painful?"

"As a matter of fact, he didn't. He was really quite civil. It's just that I prefer to forget the whole episode. I'm busy turning over a new leaf, Bill. The past is past. Period."

"Is that a fact?" he remarked rather oddly. "You don't say." He glanced over his shoulder, then looked at me with a curious expression on his face. It was the expression he had worn the afternoon Jake relieved him for tea. "I say, Rose— I've got an idea. You're starving and I'm hollow, so why don't we do something constructive about our mutual blood-sugars?"

I shook my head. I could guess what he was about to suggest, because I knew where I was with Bill. Our house at home was always filled with young men like him. "If you are imagining that I am going to produce some cocoa for you the answer's no. Juniors do not invite H.S.'s to cocoa-parties."

"Who said anything about cocoa for yours truly?" he asked plaintively. "I'm hungry; I want a man-size steak and I know where we can get one. How about it, Rose? You owe me this for standing me up at our Rugger Ball. Will you join me?"

"I didn't stand you up, and you know that quite well. I couldn't accept without breaking the last rule in the book and, having broken all the others, thought it wiser to leave that one intact. But I'd adore to come out and have a meal now—if I didn't think Home Sister would have a stroke if I asked for late leave at this hour of the night."

"She might—if we weren't so close to Christmas. Lots of things are permissible at this season. You ask her, love. Do. I'm sure I can get off for an hour or so. We won't be too late, as I have to be back at eleven for my night-rounds. But my boss is just behind us, so I'll fix my side up now. Hold it." He spun round and walked back to where Jake was walking a few paces behind us.

Bill wasted no time. "Would it be all right if I went out for an hour or so now, sir?"

Jake, possibly mellowed by the approach of Christmas, acknowledged my presence. "Evening, Nurse Standing." Then he dealt with Bill. "I don't see why not, Martin, if you're back by eleven. Fix up a stand-in and let Mr Jefferson know who it's to be. I'm going out myself for a couple of hours and he's taking over. Just let him know." He nodded to us both and walked on.

Bill spread his hands expressively and beamed at Jake's retreating figure. " You see, love? Too easy. So you nip over and tackle Home Sister, and I'll call for you in fifteen minutes."

" She may say no."

" She won't, love. Uncle knows." He tapped his chest. " Uncle is always right. Fact. So get weaving, Rose. Uncle is also raring to get at that steak."

I did not know if he was always right, but he was certainly right about Home Sister. " Do you want to go out now, Nurse? Why did you not ask for late leave earlier? "

" I'm afraid I only just knew I wanted to go out, Sister."

She opened the Late-leave book. " Well, Nurse, it is a little irregular, but you have not asked for late leave for a long time, and, as Christmas is so near, I think we can stretch a point. What time will you be back? Eleven? Good. Have a pleasant outing."

When the lift stopped at the first-year floor I stepped out into what looked like a corner of the Chelsea Flower Show. The floor was filled with my set, and all the girls seemed to be clasping bunches of flowers. Angela was holding a mammoth bunch of red roses that struck me as vaguely familiar. " What's going on, girls? " I asked. " Some one come into money? Aren't those flowers a little expensive for corridor decorations? "

" Josephine—— " began Angela, when Josephine's furious appearance in the door of her room interrupted her.

" Here—Rose! " Josephine hurled some carnations at me. " Want these? If not, chuck 'em away. I don't want to see them again! " She growled at us all. " That's the lot! Take 'em anywhere! But out of my sight! " She ducked back into her room and slammed the door.

I looked at Angela. " What's got into her? I've never seen her in such a rage. And where have all the flowers come from? "

Angela sniffed her roses. " The answer to all your questions, dearie, is Gus, Gus, and Gus again. They broke it off for ever last night, and he started this morning with these roses. Lovely, aren't they? "

" Beautiful." I looked more closely at them. " I thought I

recognized them. I saw them coming to the lodge this morning. But do you mean to tell me he sent all these to-day? The man must have spent a fortune."

"Love," said Angela tritely, "is a beautiful thing, Rose. It's also very expensive if you happen to be in love with Josephine."

"Why is she so cross? If some one inundated me with flowers like these I wouldn't chuck them out of the room."

Josephine's door burst open again. "Huh! Wouldn't you be cross too if you were told you ought to give up nursing, as you obviously aren't any good at it!" She gazed at us mournfully. "I'm not just cross—I'm flaming! How dare he say that? Even if he is perfectly right!" She retreated with another slam of her door.

I did not like seeing her so upset. I tapped on her door. "Can I come in? It's me. Rose."

"If you must!"

I went in, shut the door behind me, then put the carnations I was holding on the dressing-table. "Honey," I said quietly, "I know you're good and mad; but why get so worked up? And what does it matter if he's right or wrong? Isn't that a minor detail?" She looked at me curiously, but said nothing; so I went on, "If Gus is in love with you and still wants to marry you, well—why not? You must be in love with him or you wouldn't be so cross. You'd just be bucked about all these flowers, hang up another scalp, and have a good laugh. So if you are in love with him why hang about in Martin's?"

She said, "I so detest admitting defeat, Rose. I was so sure that I wanted to nurse, that I could make a go of it, that I didn't want to marry him. I can't face admitting that I've made a mistake."

"I wouldn't let that worry you. And I am one girl who knows what she's talking about when it comes to admitting mistakes. So you've been wrong—right. Tell him so. Say you're sorry and marry him. You don't like it here, do you?" She shook her head. "And you don't want to end your days as a sister?"

"God forbid!"

"Then, for the love of Mike, Josephine, stop play-acting

and come down to earth. Tell Gus—give it to him straight—
unconditional surrender. And leave the rest to him. I'll bet
he'll be bucked as hell."

"He'll be that all right," she replied with unusual bitter-
ness. "You should have heard him last night about this; he
was so smug, so pleased with himself. He said—I couldn't do
without him."

I looked at her. "And can you?"

She looked about to explode again, then she flopped on to
her bed and pushed her hands through her usually tidy hair.
"No."

I said, "Then hadn't I better get those flowers back in
again? You really do want them, don't you?" She did not
protest, so I opened her door. "Bring 'em all back, girls!"

Angela bounced in with her roses as if she was about to
declare Josephine's room open. "Gus back on his pedestal?
Nice work, Rose. How did you do it? And since when has
your middle name been Cupid?"

"Hey! Rose!" One of the other girls put her head round
the door. "There's a man called Martin on the inside phone
for you. He says to tell you the steak's getting cold."

"Oh, Lord!" I pulled off my cap. "I forgot I'm supposed
to be going out. Kirsty, be an angel and say I'm just changing
and will be down in five minutes."

I rushed into my own room, pursued by Angela and
Josephine. "What is all this?" demanded Angela. "Who are
you going out with so late at night? And why?"

Josephine was fast recovering her normal composure, and,
with typical attention to detail, added, "Have you got late
leave?"

"Bill Martin." I threw off my uniform and pulled on a dress.
"Because he asked me. And yes, I've seen Home Sister."

Angela said she couldn't keep up with all this romance.
"Never a dull moment on this floor—and it's still mid-winter.
What you girls will be like in the spring I hate to think!" She
noticed my legs. "Rose, you cannot go out on a date with
black stockings even if they are made of nylon. You look like
little Orphan Annie. Have you got any clean or want to
borrow a pair?"

"Heck, I forgot my legs." I sat down and peeled off my stockings. "Get me a pair—that second drawer. Thanks."

Josephine brushed my coat for me, and when I put it on continued to brush my shoulders. "You look sweet, Rose. But"—she tilted her head to survey me—"you need—— Wait here a tick." She vanished, then returned at once with one of her scarlet carnations. "Here." She pinned it to my lapel. "That just finishes you off."

I admired the flower in the glass. "Thanks. It does."

She touched my arm. "And thank you, Rose. Thanks a lot. I rather wish I had talked to you before."

"Never too late for advice from Aunty Rose," I told her smugly. "Good-bye, girls. Enjoy your cocoa."

Downstairs Bill was fuming with impatience in our Hall. "You'll be lucky if you get cold fish and greasy chips, love. Where the blazes have you been? I told you to get weaving!" He held open the front door. "I'll bet you got involved in the old cocoa routine."

I apologized humbly. "I really am sorry. I walked into a domestic crisis above stairs and couldn't get away."

He hailed a passing taxi. "Crisis over?"

"Yes, indeed. Everything in the garden now lovely."

As he got into the taxi he nodded at my carnation. "I see you've brought some of the garden with you, and very nice it looks, too. Where did it come from? You know I'm always filled with curiosity and have no shame—so tell all. Who's the ardent admirer?"

I smiled. "No admirer of mine, alas. I've never met him."

He crossed his legs. "But he sends you flowers? Better and better. I hope he's pining with unrequited love?"

"Not for me, he isn't. His name's Gus, and he's engaged to one of my set."

He said he could not admire Gus's name, but he did admire his taste in flowers. "Carnations are my favourites."

"Mine, too. Particularly red ones." I glanced out of the taxi window. "Bill, where are we going? And why are we going in state? I thought you said the steak was close by?"

"It's that, all right. We'll be there in a second. But, as

you've been on your two feet all day and so have I, I reckoned we rated the ride. Wasn't Uncle right?"

"Dead right. Thanks."

The taxi stopped outside a small restaurant in one of the little streets leading down to the river. "It looks a dive, but isn't," explained Bill, as he ushered me in.

The restaurant was warm and very clean. The small tables were covered with red-and-white check cloths. Bill chose a table by the wall, ordered two mixed grills, and coffee. "This is a favourite Martin's haunt. Been here before?"

"No. It looks very pleasant."

"It's that all right. Bert—he's the large character with the ears behind the counter—was once in Henry. He's a fervent supporter of Martin's. Soon as he suspects the presence of a stethoscope in a breast pocket he starts cutting up his best chunks of steak. He's a splendid cook, and sharp as a scalpel, but he never does us." He waved at the man as he spoke. "Evening, Bert! How's trade?"

Bert pushed up the flap of the counter and squeezed his body through the gap. "Mustn't grumble; mustn't grumble. And how's trade in the hospital, Mr Martin? I hear as they've made you a doctor now?"

Bill said he was already grey at the temples. "Can't you see the change, Bert? My carefree days are over. I'm a sober citizen now."

Bert said he thought that was all very nice, too. "Seems as I should have congratulated you, Mr Martin? Only I should say Dr Martin." He turned to me. "Grill suit you, Miss?"

"Just right, thank you."

Bill explained this was my first visit. "I told Miss Standing you'd do us proud, Bert."

Bert tugged at one of his enormous ears. "You a nurse, miss?"

"Yes. Just half-way through my first year."

He considered my face reflectively. "Thought as I hadn't seen you before, miss. But I hope as now you've come here you'll come again. Ever you're on your own like, and wanting a good hot meal, just you drop in here. Of a morning or of an evening. I'll see you get it; and I'll look after you. There won't be nobody as'll bother you if you likes to sit at a table by yourself and just drink a cup of coffee and have a quiet read. You young nursing ladies can do with a quiet sit down every now and then, I know. I mind "—it was a wonder his ear did not come off the way he was maltreating it—" as how those young ladies was running round that Henry ward when I was in. Never off their feet, they weren't, and always a smile and a bright word. Lovely lot of young ladies they had in that Henry ward, and I tell them just what I tell you, miss. If you want a quiet sit down and a cuppa or a meal any time you just come along to Bert and he'll take care of you."

I thanked him warmly. He gave me a broad smile, smoothed his white apron over his substantial middle, and strolled back to his counter.

Bill leaned forward. " He means that, Rose. And heaven help any character who tried to give you the green light in here. Bert was once a professional fighter. Told you he was a good type." He sipped his coffee. " You may not be aware of it, love, but you've just been accepted as a member in the most exclusive club in Martin's." He raised his cup. " Here's to you." He glanced over my shoulder at something behind me, then smiled into my eyes. " And here's to your carnation too. Down the hatch." He lowered his cup and nodded at some one I could not see—another student or houseman, I supposed. Then he leaned forward again, propped his elbows on the table, fixed his chin in his hands, and gazed at me. " You know," he said softly, " this is really very nice. Why haven't we done this before, Rose? "

His tone and whole attitude had suddenly changed, and both surprised me. I certainly did not know him very well, for all that I knew him better than I knew any other man in the hospital and recognized his type; I had never heard him speak like that or look at me like that before. I did not answer immediately, as I was tired, and I half wondered if I was imagining all this. Then he said, " Rose, love, I asked you a question. Why—haven't—we—done—this—before? I wish we had." He moved one hand and flicked at my carnation. " And I wish I had thought of giving you that flower. You look so like a flower yourself to-night. You look just like a rose."

I thought, Blimey! What's come over the man!

I answered literally, "We haven't done this before because you never asked me before."

He looked down at the table. I noticed his eyelashes for the first time. They were very long and very thick. "Would you have come"—he raised his eyes and looked into mine—"if I had asked you?"

I hesitated, then again gave him a literal answer. "I expect so. Our food's pretty good, but I'm always hungry. And this is the best mixed grill I've had in years."

"Rose, dear," he looked hurt, "don't joke. I'm serious."

He sounded serious. I considered him thoughtfully. If he was serious, then I really was out of my depth. I had told Angela the truth when I said I was used to being dated by young men who wanted to talk to me about their love-life. No one I had ever wanted to say these sort of things to me had ever said them; they just asked me to be an extra sister to them. I knew exactly how to deal with them; I had been dealing with brothers all my life; but I did not know how to deal with this. And somehow, although Bill seemed sincere, I just did not believe that he was. I once again had that instinctive reaction that this was some kind of a line. I might have had that reaction because of another bit of fraternal advice I had had from Hector: "Beware the smooth chaps with lines, Rose. A chap only uses a line when he's playing around. When he's serious he's so dead keen not to put his foot in it that he does that all the way along. And another thing, Rose, when a chap looks you straight in the face, clasps his hand to his heart, and sighs deeply, before you return his sweet nothings take a good look round and see why he's so anxious to keep your attention fixed on his face. There's generally something behind you he doesn't want you to see."

Recollecting this, I said with a horribly arch simper, "But I am serious, Bill; this grill is superb," and, to amuse myself by testing Hector's theories, I glanced back over my shoulder. When I saw who was sitting at the table directly behind our own I nearly dropped my coffee-cup. I put it down unsteadily and some of the coffee spilled over on to the red-and-white tablecloth.

Bill mopped this with his napkin. "Wouldn't you two be on speaking terms, love?" he murmured. "Or are you unaware that you've just cut our S.S.O. stone dead?"

I met his eyes. "Oh, him? Why, we always cut each other dead off duty. It's the done thing. You must know that, Bill. First-years don't exist."

"They don't?" He narrowed his eyes. "I know of one first-year who exists, so very much, for a certain character of an H.S." He sat back. "And don't pretend I haven't said that, love, as you did before. You know quite well what I've said —and why."

I said quite honestly, "I don't know why."

"Rose"—he moved again, and this time took one of my hands in both of his—"be your age. Please, this is important. I'm trying to tell you"—he sighed—"just how important it is—to me. Try, try, to understand."

He spoke so genuinely that I was more than half convinced that both Hector and I were wrong, when I noticed that between the long, searching gazes into my eyes he was glancing over my shoulder, then back at my face, as if he was checking on his audience reaction. I could not conceive why he should do this; but when he did it for the third time I was quite certain that for some unknown reason it was amusing Bill to play to the gallery. If there had been anyone else but Jake behind us it might have amused me too. But I had seen the coolly amused manner in which Jake had been watching us, and I did not care to provide any further light relief to his mixed grill.

I flapped my eyelashes at Bill. They were nothing like as long or thick as his, but I hoped my flapping would be fairly effective. "I'm afraid I'm terribly bad at understanding anything, Bill," I said plaintively. "My brothers are always narking at me about that. Hector—he's the eldest—says I have the sensitivity of a stuffed doll. I haven't told you about Hector, have I?" I beamed at him. "I've been meaning to tell you, because you remind me so much of him—in fact, I always think of you as rather like a brother."

He looked at me for a long time. His grip on my hand relaxed a little. "You—er—regard me as a brother, eh, Rose?"

"Yes, indeed," I assured him brightly, "just like a brother. I can't help it. You are so like Hector to look at." Which was a lie if ever I told one, as Hector was as fair as I was.

"I see." He let go of my hand and took out his cigarettes. "Tell me, love," he took out a cigarette slowly, "has it ever occurred to you that, although all men are technically brothers, that relationship doesn't automatically apply to women?"

"Of course it doesn't. Women are sisters."

His hand shook and he had to light a second match. He inhaled, then blew the flame out quickly. He said simply, "Good God," and was silent.

I decided to end our party. I looked at my watch. "Bill, I'm awfully sorry, but I think we ought to go. I've got to be back by ten-thirty."

"But you knew I was off until eleven," he remonstrated.

"Till eleven? Oh, dear. I'm terribly sorry—I got muddled." My beam reappeared of its own accord. "You know how dumb I am. Anything muddles me, and I told Sister half-past ten. I'm afraid we'll have to go. I don't dare be late."

He deposited his stained napkin on the table. "I'm not sure that I go along with you in all your statements, Rose; but if you have to be back we had better get cracking." He beckoned Bert, paid the bill, and we all exchanged more expressions of mutual good-will. As we moved from our table Bill stopped beside Jake's chair. "Grill's pretty good to-night, sir."

"Very good." Jake stood up and for the second time that night wished me good evening. Bert, taking us all for old friends, remarked pleasantly that it was the young lady's first visit, but he hoped not the last! "You get Mr—beg pardon—Dr Martin to fetch you along again, miss. Want to come regular like Mr Waring, you do! I was only telling my missus this morning, 'Friday won't be Friday without that Mr Waring sitting at his table reading his paper.' How much longer you got, sir?" he asked Jake. "Getting near the end of your time, ain't it? I mind as you told me when I was in that Henry ward as you'd got another two years to go. Getting close now, ain't it, sir?"

"It certainly is." Jake smiled down at Bert's wide, shining face. "I'm going to miss your good cooking."

Bert wagged his head. "An' they'll miss you in that hospital of yours, I reckon. You been there a tidy time in all, they say."

"Fourteen years on and off," replied Jake. "I was away five years in the War."

Bert flicked his dish-cloth over Jake's table and said where the years went to he couldn't say, he was sure, but he'd best be getting back to his counter. "See you later, sir." He added another set of farewells to Bill and myself, and ambled back to his grilling.

Bill slipped his arm through one of mine. "And I had better take you home, Rose. Nurse Standing," he explained to Jake, "has to be in shortly. Excuse us, sir."

"With pleasure. Good night, Nurse." We moved on, and Jake sat down again and picked up the paper that lay at present unopened beside him.

Outside, I turned on Bill. "You shouldn't have called me Rose in front of him. I'm sure he didn't approve."

He laughed and held my hand as well as my arm. "He probably didn't. So what? You're off duty, in mufti, and so am I. Relax, sweetie. Not even Matron could object to what you do away from the hospital in plain clothes. You're a private citizen for another quarter of an hour. She couldn't even object if I——" He broke off, let go of me, put his hands in his pockets, and rocked on his heels. "Now why didn't I think of that in there? Old Bert would have been delighted— he's incurably sentimental. Sink me, Rose! Uncle's losing his grip; but, by God, who wouldn't lose his grip when a character tells him that he looks like her brother. Still thinking of me as one of your dear brothers, Rose?" he asked smoothly.

"But, of course, Bill. I told you—you're just like Hector."

"Am I?" he murmured, then caught me by the shoulders and kissed me as I had never been kissed before. "Hector kiss you like that?" he asked a shade breathlessly as he let me go.

I was a little breathless myself and a little annoyed—with myself. "No, he didn't."

Bill asked, "Still thinking of me as a brother?" But without waiting for my answer he added, "Block your ears now, love, because I'm going to whistle a mighty whistle. There's a taxi-rank just round the corner, and they can hear from here." He did as he said and almost immediately we heard a car engine drawing close. The taxi wheeled round into our street, and Bill opened the door as it slowed. "Hop in, Rose, and relax. I don't fool around in taxis. You're quite safe. And don't look so old-fashioned, love. You don't fool Uncle. I'll admit you did—for a short while; but I'm not as dumb as you like to make out that you are, Rose. I know you really aren't shocked—and no harm's done to your career. Matron wasn't looking and Jake's not the type to tell tales out of school even if he had been watching, which he wasn't. I noticed that he was looking at his newspaper just now when I looked back at him through the window before I kissed you. So you can't say Uncle hasn't thought of everything from your angle."

I said, "No, I can't." I was not going to give him the pleasure of knowing that he had had an audience to his embrace. Jake had put down his newspaper again, and was staring out of the window at us. I had seen him as I turned away after Bill let me go. Of course, I now thought, the street had been fairly dark and he might not have seen us at all, even though we were standing only a few feet from the window. Certainly he had not looked shocked or even interested; he had only looked anxious. Very, very anxious. The recollection of his expression kept me quiet all the way back to our Home. I could not understand his expression. Then I closed my eyes, and the light dawned. He was obviously not thinking of us at all, but worrying about his own affairs; his future. It must be a big step for him, leaving Martin's; he might well be anxious about it all—and so was I.

"Rose." Bill touched my hand. "Wake up, love. We're here." As he helped me out of the taxi he added, "You still haven't told me what you thought about my kissing you."

I sighed. I suddenly felt terribly tired. "Bill, I'm sleepy. Do I have to make a Federal Case out of it? But thanks for the grill. I enjoyed that. Good night."

# 10

## *Nurses may not be kissed in Casualty*

NEXT afternoon Angela and I helped Home Sister decorate the junior sitting-room in the Home. After we had worked for about an hour we ran out of drawing-pins. Home Sister went for a fresh supply while Angela and I sat on top of our respective step-ladders and discussed Bennings, Josephine, marriage, men, and whether the laundry would come back before Christmas Day, as we did not dare ask Home Sister, since that would mean my admitting that I had forgotten to send my soiled uniform in the last laundry collection.

Angela stepped down to the floor. "I can lend you three aprons, but only three, as I need the rest for myself." She surveyed the paper-chains. "Rose, your last one is crooked. You've fixed it about a foot below mine. Lift it up."

"Right." I pulled out the pin and held up the chain. "How's that?"

"That's straight." She descended her ladder slowly. "By the way, how did you get on last night? I forgot to ask."

"All right in parts." I answered absently, looking out of the high window at the end of the room. That window was too high to look out of if you stood on the floor of the room, but my ladder gave me a clear view of the road. I watched the road—at first incuriously, then incredulously. "Angie, get up your ladder—look out there! Do you see what I see?"

She went quickly to the top and stood on the step. "What? That kid? I say, Rose, what—?" But I did not stop to hear more. I shot down my own ladder, out of the sitting-room, nearly knocked down Home Sister, who was returning with the drawing-pins as I ran down the corridor, through the front hall, and down the steps leading from the front door of our Home. I heard irate voices asking me what I thought I was doing, and telling me to stop that at once! I ignored them all. When I reached the pavement I ran as fast as I could to the spot where the small boy I had seen from my perch on the ladder was dodging on and off the pavement in front of the oncoming traffic. Just before I reached him he deliberately screwed up his eyes and stepped into the road. I leapt the last couple of yards, grabbed his coat, and hauled him back to the pavement as the car that was coming directly towards him on this side of the road swerved widely, avoided a bus by inches, and stopped with a scream of brakes about twenty-five feet on. The driver jumped out and slammed his door. He came towards the child and myself, looking very shaken and very angry. He was not nearly so angry as the child squirming in my arms.

"You didn't ought to 'ave pulled me! You didn't ought to 'ave pulled me! You didn't! You didn't! You didn't!" His tight dirty little fists thumped my apron. "I wanted to get run over a bit! I wanted it! I did! And you didn't," he began to sob, "you didn't ought 'ave stopped me!"

The motorist had joined us. "I'm more obliged to you than I can say, Nurse. But did you see what that child was doing? Here! You! Boy!" He shook the boy's shoulder not ungently. "What do you think you were doing? Don't you realize a car is a heavy and dangerous machine? You can't stop a car just like that. See where I stopped"—he pointed down the road—"see? Over there! And I had my foot hard on the brake! But I still had to go all that distance. If this young lady had not seen what you were up to you'd be under my car now."

I tilted back the furious little head and recognized who it was. "Trevor! It's you! Trevor, you should have known not to do that."

He was sobbing, uncontrollably. "But I wanted to get knocked down a bit like I said. I wanted to! I did! I did!"

The motorist stared at me. "What did he say? Did he do it on purpose? Do you know him, Nurse?"

"He came in with a cut a little while ago."

As I spoke Home Sister and Angela appeared on the pavement beside us. Home Sister looked pale. "Is the boy hurt, Nurse Standing?"

"I don't think so, Sister—just shocked." I tried to disengage his arms from my waist, but he would not let go. "Trevor," I said quietly, "let us have a look at you—there's a good boy. We just want to see if you are all right."

"Course I'm all right," he wept, "but I wouldn't 'ave been all right if you'd let me be. Then I could have gone in—in" —he let go with one hand and smeared the tears over his face—"gone in and 'ad me Christmas—proper—like last year." And more tears pelted down his poor little face.

Home Sister grasped the true situation first. She laid a hand on his shoulder. "Were you in Christian last Christmas, sonny?"

He looked up at her and nodded. "You been in there, Sister?"

The motorist gazed at us blankly. "What is all this about?"

Sister took control. "I believe I understand. He wants to come in to hospital for Christmas, so he thought he would come in"—she glanced at the road, then back to the man—"this way."

Trevor, sensing that he had, if not an ally, an understanding adult, detached himself from my waist and caught hold of Sister's apron. "I didn't want to be 'urt bad, see; but I reckoned as if I got sort of knocked down a bit they'd 'ave to take me in. They would, wouldn't they?" He appealed to Sister. "And then they wouldn't send me out again until— after, see. It's only three days—an'"—he sniffed and dried his eyes on his coat-sleeve—"I just wanted to come in— honest, I did."

The motorist looked more shocked than ever. "But, boy, you might have been killed."

Trevor began to cry again. "I only wanted to go into 'orspital. I only wanted that."

"But your mum, Trevor, what about her?" I asked. "Won't she be upset if you're not home for Christmas? You wouldn't want that."

He produced a surprisingly clean handkerchief from a

pocket and scrubbed his face. "We don't 'ave Christmas at 'ome," he replied flatly. "My mum says as she's too busy to worry with all them goings-on; she says as I can see Father Christmas on the telly, and, anyway, she says as there ain't no real Father Christmas—it's just kids' stuff. But I see 'im," he insisted. "I see 'im last year when I was in that Christian ward, an' 'e come round an' fills all our stockings. An' when I tells me mum that she says as there might be a Father Christmas in 'orspitals, but 'e don't come to our 'ouse and, anyway, Dad can't be doing with all that dressing-up, what with his over-time, and she says I'd better see it on the telly. But I wanted to see 'im, and I wanted to come in and she "— he jerked his thumb at me and gave me a hideous scowl— "she stopped me."

The motorist said curtly, "You should thank the young lady for saving your life, boy."

Sister put up a hand. "He is only a very little boy and he is very upset. I am just going to take him into our Casualty department to let one of our physicians have a look at him. Perhaps, sir, you had better come with me. I am sure you feel very shaken yourself and could do with a cup of hot tea. We all witnessed what happened and saw that you were in no way responsible." She offered her hand to Trevor. "You come with me, sonny. You'll be quite all right with me." She told Angela and me to return to the Home. "Straighten your cap first, Nurse Standing. You have displaced it." And she walked off, leading a docile Trevor into Casualty.

The man lingered. "I cannot tell you how grateful I am to you, Nurse." He shook my hand. "How did you grasp what he was about?"

I explained that I had been on a step-ladder. "At first I thought he was playing that awful 'last across' with another child. Then I realized he was alone and just thought he had lost his nerve and didn't dare cross. I hurried simply because I was afraid he'd cross at the wrong time; I never dreamt that he was doing it all on purpose until I saw him shut his eyes and deliberately step out into the road. You know the rest."

He asked for my name. "I may need it. I doubt if I will, but it is as well to have it. And your address is St Martin's Hos-

pital? Thank you." He fingered his collar as if it choked him.
" I think I am going to pay a call on that boy's mother. I
think she requires to be told how nearly she lost her son—
and why."

As we walked back to the Home Angela said, " Think he'll
do any good? How old's that kid? "

" Six."

She surveyed the endless traffic. " And she lets him wander
around London alone and doesn't let him believe in Santa
Claus. Why do some people have children? "

" I dunno." I was very upset now it was all over. " I wonder
what they'll do about him."

She said she did not know, but was sure Home Sister would
cope. " Did you notice how the old dear stopped being an
elderly housekeeper and snapped back into an efficient nursing sister? She'll fix it up, you see."

I went to wash the mud off my hands and arms, and change
my apron and cap. When I returned to the decorating Sister
was handing up drawing-pins to Angela. She said she had left
Trevor with Dr Spence. " The poor child is now very shocked
and frightened. I do believe he at last understands what might
have happened. Dr Spence talked to him very seriously."

I asked unhappily, " I suppose he has to go home, Sister? "

Sister studied her drawing-pins. " Naturally that kind of
behaviour cannot be encouraged, Nurse. Children have to
think before they act, and we have to teach them to do that,
although occasionally "— she looked at me—" one has to act
and think simultaneously, as you did this afternoon, Nurse
Standing. You acted most promptly and creditably. But that
little boy appears to have had to learn far too much already; he
needs to relax and behave like a child again. He is very shaken
and will certainly have a high temperature to-night; children
almost inevitably produce temperatures after bad shocks, so
Dr Spence and Sister Casualty both feel that he needs to be
warded." Her old face relaxed into a genuinely mischievous
smile. " One has to watch any child with a temperature,
Nurses. You can never foretell what that temperature may
herald. I do not doubt that Dr Spence will want to keep an
eye on Trevor for a few days."

We both smiled back at her. I said, "Sister, I am pleased."
Angela asked, "Do you think his parents will object, Sister?"

Sister's expression altered. "I understand," she said rather
grimly, "that Dr Spence is most anxious to speak to Trevor's
parents. I am sure they will not object. Dr Spence," she added
not inconsequentially, "is a father himself."

Casualty was very quiet when I returned to duty that
evening. Both staff nurses were on duty in the Hall; three
of the Cas. nurses were working in the half-empty dressing-
rooms; Astor was dressing a fairy doll for the Christmas-tree
in the stock-room, and I was told to return to my painting in
the plaster-room. "If we have a crisis, Standing," said Nurse
Davis, "we'll call you out; but unless I do that carry on with
your decorations until supper. I don't expect we'll need you in
the Hall; we've got the whole staff on to-night with the
exception of Sister." She took off her glasses and rubbed her
eyes as if they ached. "About an hour ago I didn't think either
Astor or yourself was going to be able to finish your things
this evening; we were packed with patients, even though it's
Saturday. We suddenly cleared in the last half-hour. I'm very
glad, not only because we want those decorations finished
to-night, but because it lets Sister go to her sherry party
with a clear conscience. So off you go to your ducks."

It was peaceful in the plaster-room; peaceful and rather
lonely. I had never felt lonely in there before, so I decided
that it was the party that was responsible for my Cinderella-
ish frame of mind. I applied myself to my painting, but,
although penguins—I had finished the ducks—are pleasant
birds, they do not engross your entire mind; at least, my
penguins did not. Once I had painted one with Indian ink I
had painted the lot, mentally; only I had twenty-seven to do.
I played games with myself, painting a row of left flippers,
then five heads, five feet, back to flippers again. I was not sure
that this increased my speed, but it partially occupied my
mind. Only partially. After an hour or so I was nauseated
with penguins; I never wanted to draw another in my life,
and I still had eleven to finish. As a relaxation I picked up
a pencil and began to doodle on a spare sheet of paper. I drew
Josephine throwing out her flowers, Bennings in that bubble-

bath of detergent powder. I surrounded Bennings with little penguins, then decided I was going quite obsessional about the wretched birds and scratched them all out. Then, without planning what I was drawing, I let my hand—and mind—wander. I drew a head, outlined the hair-line and contours of the jaw. I nodded at the head as if it was an old friend, and filled in the face. He had highish cheek-bones and hollows—here—and two lines running down the side of his mouth and dozens of little lines under his eyes. Laughter lines or tiredness? I wondered. He must surely often get very tired. I studied the drawing, then worked on the eyes, studied it again. It was not right. I remembered how he had looked through the window last night and altered the curve of his mouth. I had given him too much of a curve; I straightened it, shaded the whole thing and put down my pencil. " That's not bad," I said aloud, as I was alone. Like most people, I often talked to myself when alone.

But I was not alone. " It's not only not bad—it's very good," said an amused voice from behind me. " You seem to be a girl of parts, Rose. You have a strong talent for repelling boarders, spring a rival effort to the four-minute mile for Martin's, and then turn out to be a portrait artist in disguise." Bill bowed to me. " A charming disguise, love. Just a moment!— " And before I grasped what he was about he tore the little drawing off the sheet of doodling paper. " You've got the boss exactly. I must show this to the chaps. It's really good."

" Bill—please." Once again I was annoyed with him and myself. " It's not good at all. Tear it up. I was just doodling."

He shook his head with maddening calm. " Can't destroy a masterpiece, Rose. Sheer vandalism. And I want you to sign it for me. Who knows—one of these days it may be worth good money. You've really got a talent for drawing, love. What ever made you take up nursing? "

" I often wonder," I replied drily. I was growing genuinely concerned. I did not want him to guess how important that drawing was to me, but I did not want him to have it to show to the boys. I tried a new approach.

" What are you doing in here? Are you on duty? Do you want Davis? She's in charge."

He flicked at his jacket cuff. "Note the tweed suiting. The white coat is in the cupboard. Uncle is off duty for the week-end, and that's official even if my week-end didn't start until twenty minutes ago. I came down to congratulate you on sprinting down the road and hurling young Trevor Brown from the Pearly Gates. Davis said you were in here turning out high art, and gave me permission to come in and ask you, as one artist to another, whether you have any views on cottage roofs. I'm O.C. cottage and want red tiles; the chaps say green. What's your view?"

"I haven't any strong views; I prefer red as a colour. Look, Bill, if that was all you wanted to see me about you'd better move off. You may be off, but I'm on duty, and Davis won't like it if you're in here too long."

"My love," he said, "you really must stop being such a dead bore about etiquette. I told you Davis said I could come and talk to you. The door's open—so relax. And, incidentally, may I remind you that if you were the prim little soul you are trying to make out you would be sitting here turning out penguins and ducks non-stop and not taking time off to draw snappy little pictures of old Jake." He took the scrap of paper from his pocket and grinned at it. "The chaps'll be tickled pink. This is exactly Jake in his most S.S.O.-ish mood."

I had an inspiration. "If you're so keen to have it hold on a second and you can have the pair. I've done the S.M.O. before," I lied, "so I expect I can do him again." I drew quickly and produced a rough caricature of Dr Spence's face with his hair on end, which was not nearly so good as the one I had done of Jake—not only because of the speed with which I had just drawn the S.M.O., but because I had not watched his face as frequently as I had watched Jake's and so did not know every line by heart. I tore off the drawing and gave it to Bill. "If there's anything else you want just ask."

He raised his eyebrows. "You sound really peeved with me, Rose. Would you be cross about something? Last night, for instance?"

"I'm not peeved," I said evenly. "I only get peeved about important occurrences."

He smiled. " My, but what long words you use! What do they mean, love? "

I took up my paint-brush. " That I think it's time I got on with my penguins."

He said quietly, " You are peeved, aren't you? Don't you like being kissed? " He moved a little closer. " Or is this no-touch technique part of your let-me-be-a-sister-to-you-boys angle? "

I glanced up from the flipper I was inking. " You talk about my being a dead bore on etiquette. Wouldn't you be a little obsessional yourself about my reactions to last night? What did you expect me to do? Slap your face in high dudgeon? Or fall into your arms with glad cries? You told me to be my age last night—I forget why; mind if I suggest you do the same? Who on earth," I added deliberately, because I felt like irritating him, " takes a hit-or-miss peck like that seriously nowadays? I was only put out at the time because of the hospital. This first-year business has got under my skin at last, and I find myself getting worked up about what I'm doing when I really have no need; but I'm only worked up wondering what Sister or Matron will say when they find out. But, as you reminded me, I was a private citizen last night, and, as such, I don't give odd pecks a second thought."

I wanted to irritate him, and from his expression it was obvious that I had succeeded. Not that he frowned or ground his teeth; he just smiled far too brilliantly and showed most of his teeth. " So I peck, do I, love? And you don't give that a second thought? Interesting," he remarked mildly. " One wonders what one has to do to produce your second thoughts? For instance—this? " He took hold of my shoulders, spun me round, and kissed me again; not once but several times. And, like last night, he did not peck, as I had untruthfully said, but kissed very well. So well that I had no breath with which to raise the necessary strength to push him away; it was not emotion that left me breathless, but the physical circumstances of the position in which he held me. When a strong, large, young man embraces you tightly the combined pressure on your chest-wall and mouth pretty well cuts off your air intake.

In an academic fashion which is common to any young

woman who gets kissed by a man who leaves her emotionally
cool, I was able to think all this out while he was kissing me
and to wonder if the added constriction of tight-lacing was the
reason why Victorian maidens swooned on such occasions. If
I had been wearing a corset, I thought as I began to see
sparks and black dots racing round my eyelids, I too would
have had a complete blackout.

Eventually, as he had to breathe too, he let me go.

I leant against the table. "You really are daft, Bill," I said
breathlessly, "in more ways than one. I know you're in mufti,
and I'm only painting birds in the plaster-room, but I am on
duty. There'd be hell to pay if anyone had walked in on
us."

"There would indeed," said a frigid voice from the doorway; "so it might have been a good idea had you recollected
that you were on duty previously, Nurse Standing."

It would have been hard to say who looked the more
astonished—Bill, Jake, or myself. Bill's dark face turned
purple; I felt myself going white as I do when really shaken;
Jake's colour was normal, but his expression was more for-
bidding than I had ever seen it.

Jake looked Bill up and down. "I'll see you later, Martin,"
he said ominously, then stepped aside from the doorway. His
reason for stepping aside was unmistakable. Bill murmured
something I did not catch, and walked quickly from the room.

Jake remained where he was, and for a few seconds that
lasted hours said nothing at all. Then he looked at his feet.
"I came down for my car-keys; I left them in Sister's office
last night. I happened to glance in at the open door of this
room as I walked past. I'm not on duty"—he looked up from
the floor now, and a small flame of anger lit his grey eyes—
"but there are certain things I cannot pass in this hospital.
Can you imagine, Nurse, how your behaviour would have
appeared to a patient? The fact that there are temporarily no
patients about excuses neither of you. You may be very junior,
Nurse Standing, but you are not now so new as to claim
complete ignorance of the conventions and standards expected
of members of this hospital. I am well aware"—he was looking me over now as he had done Bill—"that you take your

responsibilities far too lightly. What you do in your own time —outside the hospital—is your own concern. What you do while wearing a Martin's uniform is the concern of every one here. Fortunately, to-night I was the only spectator to witness the manner in which you saw fit to disgrace your uniform. And if you think I am being quaintly antiquated, Nurse, may I remind you that to the general public there are only two kinds of nurses. Only two," he repeated. " The sinners and the saints. Have you not heard that? "

I had; many times. I said, " Yes, Mr Waring."

He looked at the floor again. " We are proud of our nurses here," he said quietly, " with reason. And we are jealous of the reputation that a Martin's badge gives a nurse in any hospital in the world. Just how long do you think that reputation would last if the average Martin's nurse behaved as you do? " Without waiting for my answer, he turned his back and walked across the hall towards Eyes and the main corridor.

My immediate thought was, he's forgotten his car-keys; he's gone the wrong way. That thought was a defence, but the mechanism broke down instantly and his words sank in.

My knees shook, so I sat down hastily at the drawing-table. No man had ever been so angry with me in my life before; and being spoken to like that by a man shook me quite as much as what he said, even though I knew he was perfectly right in all he said. My father had always left the reprimands I gathered in childhood to my mother; my brothers' occasional outbursts of rage never touched me; but their outbursts were not comparable to the honest anger I had seen and heard in Jake's expression and tone. I relaxed against the back of my chair and closed my eyes. What would he do about this? Tell Sister Casualty? I imagined he would have to. And if he reported me she would have to tell Matron. I opened my eyes and looked at the penguins. I wondered if I would ever see them hanging up.

I was too miserable and worried not to tell the girls. They were kind, sympathetic, and gloomy.

" That wretched Bill Martin! " groaned Josephine. " Why couldn't he be more careful? "

"Why does he have to go round kissing people?" I demanded bitterly.

Angela said she didn't suppose he meant any harm. "He sounds a mad type, Rose. Just like you. I don't expect he thinks before he acts, either."

"Well, if it's any consolation, I've acted without thinking for the last time. And Bill's caught me unawares for the last time. I'm damned if I'll have anything to do with him again!"

Josephine said she doubted if Bill would risk so much as looking at me again. "If Jake Waring said all that to you you can bet he'll say double to Bill. The S.S.O. keeps a firm grip on his boys. Bill won't get off with a laugh."

Angela asked mournfully why we thought there was any chance of my being in a position to have anything more to do with Bill. "I'm sorry, Rose, but I'm sure you've really overshot the mark now. If Matron gets to hear of it you're out. No two ways about it with your past history as a junior. If you had been a senior with a row of sterling reports behind you she might have given you the father and mother of all rockets and let it pass—as a first offence. Not for you. Why, why, why, did you have to let it happen?"

"I didn't. It just happened."

They looked at me and then at each other.

Josephine said, "Rose, we know you—so we know that. But it's no good pretending that anyone else in the hospital is going to believe that you were taken unawares. They'll all think the S.S.O. walked in on your having a necking session with Bill Martin. No, wait," she added as I was about to protest, "I haven't finished. I know you know a lot about brothers and you gave me some good, and very surprising, advice last night. I guess you were speaking instinctively. You must have been, because you're so green about most things. But even you must know that on the whole no girl gets kissed by a man unless he senses that she wants him to kiss her. Right or wrong—and for my money it's right—that's a generally accepted fact. And before you say no girl would be daft enough to have a necking session in Cas. do remember that that sort of thing has been heard of before—even in Martin's."

I said, "I didn't know that. What happened?"

Josephine shrugged. "According to rumour, it happened a couple of years ago. Some girl called Ellsworth."

"She get chucked out?"

Josephine nodded. "Next day."

We sat in an unhappy silence. Angela broke it. "I expect the memory of that and the thought that you were the acquiescing type combined to make the S.S.O. so cross. If he had honestly known that Bill had swooped on you out of the blue he wouldn't have been so annoyed with you. Jake's a fair man—every one says that."

I said wildly, "What does he care if I want to be kissed or not?"

"He doesn't care at all—off duty. He as good as told you that. What got him was your being on duty. And he's dead right, Rose. I'm sorry to say it, but he is. He couldn't look the other way about something like that. Martin's would be a riot of a place with all the boys and all of us meeting constantly in little empty rooms if authority didn't clamp down instantly at the mere suspicion of sex rearing its ugly head."

"The maddening thing, Angie," I protested, "was that sex didn't come into it. Bill didn't want to kiss me—any more than I wanted to be kissed by him! I'm quite sure of that. It was just done, because—oh, I don't know why—for a laugh or something."

Angela looked exasperated. "Rose, for goodness' sake grow up! Stop talking like an idiotic two-year-old. Don't tell me Hector hasn't told you something to cover this?"

I calmed down. "Yes, he has." Yet, although I accepted that she was talking sense, I could not accept the idea that Bill had feeling at all for me. That was what made all this so hard to take. If I was going to be a slaughtered lamb, at least, it would be some consolation to feel that that stupid embrace had been enjoyed by one of us. I was certain he had been as cold as I and merely kissing me with apparent passion to prove what he could do. Why he wanted to prove that I was not clear; but now, at last remembering my own boys, I realized how when you goad any young man you are asking for trouble. I had certainly got it. And the worst thought of all was the one I had to suppress from the girls, which was that Jake's opinion of me, always pretty low, must now have sunk beyond recovery.

I asked for their verdict. " Think it'll get to Matron? "

Angela did not answer; her expression told me more than enough.

Josephine surprised us both by saying that now she really thought it over she was not so sure. " I don't think the S.S.O.'s the type to get some one chucked out. I should think there is a hope that he'll prefer to deal with you both himself. And Christmas is round the corner. That may make a difference. And he had just been to a party. The sherry may have mellowed him."

" He didn't look or act mellow. I don't believe either Christmas or the party'll affect him at all."

I slept badly that night; and when I slept I dreamt that I was back in the plaster-room, and my dreams changed into nightmares in which I kept knocking things over, breaking china, drawing enormous penguins who all had fair hair and Jake's face. I was really relieved when the getting-up bell rang. I got up and dressed slowly, as, for once, I had plenty of time.

Casualty was moderately busy for Sunday, but the morning dragged by. Sister did not come on until nine, as it was Sunday, and from the moment she arrived I expected a summons to her office and then her voice to tell me to come in and close the door, please, Nurse. Then, as the time passed and eleven came, my hopes began to rise; perhaps Josephine was right. He was going to leave things in his own hands.

At 11.15 Astor called me from my glove-mending.

" Standing, Sister wants to see you now."

I straightened my cap, smoothed my apron and knocked at Sister's office door.

She did not tell me to come in and shut the door, please, Nurse.

She looked me over and said instead, " Nurse, I think you had better go and get another apron if that is your clean one."

My mouth felt dry. "Yes, Sister. I changed into this one at nine."

She nodded. "Go now, and then will you go straight to Matron's office? She has just telephoned to say she wishes to see you herself."

"Yes, Sister."

"Before you go, Nurse," Sister Casualty added soberly, "I should like you to know that I am very sorry that this has had to happen."

# 11

## Sister Margaret is not Pleased

MATRON said, "Come in, Nurse Standing, and close the door, please."

My hand was wet and the door-knob slipped under my fingers. But when I turned round to face Matron my knees nearly gave way beneath my weight. My knees had had a bad shock. Matron was smiling at me.

"I do not," she told me, "normally interview my junior nurses before sending them on night-duty; but normally I try to avoid removing any nurse from her ward or department immediately before Christmas. Sister Casualty has told me that you have been enthusiastic in the help you have given with her preparations for her party, and I do assure you that I am most reluctant to have to transfer you to-day. Unfortunately, I have no option. I must have another junior on night-duty to-night, and I do not want to move any ward nurse, since if I did so it would mean that the patients in her particular ward would lose a nurse to whom they have grown accustomed, and that might mar their own enjoyment of Christmas. Patients," she added, "do so dislike changes of staff. The only possible alternative to yourself is Nurse Grey, the day junior in Margaret ward. However, as Nurse Grey has already spent three months in Margaret ward, when she is placed on night-duty she should have a change of experience. So I want you to go on duty as night junior in Margaret ward to-night, Nurse Standing."

The most wonderful wave of relief I had ever experienced swept over me. I was not in dire disgrace or about to be dismissed from Martin's; I was merely going on nights. I was too grateful at this respite to feel any disappointment yet about missing Christmas in Cas.

Matron explained the reason for my transfer.

"Nurse Sharp, the present junior, has just been admitted to Nightingale with influenza. Margaret, being a very heavy medical ward, requires a permanent night junior. Night Sister cannot be expected to manage by borrowing junior nurses from the other wards to tide matters over; she must have a proper substitute." She smoothed her organdie cuffs and smiled at me again. "It will be excellent medical experience for you, Nurse, and make a complete change from the first-aid and administrative experience you have been gaining in Casualty. I have explained the situation to Sister Casualty. Sister is going to send you to first lunch and then off duty for the remainder of the day. Go over to your room after lunch and pack your belongings; Home Sister will arrange for them to be moved to your new room in the night-nurses' home this evening. You must be in bed by three o'clock this afternoon. Try to sleep. You have a busy night ahead of you. Is that all quite clear?"

"Yes, thank you, Matron."

She inclined her head, and the lace frills on her cap swayed.

"That will be all, Nurse. I hope you have a pleasant Christmas in Margaret ward. It will not, naturally, be the merry Christmas you would have had in Casualty, but I know that now you are aware of the circumstances you will be quite content with the knowledge that you are being transferred at such short notice because your presence is necessary to the comfort of the patients. That comfort is ever our one consideration." She nodded at the door. "Close it quietly when you go out, please, Nurse Standing."

When I returned to Casualty Sister's genuine sympathy made me feel hollow with guilt. "It is a shame that you have to move to-day, Nurse. I am really sorry that you should miss our party after all the work you have done for it. Come and see us on Christmas morning if you are not too tired. And, as you are now leaving my department, Nurse," she continued gravely, "I will tell you, as I tell all the nurses who pass through my hands, of the report I am going to make on you to Matron."

I braced myself. "Yes, Sister. Thank you."

She smiled faintly. "You would do better to wait until you hear what I have to say before you thank me, Nurse." Then she allowed herself to smile properly. "It is all right, Nurse. I am quite pleased with your work and your conduct in Casualty. You have made several mistakes—one very serious one; but you have tried to improve, and I can understand that at your age and with your somewhat light-hearted temperament it is not always easy to take life and your work seriously. But I am going to tell Matron that your work is showing some improvement, and I know she will not expect more than that from any nurse at this early stage of her career. Now, be off to your lunch, and good luck in Margaret. I think you will enjoy working there. Medical wards are pleasant places, and medical patients really need nursing."

I did not understand that last remark, but did not like to question her. I was now not only feeling guilty, but stricken with remorse. She could not have been nicer—and what would she not have said had she known about last night! There was now no doubt that Josephine had been right: Jake must be keeping this to himself, which was incredible and wonderful and disturbing. And then I thought, not incredible at all. He is such a nice man; and nice people do things like that.

Angela was already in the dining-room when I got there. I sat down beside her. "Angie, I've left Cas."

She choked over her glass of water. "Rose!" she gasped as I banged her back. "You've not been thrown out?"

"No! Isn't it wonderful!" I beamed at her scarlet face. "I'm on nights to-night. Matron says some one called Sharp——"

"Matron?" she interrupted me anxiously. "Rose—he did report you?"

"If you'll only listen, honey," I said soothingly, "you won't have to choke again. No. He can't have reported me to anyone. I've seen Matron and Sister Cas. this morning, and neither of them said one word about it. But there's a crisis on in Margaret, and as the one wardless pro. I'm the answer."

"Answer to what?" Josephine sat down on my other side. "What have you done now, Rose?"

"It's not what I've done but what I'm going to do. I'm on nights in Margaret to-night." And I repeated what I had just told Angela.

Josephine was delighted for me. "Rose, what a stroke of luck! It gets you out of Cas. before you can put your foot in it again—and will keep you out of Bill's way. The surgeons don't go near Margaret. It's Martha, plus. You'll see nothing but physicians for the next three months. Aren't you thrilled?"

I had intentionally avoided looking at the change from that angle. It had occurred to me directly Matron mentioned Margaret, but in her office I had been too relieved at discovering what the interview was about to worry over anything else. The moment I got outside her office I had realized that in Margaret on night-duty I should see nothing at all of Jake. And by the time I came off nights he might very likely have left the hospital.

"Aren't you thrilled?" demanded Josephine again. "You ought to be. Don't look so glum. This really is a break with a vengeance."

"I know." I assumed a wide smile. "And of course I'm thrilled. I can't believe my good luck. I do think it best that I should leave Cas. quickly. I'm only a little gloomy at the thought of missing Christmas in Cas. and that party. I was longing to see the S.M.O. shoot in in his jet."

Josephine said that, if it was any consolation, from what she had heard of Margaret I would not have a spare second to remember the date once I got there. "Sister Martha was saying only this morning that Margaret is now the heaviest ward in the hospital. But there's Gill Grey"—the junior Matron had mentioned to me and another member of our set—"she'll know more. Gill," she called down the table, "what's Margaret like at night?"

Gill Grey was a plump, phlegmatic North Country girl. "Why? Who's coming on nights?"

"I am. To-night. What's it like, Gill?"

For the second time she evaded the question. "What's up with Sharp?"

"She's got 'flu. I'm taking her place."

"Then, if I were you, love," replied Gill grimly, "I'd get

the 'flu too—or the measles. Either would be a piece of cake compared to night-life in Margaret, so Sharp's given me to understand."

I said, " Gill, it's not as bad as all that? "

She nodded calmly. " Aye. It would be. But you'll find out, Rose."

I closed my eyes. " I can hardly wait."

" Nurse Standing! " Home Sister called to me sharply from her seat at the head of our table. " You are not yet a night-nurse. Will you kindly remain awake at meals until you become one? Thank you."

Sister Casualty had been kind enough to say she was sorry to see me leave her department at this period; that night I discovered that Sister Margaret also had her regrets. She announced very frankly that she was extremely sorry to see me in her ward. " I do dislike sudden changes of staff, Nurse. They are so upsetting for my patients; particularly on the night before Christmas Eve. And I understand "—her eyebrows met over her nose—" that this is your first night-duty, Nurse Standing? "

I said, " Yes, Sister."

She looked meaningly at my night senior, Nurse Jones. " And I also understand," she continued, " that you have not previously worked in a medical ward, Nurse Standing? "

I said, " No, Sister."

She looked me over and did not appear to find pleasure in what she saw. " You have recently been working in Casualty? "

" Yes, Sister."

" And what were you doing in Casualty? " she demanded. " You are very junior to have worked in that department."

I walked in to that one. " I don't know, Sister."

She took me up at once. " So you do not know what you have been doing for the past three months, Nurse? Indeed? I must say, you are going to be a lot of use to me if you are capable of spending three months in a department without discovering what you were supposed to be doing! Allow me to tell you, Nurse, that I expect every nurse in my ward to be able to account intelligently for every minute she spends on duty."

I took a deep breath. " Yes, Sister."

She thrust a large cardboard diagnosis list at me and told me to take the seat opposite to her own at her table. " Keep your eyes on that list, child, and try to follow the report I am about to give Nurse Jones. You will possibly not understand a word I say, but sit still and listen." She pushed back the chair next to her own. " Sit down, Nurse Jones, and I'll get on. We have had a very heavy day, and how you are going to cope to-night with all these ill women and a brand-new junior I cannot conceive. However, as there is nothing to be done about it, you will just have to manage."

Nurse Jones sat down. " I expect we will, Sister," she replied mildly. " Thank you." She folded her hands in her lap and tilted her head slightly to one side to listen to the day report.

Sister's table stood in the centre of the long, silent, dimly lighted ward. The table was partially hidden behind red screens at night; the light above the table had been pulled right down to the extent of the flex; it hung only a few inches above the lace in Sister's cap. The china shade of the lamp was covered with a red shade-cover—the same red as the screens, and the two women opposite and myself were bathed in a soft rose-coloured glow. I had not met either Sister Margaret or Nurse Jones until ten minutes ago, and as Sister read her long, detailed report I glanced up from my list every now and then to see what they both looked like.

I decided that it was just as well to see Sister Margaret in a rose-coloured light. One look at her explained why Gill had said 'flu or measles would be preferable to night-life here. I guessed her to be in the late thirties or early forties. She had short thick ginger hair, a square jaw, pale complexion, and thin, pale lips. Her eyes were her redeeming feature. They were not large, but beautifully shaped, deep brown in colour, and her lashes were as thick, dark, and long as Bill Martin's. She was a tall woman and she had the good figure that all modern hospital sisters seem to acquire with their blue dresses. She was really a very striking woman in a spine-chilling way.

There was nothing at all striking about Nurse Jones. She

was small and thin; her complexion was not good, and her features too irregular to approach moderate prettiness. Yet somehow her whole appearance was attractively homely. She wore a hospital badge and a fourth-year belt, which showed she was over the final-examination hurdle and a State Registered Nurse. I should have been surprised at finding a nurse so senior on night duty as a ward nurse had not my fellow night juniors at supper told me that Margaret had even been known to have a permanent staff nurse in charge at night. " It's such a busy ward that Matron only sends very senior girls there. As Jones is in her fourth year, she would normally be free of nights for good, but she's doing an extra spell to oblige. She doesn't mind what she does for her last couple of months, as she's leaving to get married directly her contract finishes. Of course, if she wasn't leaving she'd be a staff nurse for sure, as Matron thinks a lot of her—and she won the bronze medal in her hospital finals."

The prospect of working with a medallist did not cheer me. I remembered Bennings and her gold medal only too well. I asked the question that is all-important when you are going to work with the same person for at least two months. " What's Jones like to get on with? "

The night juniors said they had heard from Sharp that Jones wasn't too bad. The girl next to me said she thought Jones was considered fussy over details. " But she's a good worker and the best thing about her, according to Sharp, is that Sister Margaret likes and trusts her. You really run into trouble on nights when the ward sister and your senior don't hit it off. Then it's hell on earth; every report is agony, as the sister does nothing but pick holes in what the night girls have done."

I asked, " Do we see much of the ward sisters? I thought Night Sister ran us at night? "

" So she does, during the night and in the Night Home. But you have to face the ward sisters every morning and evening. That can be a lot of meetings. But, of course, the brunt of the night is born by the senior. She has to answer to sister and carry your mistakes as well as her own."

I said I was glad to hear Jones wasn't considered too bad.

"Must be tricky if you're thrown with some one with whom you can't get on."

"Not tricky at all," replied my neighbour placidly. " Night juniors have to get on with their seniors, and that's all there is to it. It's part of the job of being a night stooge, like counting laundry and cutting bread-and-butter."

I thought about this as I risked another glance at Jones, and saw she was summing me up as I was summing up her. Her expression was curious but not unfriendly. I decided I liked the look of Jones. I shot another glance at Sister Margaret and decided to try to acquire some of Gill Grey's North-country phlegm—and to give my full attention to the diagnosis list.

When Sister had finished her report, without looking up from her log-book, she demanded to know of the pages whether the new night junior intended to sit at her table all night.

I bounced up. " No, Sister."

She said she was glad to hear it. " Go and put the milk on to heat, Nurse; then set the kitchen for the night. Nurse Jones will be ready for you directly. And mind you do not burn the milk. I do not allow milk to be burned in my ward."

" No, Sister. Thank you." I walked as quietly and as quickly as I could towards the ward door.

I was not quiet enough. Sister called me back.

" Nurse Standing, I also do not allow a herd of elephants to run rampant in my ward. Kindly tread more softly in future."

In an effort to do the right thing, I replied in a whisper, " Yes, Sister. I'm sorry, Sister."

That was the wrong thing. She asked if she was whispering. " No, Sister."

" Then why do you do it, Nurse? Perhaps you feel you know more about such matters than I? "

" No, Sister. I'm sorry. Sister."

She said, if that was the case, would I be good enough to learn to modulate my voice to the right flat pitch for night-duty. " The tone I am using does not carry as a whisper would do, nor is it so irritating to the patients. I do not allow my patients to be irritated, Nurse Standing. Now go and do those drinks."

I said flatly, and thankfully, "Yes, Sister," and tiptoed out of the ward as quickly as I dared.

I took another deep breath when I reached the kitchen without being called back, filled the milk saucepan, lit the gas, and put the milk on to heat. I recollected how the night junior in Francis laid out an assortment of cocoa, tea, coffee, meat extracts, sugar, glucose, and so on, and arranged the various tins in a straight line on the dresser, then set the large wooden tea-trolley with thirty-six cups and saucers.

Jones came in as I added the teaspoons. "You can't use that trolley at night, Nurse; it's far too noisy. You must always set everything on a tray covered with a cloth or the cups will rattle." She laid a small tray rapidly. "Like this. And don't put the spoons in the saucers for the same reason; leave them on the cloth until you need them. Noise is the one thing we don't have at night; anything that may possibly make a clatter or clash is out, even if it does mean extra work. And be very, very quiet when you are working in here during the night. Make sure that serving-hatch"—she gestured to the hatch that opened into the ward—"is closed when you are in here alone. If for some odd reason we are both in here for more than a couple of seconds then it has to be open, as we can't otherwise hear the patients. Now"—she removed the milk from the gas—" as you're new, I'll help you with your drinks to-night and take you round at the same time. When we've settled the women we'll go through the report together, but that won't be until much later, when the men and Night Sister have done their rounds. The rounds are my concern; all you really need to know at this stage is that you must not make a noise, and you must never, ever, attempt to lift anyone up in bed by yourself. We've a lot of acute cardiacs in here, and they must not help themselves. If you attempt to move them alone they'll insist on helping you and harm themselves; so remember, whatever else you may forget, don't forget to come and get me every time anyone wants heaving up the bed. Got that? Good. Then let's get going."

We got going and we did not stop all night. The only time

I sat down was during my meal-hour in the dining-room. Jones gave me her promised run-through the report, in writing. "Read it while you eat your meal, Nurse. I had a feeling we wouldn't have time to talk it over, so I wrote it in bed this morning when I heard Nurse Sharp had been warded. I'll try and elaborate on it another night, but it will help you to get a general idea of what's wrong with our ladies, the treatments they are getting, and why."

At five in the morning Jones cheerfully announced that it was time to start work. "Finished your routine? Good. Then let's," she repeated, "get going."

Jones switched on the ward lights; I carried in the early-morning tea, handed out cups to those who could feed themselves, and held the feeders of tea for the eight women who were too ill to hold a feeding-cup to their own lips. Then I helped Jones with her washing of the very ill women, and gave out washing waters to the remainder—about half the ward. Between assisting Jones I scampered round with mouth-wash mugs, empty cups, used washing-bowls, stripped and made beds; collected used mouth-wash mugs and kidney dishes; made more beds; removed the screens from the centre table; tidied the table and refilled the ink-wells; removed shade-covers; pushed up lights; tidied the rows of wheel-chairs and the centre of the ward; cleared treatment trolleys; boiled used kidney dishes in the sterilizers, then removed them from the sterilizers and switched off the electricity so that they might be cool when the day juniors came to clean them; pulled all the beds away from the walls so that the ward-maid might sweep behind them, then pushed them all back again, clicking the castors correctly inward; replaced sponge-bags; used night-dresses, bed-jackets, and biscuit-tins in lockers; fluffed pillows that had become flattened since we made the beds; and then, suddenly, the ward was full of day nurses, and Jones told me to go and change my apron.

She joined me in the changing-room and unbuckled her belt quickly. "The first part of the night was a bit hectic," she admitted, as she buttoned a clean apron round her narrow waist, "but I'm glad we'd a quiet morning. It makes it so much easier for you to find your feet if you don't have to hurry."

I had only enough breath left with which to gasp, "Yes, Nurse"; then we smiled spontaneously.

Her smile ended in a yawn. "I believe I'm tired." She sounded surprised. "But, truthfully, Standing, it hasn't been a bad morning at all. All acute-medical wards are heavy in the morning; far heavier than any surgical ward can ever become, as medical patients are really ill and need to have so much done for them. They don't just need a few days' post-operative nursing, but all the time they're in. It makes medical nursing hectic, but far, far more satisfactory. In fact, I don't think you can know what nursing really is until you nurse medical cases. I like working in Margaret. It's my favourite ward here. Now I've got to give Sister my report. All you have left to do is take a last look round to see every-thing's tidy when Sister comes in for Prayers."

The ward looked perfect to my sleepy eyes when Sister swept out of the duty-room ten minutes later. She stopped in the ward doorway. "Where's the night junior?" she barked.

I moved to her side. "Here, Sister."

"Nurse." With a magnificent gesture she pointed up the ward. "Look at that."

I looked obediently, but could see nothing out of place. "At—er—what, Sister?"

"There is an empty cup on the locker beside Bed No. Nineteen," she announced in a voice of doom, "so will you kindly remove it at once and remember in future that I do not allow my night juniors to leave their work unfinished!"

"Yes, Sister. I'm sorry, Sister." I scuttled up the ward and seized the offending cup and saucer. The woman in 19 whispered anxiously, "Ever so sorry, duck. I tried to get your eye, but you was busy."

"That's all right, thanks. Don't worry," I murmured and shot back to the kitchen, watched by all the patients, Sister, her day staff, and Nurse Jones.

When Sister dismissed us I apologized to Jones. "I'm sorry I missed that cup, Nurse."

She swung her cape over her shoulders and buttoned the collar. "Don't worry about that, Standing. It wasn't a serious slip. In fact, it was proof that you had the ward looking very nice. Sister Margaret couldn't find any other fault. And if she had you'd have heard about it. Sister Margaret never lets anything by, which is another reason why I like this ward so much. You know exactly where you are with Sister. With her silence means approval. If she disapproves she says so at once. It makes Margaret a very restful ward to work in."

Restful, I thought as I limped to breakfast. She called Margaret restful! I was very tired, but I smiled at my porridge. The girl who had told me so much last night was sitting by me again. "Hallo, Standing. You look very bright and cheerful for a morning after. What's the joke?"

I told her. She smiled wearily. "That's Jones all right. Sharp said nothing ever puts Jones out. The more Sister Margaret bulldozes the more placid little Jones becomes. And she's a bright girl." She tapped her head. "Got it up there. But I expect," she sipped her tea, "a lot of it's love."

"How do you mean?"

"Love," she repeated. "Her engagement—future—all this and heaven too sort of thing. It must make a difference to a girl; it must take the edge off things—and people like Sister Margaret." She sighed. "Maybe I ought to fall in love. Then life in Henry might be bearable at night."

I asked what was wrong with night-life in Henry? "I thought it was meant to be a pleasant ward?"

"It might be all right," she glanced round cautiously, "with another senior. My senior's not a bad sort, as far as I'm concerned, and she's quite a good nurse. No medallist but decent-certificate type. But she's just fallen in love, and the problem there is that I'm fairly sure Sister Henry has caught on about the affair and disapproves, plus."

"But why? If it's all right for Jones?"

"Jones's young man isn't in Martin's, and she doesn't have to meet him nightly on his rounds. Also, Jones's love-life is properly organized, tied up with pink ribbons and an engagement ring. My senior's affair is totally different; I don't think it's yet anywhere near the engagement stage—and, knowing the man even slightly, I'll be very surprised if it ever progresses beyond a normal hospital affair. I don't think he's really serious about her. But that," she added "makes it hard for my senior, who is pretty nearly crazy about him and can't get him out of her mind or conversation to me at night. We talk her beloved Bill non-stop at every possible occasion in the night. And, being so preoccupied, the poor girl makes mistakes in the ward, which drives Sister Henry up the wall and makes it hard for me, because I always seem to be around when Sister Henry is going up the wall and have to carry the can."

I was having a little difficulty in following what she said. A night-nurses' haze had settled over my mind after one night in Margaret, but I did catch the Christian name she mentioned and, although Bill is a very common Christian name, I was curious to hear more.

" What's your senior's name? "

" Dingle." She looked round again. " She's not down yet. She's a nice soul—when not in love. Pretty, too."

I said I did not know her.

" That's not surprising. My set's only six months senior to yours, and you're the first of your set I've seen. Martin's is so huge that until you work with a person you really only meet your own set—apart from nights. The night staff, being smaller, get to know each other fairly well. Incidentally, I'm Ellis. I know you're Standing, because last night we all heard Night Sister telling Sister Dining-room that you were taking Sharp's place."

I said, " Sister Margaret aside, I rather think I'm lucky to be doing that. I like the look of Jones." And, to turn the subject back to night-duty in Henry, I added, " And lucky she's safely engaged to her young man. Is he a Martin's man? "

She nodded. " A G.P. now. Assistant with view. Nice man, so Dingle says. She knew him; I didn't."

" Do lots of girls marry Martin's men? "

" About seventy-five per cent.—and that's putting it low. Maybe more. The marriage rate is terrific. Inevitable, really, since the only men we see are our own men and vice versa. None of us have any time for a social life outside the hospital."

I could understand that. I asked, " Then why shouldn't your Dingle eventually marry her—Bill, was it? "

" Is it not Bill! " she retorted sourly. " It's Bill, Bill, Bill—

and am I sick of him! I tell you, Standing, what I don't know about Bill Martin isn't worth knowing. And if it weren't for Dingle shoving him down my throat all night I'd quite like him. Know him? "

" One of the new H.S.'s? Yes. He was a C.O. in Cas."

" That's the man. Didn't you think he was rather nice? "

I said I did not know Bill Martin very well.

" Suppose not, being Cas. junior. But he's fun, Standing, although not, I should say, fun to fall in love with. He's quite crazy and very much a one for the girls. Also, like most crazy people, he strikes me as being fundamentally sensible, and it isn't sensible to get yourself matrimonially tied up when you've just started your first house-job. I'm afraid poor Dingle is asking for a packet of trouble by falling for him."

" Because he's got a roving eye? Or dishonourable intentions? "

She grinned. " The first. He's too bright to have the second in the hospital. Remember, we all have to go on living with each other. And there's something else. You can probably tell me more about this than anyone, as you've just come off days. We've heard a rumour at night that he's now running round in the daytime with one of the first-years. Know anything about that, or who it is? "

" Oh? " I helped myself to another roll. " No one's mentioned that rumour to me. But—er—do housemen even notice first-years? "

" Not as a rule. Unless they are already engaged—the rare young widow—or some one else has noticed them first. From what Dingle and the girls say, Martin is one of those men who only take note of a girl when there's another man in the offing. Bill Martin seems to make a hobby of cutting in and cutting out. He certainly did that with Dingle. She was almost engaged to Fred Lang, one of the pathologists, when Bill appeared on the scene and swept all before him. But now he's succeeded in getting rid of Fred Lang he seems to have lost interest in Dingle. Which makes life exceedingly difficult for me! A senior who doesn't get on with Sister Henry is bad enough; but when on top of that the poor girl is in the process of being crossed in love it makes life grim. You can't imagine what I'm going through," she ended petulantly.

" Must be grim." I did sympathize with her as a fellow junior, but I could not help feeling even more sympathetic towards this unknown Nurse Dingle. " And you can't help seeing a lot of Martin, as he's the S.S.O.'s houseman? "

" No. They are both in and out of Henry all night, particularly now that we, and not Albert, are the official overflow from Francis." She looked at me. " I suppose you're well up in the surgeons after Francis? "

" With all the firms after Cas. It was the crime in Cas. not to know who was who. You had to have the resident staff taped."

" That reminds me—as you've come from Cas. you must know even if you were the junior—is there anything in all the new talk about Sister Cas. and the S.S.O.? "

I shrugged. " I honestly wouldn't know. He did take her to the Rugger dance, and they are obviously great friends, but whether things are working up or not—I don't know."

" Don't mention that dance to me! " She gave an exaggerated shudder. " How I suffered over that dance! Dingle nearly had a nervous breakdown. First she took it for granted he'd take her and badgered Night Sister into changing her nights off so that she'd be free; then he didn't ask her for ages, and poor Dingle got glummer and glummer, and wept on my shoulder most nights; and then all was sunshine, because at the last moment he told her that of course he was taking her and hadn't bothered to mention it, as he simply took it for granted that she'd be going with him. But talk about my nerves! I was worn to a shred calming Dingle by night and Sister Henry in the morning. Actually," she added sanguinely, " I was certain she was flapping for nothing. I knew he was going to ask her. He may be a gay lad, but I wouldn't say he was unkind and he has got charming manners."

I looked at her and added mentally, And a fresh scalp, obviously. I merely repeated that I did not know Bill well.

She gave me an arch smile. " Then you've a treat in store. He goes for blondes." She was fair herself, and the knowledge clearly pleased her.

I stood up. " That's too bad, because so do I." And then I

wished I had not spoken so sharply or so thoughtlessly. Luckily, she was no longer paying attention to me; she was waving to a very pretty, very fair girl with a harassed expression who had just come into the dining-room. As soon as she caught sight of my companion the newcomer came over to our table. " Nurse Ellis, have you got the stock-cupboard keys? "

Ellis stood up. " No, Nurse. I didn't go to the stock-cupboard last night. But I saw them hanging in the rack in the duty-room when we went on last night."

The girl, who was obviously Nurse Dingle, sighed. " Oh, dear. I did open the stock-cupboard about midnight. I must have put them down somewhere. I'll have to go back to Henry. Sorry to disturb your breakfast, Ellis."

Ellis shook her head over her fifth buttered roll. " That means Sister Henry up the wall again! Ah, me. Not even the fact that it's Christmas Eve is going to make Henry a ward filled with good-will to-night. Roll on, next month, when I come off." She glanced up at me. " How does the thought of three months on nights appeal to you, Standing? "

I said at the moment all that appealed to me was the thought of a bed. " I even forgot it was Christmas Eve."

" If you weren't a junior," she announced cheerfully, " I'd say you were in love too. You look in a trance—like Dingle does at night. Must be night-duty. Juniors don't fall in love, because no one loves juniors."

I said I was quite happy to go to bed and eat worms. " I'm too tired to go out into the garden to find 'em."

" Sleep well. In case I'm not sitting by you at supper to-night—Happy Christmas."

" It's not that until to-morrow."

She took a sixth roll. " It starts at midnight. Remember? And you'll be there to greet the dawn. Won't that be nice for you? "

" Very nice. Sleep well yourself."

I was very thoughtful as I crossed the park. I had heard so much about the hospital grapevine; it was hardly surprising that that grapevine was so efficient if there were many girls like Ellis around. I had never met anyone who was so chatty on first acquaintance. I did not then appreciate the part night-duty played in her chattiness; night nurses—in the morning —become complete extroverts. The night nurses' breakfast is always the noisiest meal in a hospital, and that was possibly why it was the one meal over which no sister presided. Even Sister Dining-room, I had noticed this morning, had retired into her office and made no attempt to quell the talk and frequent shouts of laughter coming from the tables. Possibly extreme physical fatigue stimulates uninhibited conversation; it certainly makes you light-headed. After only one night I had merely reached the peak of tiredness; later I discovered that you pass that peak and grow beyond fatigue, and feel, not drunk, but as if you have drink taken. It is quite a pleasant sensation and must be the main reason why Night Sisters and Home Sisters have to be so adamant at chasing night nurses to their beds. Without an irate sister to insist on that, most junior night nurses would remain chatting at the break-fast-table until it was time to go on duty again.

This morning, however, I was only surprised that Ellis should have confided so much to a total stranger; I was also surprised about Dingle; I was not at all surprised to hear that Bill had another young woman. I thought it more than likely that he had two or three. What surprised me about Dingle was that she should have taken him seriously. Surely no young woman in her right mind could believe a word that man said? Then I recollected the advantage that the possession of brothers of your own age gave you; if it had not been for Hector, Piers, and Godfrey, I might have been taken in by Bill. Particularly on that night at Bert's. That raised an old question: why had he bothered to ask me out at all? I had no pathologist in trail; I was not even engaged to an outsider like Gus—so why? I reached an answer fairly easily: I was a blonde and a young woman; Bill was the type who had to have a woman about. My second brother, Piers, was of the same calibre. Piers always had some girl with him—if he was only going to post a letter.

Then I stopped bothering about Bill, who was unimportant, and thought about Jake and how desperately important he was to me, and how I had now been removed from any possibility of coming into contact with him again on duty. I wondered when exactly he would be leaving. I wanted to know—and yet did not want to know—the exact date. Would I see him again before he left? Would I even know that he had gone? Sooner or later, I thought wearily as I undressed, some one will tell me. Sooner or later some one always tells you everything here; all you need is patience. I was not naturally a patient person; I decided to try to acquire patience.

To keep my mind off Jake, I thought about the party due to take place in Cas. this afternoon. I fell asleep thinking about my penguins. When I woke some hours later the pale December afternoon sun was shining on my face. I could not go back to sleep, so I lay half-awake and watched the sun slide slowly down the sky. Soon the short afternoon was dead, and it was quite dark. The vanishing sun reminded me of something Sister P.T.S. said on our last day in the school: ". . . In your modern phraseology, you are going on a one-way ticket." The sun would be back in the morning, but as we moved on through the hospital we seldom returned to the same ward or worked twice with the same people. I had met him and moved on. I knew that I should never forget him; I doubted if he had noticed my absence.

# 12

## A Bunch of Carnations

MARGARET was full of stars that night. Large, shining golden stars hanging over every bed, down the centre of the ward and across the doorways. Bunches of holly and trails of ivy were fixed all round the walls; long green and gold streamers stretched across the ward from window to opposite window; and at the far end, hiding the wheel-chairs, was a tall slender Christmas-tree that nearly reached to the high ceiling and was bright with electric candles, coloured balls, a multitude of small red-wrapped packages, cotton-wool snow, and glittering Epsom-salt frost.

I admired the scene from the ward doorway before going on duty. "It's perfectly lovely."

"Well, Nurse Standing?" Sister Margaret bore down on me from the sterilizing corner on the right of the ward door. "Do you propose to favour us with your presence to-night, or have you taken root in that doorway? Hurry along, child! What's the matter? Have you never seen a star before?"

"Not in a ward, Sister."

"You haven't, eh?" She stood squarely in front of me buttoning her sleeves. "Well, you should have! There are plenty of stars in the wards, and not only on Christmas Eve. In our profession, Nurse, you have got to make up your mind which you are going to see. The mud or the stars. Both are there. It's up to you to make your choice. Now, take off that corridor cape and come along to my report. I have work to do if you have not!"

"Yes, Sister." I retired to the changing-room swiftly, hung up my cape, and joined Nurse Jones, who was waiting by the red screen on the near side of the centre table.

The women were enthusiastic when I took round their nightly milk. "It's been ever such a day, Nurse! You never saw such a carry-on! That Dr Ross was on top of a step-ladder all evening. And him and that Dr Linton! The things they'd say with ever such serious faces! I declare, Nurse, it was as good as a turn on the telly! And the nurses have been busy all day hanging up them lovely stars—made them all themselves they did—aren't they sweet?"

Jones helped me collect the empty cups. "We'll settle but not tuck down our ladies. The P.T.S. are going to do this ward early, as we've so many ill women. I do hope they are all able to enjoy it."

"Enjoy what, Nurse? And why do the P.T.S. come here?"

She said she had forgotten it was my first Christmas here. "I won't tell you, and then it can be a surprise for you as well as for the women. Just make sure the ward is ready by nine-thirty; leave all the outside routine until later. To-night is the one night in the year when it is permissible for your routine to go haywire. But one thing I must tell you; get on with things as fast as you can, because in the small, dark hours you and I are Father Christmas in Margaret. Let's get going."

The women were settled by 9.25. One of them, a lady named Mrs Yates, called to me; "Nurse, what is going to happen? Sister said we were going to have a nice surprise this evening. What is——" She broke off and held up her hand. "Oh—listen."

Very softly, from a long way off, we heard the girls singing. In a few minutes, still singing quietly, they walked in pairs into the ward. They walked slowly, they wore their capes reversed with the scarlet lining uppermost, and they carried small lighted lanterns. They stopped when they reached the tree, grouped themselves round it, then sang three of the quieter carols. I guessed they had been asked to sing those particular carols, because so many of our women were very ill. The soft light from the electric candles on the tree mingled with the rose-coloured night lighting, and illuminated the young, serious faces of the P.T.S. pros., and the thin, plump, broad, and narrow faces of our patients, who turned their heads towards the tree and watched the girls with eyes from which the dullness of illness had momentarily faded. I noticed that even Mrs Simmonds, our most ill patient among so much illness, was smiling. Jones had told me last night that Mrs Simmonds would not only not see another Christmas, but it was doubtful that she would see the New Year. She was very young to die—only twenty-eight; but her heart was old, very old. She had looked old this morning; somehow she did not look old now. She caught my eye; I was standing near her. She said, "This is lovely, isn't it, duck?"

The P.T.S. girls cast sidelong and respectful glances at Jones and myself; I felt very much an experienced old hand at nursing. To increase this novel sensation, when the singing was over, Sister P.T.S., who had been standing with Sister Margaret in the ward doorway, came forward to wish Jones and me a Happy Christmas. She smiled at me. "Night-duty already, Nurse Standing? Really, how time passes! Your first year will be over quite soon."

When they all left Jones and I tucked down the women. "It was ever such a nice treat, Nurses," they told us; "and they sang real pretty. Soothing it was. Nice to hear a carol or two even if you are in hospital. Expect we'll all sleep ever so well to-night."

At midnight Jones's head appeared round the kitchen door. "Come into the duty-room, Standing. There's something I want to show you."

I dried my hands and followed her across the corridor. On the duty-room table was a stack of bulging operation stockings.

"If I get held up over anyone will you take these round? They are all labelled with names and bed-numbers, so you can't go wrong. And try not to let them see what you are doing, or it'll spoil their pleasure when they wake in the morning. They have to be round before we put the lights on." She yawned. "Sorry." Then she smiled. "You may have missed a lot of fun leaving Cas., but you'll get quite a kick in the morning. We've no one in who's been in before for Christmas, and they aren't expecting this. You'll be surprised at how thrilled they get."

"Do all the patients in the wards get stockings? And do the P.T.S. go round everywhere?"

"Yes. Both are traditional customs. I thought the pros. sang very well this year. How about you?"

"Like the women, I thought they sung real lovely. Nearly made me want to cry."

She smiled again. "You're one up on me. I did weep—always do, like a tap." The telephone that was buried under all the stockings on the table jangled with the urgency that telephone-bells have at night. Jones reached for it, murmuring, "Now what?" In a different tone she said, "Margaret Ward. Nurse Jones speaking," and listened. I was going to leave her when she beckoned to me to stay where I was. She said, "Yes, Sister . . . Yes . . . No, we haven't a spare bed. . . . Yes" —she looked at me—"we can put up a spare. There is room between 18 and 19." She listened again. "Acute lobar pneumonia. Do you know her age, Sister? Thank you." Pause. "Yes. I see. . . . Thank you, we can manage." She replaced the receiver. "Get all that, Standing?"

"Most of it, Nurse. Where do we find the spare bed?"

"Back of the linen cupboard. I'll help you put it up straight away. She'll be up in about ten minutes. Then will you set for a straight pneumonia, stat. You know what to get? Oxygen, mask, extra pillows, fracture boards, cradle, electric blanket, personal blanket, bed blocks, hottie bottles. Got that? Good. Oh, just one thing more"—she glanced at the stockings— "this girl is twenty-five. Do a stocking for her sometime, will you? There are some spare boxes of toilet soap and talcum powder in that lower drawer; give her one of each and one of the charm bracelets that you'll find in the blue box behind the soap. See what she looks like and give her the kind of thing you think she'll like; if in any doubt give her the sort you'd like to get yourself. We can't leave the poor girl out. She must be feeling miserable, apart from springing acute pneumonia to-night. Got that too? Good. Then let's," she ended inevitably, "get going."

We did so, quickly and silently. We were just ready when the porters appeared with the long, rubber-wheeled stretcher-trolley. One of the porters gave Jones a sheaf of notes. "S.M.O.

said to tell you he'll be back to see her in half an hour, Nurse."

The young woman with pneumonia was called Jean Mason. She had pale-brown hair, a thin, pinched face, and very frightened blue eyes. Her breathing was obviously painful, much too rapid and shallow. The porters helped us lift her into bed, then disappeared with their trolley as quietly as they had arrived.

Jones took Jean's temperature, then showed her the oxygen-mask, and explained its purpose. "You will feel much more comfortable if you wear this, my dear. It will help your breathing a lot. May I slip it over your head?"

The girl licked her dry, cracked lips and gave a tiny nod. "If you say so, Nurse," she gasped flatly.

Jones gave her a shrewd look, but said nothing. When the mask was in position she checked the rising bubbles of oxygen in the flow-metre attached to the oxygen cylinder, then beckoned me to her side of the bed. "It must go at that speed, pro tem. Keep an eye on it." She touched one of the figures marking the metre. "There."

"Nurse!" Mrs Yates' voice called urgently from the other end of the ward. "Nurse, can you come?"

Jones replied instantly, "Coming, Mrs Yates." She looked at me again, "You stay here, Standing." And she shot down the dim ward.

I watched the oxygen; the girl in the bed watched me. "You—busy—in—here, Nurse?"

"A little," I smiled at her. "Is that stuff easing your breathing?"

"Think so." She touched her chest experimentally. "I got a pain—here. It was bad, but they give me something for it downstairs, and it don't feel so bad now."

"That's good." I smiled once more and checked her pulse. Her pulse was racing, her skin burning with her high fever. I was not sure what to do. As far as I knew, Jones had done all we could do for the moment for Jean; no treatment could be given until Dr Spence arrived to order it. I could hear Jones moving round the ward; two other women besides Mrs Yates had called to her, and I wondered if I should go and help her. But she had said, "Stay here"; so I waited.

Jean had not taken her eyes off me. "Expect you get used to people coming in all night?"

I sensed the appeal behind her question. "Oh, yes. Lots of people come in at night."

Her blue eyes widened. "Don't it frighten you, duck? It would frighten me. It—does"—her voice was nearly inaudible —"frighten me."

Instinctively I held her hand. "Your first time in hospital, is this? Don't be frightened. There's nothing to be frightened of here. Honestly."

Her hand gripped mine. "Nurse," she said quite clearly, " am I going to die? That doctor at home to-night, I heard him tell my mum that I had to come straight in—and Mum, she didn't want me to come, what with it being Christmas to-morrow—and she said, did I have to? They didn't think I could hear, but I could, and I heard him say, ' She's got to go into Martin's or . . .'" She left her sentence unfinished, but the expression in her eyes showed what had been left unsaid.

I did not stop to wonder what I should say—I just said it. " You aren't going to die, Jean; you aren't, truly. I expect your own doctor had to make your mother grasp how important it was that you should come in, and so perhaps he put it very strongly. But you aren't"—I was perfectly definite—" going to die."

She asked simply, "Why not?"

" Because no one here is going to let you die. That's why you are here. To get well."

She looked up at me. "You look ever such a kid—but you talk—as if you know." She put up her free hand and fingered my apron skirt. "Course, you're a Martin's nurse, so you must know. You nurses here are good. Every one knows that." Then, to my astonishment and sheer wonder, some of the fear faded from her expression. "I'm glad that other nurse told you to stop with me. I feel better with you here. I don't feel so—alone."

And I felt filled with admiration for Jones's shrewdness. " I'm glad about that, Jean. The doctor will be up to see you soon; he'll probably give you something else for your chest, and then you may be able to have a sleep."

She said she would like that. "I didn't get no sleep last night. I got that pain in my chest, see—and it hurt every time I coughed and I kept on coughing. I haven't coughed much since I had that stuff they gave me downstairs, and that little fat doctor, he said as the pain would go right away soon."

"That was Dr Spence. He's the Senior Medical Officer here and the man who's coming up to see you. So you can be quite sure that you needn't worry any more. Dr Spence is a very clever doctor and he never pretends; if he says the pain'll go right away it will."

"I thought as he said it just to cheer me up. I didn't believe him—till you told me just now as I'd be all right." She glanced up at the ceiling, then stared. "What are all those things, duck? They look like stars."

"They are stars. Which reminds me, it's after midnight. Happy Christmas, Jean, and may you get well very soon."

She turned to me. "It's not Christmas yet, dear. It's still dark—the night."

I said, "But Christmas Day is like all other days in one thing: it begins in the dark."

A faint smile flickered through her eyes. "Well, I never. So it does." Her hand tightened in mine. "Ta, duck. And a Happy Christmas to you, I'm sure."

Jean and I became friends that night, and our friendship increased in the nights that followed. After a couple of weeks on night-duty I forgot that I had ever had any other existence and in many ways felt as if I had begun nursing again in a new hospital. I saw nothing of the girls in my set, as I was the only one of our number on nights. We night-nurses slept in a different building, ate meals at different times, and made different friends in our own small circle, that seemed so alien and removed from the normal world of people who went to bed at night. I discovered that I enjoyed being an alien; I liked getting up when the world was going to bed; and, above all, I adored packing myself into bed between three hot-water bottles on those cold January mornings and drinking hot cocoa and reading until I was too sleepy to see the print clearly and could then drop the book and turn over and go to sleep without even having the bother of turning off a light.

Another pleasure I discovered was that of finding that Margaret belonged to Jones and me, and we belonged to Margaret, not just for an odd half-hour, but for eleven hours every night. I had been fond of the men in Francis, but I never felt as at home in Francis as I did in Margaret; nor was I allowed to do so much nursing of the men as became part of my work for the women. Very little cleaning is done in the wards at night; the nursing of the patients was our sole concern. Jones was a good nurse and a patient senior; she enjoyed teaching, and while she taught me she had the gift of making me feel that I was not just a useless, ham-handed pro., but another young woman, who did not yet know as much as she did, but would as soon as I had had her experience. She never talked down, and she never lectured unnecessarily. Very soon I looked forward to going on duty at night and was quite disappointed when my nights off arrived and I had to hand over my beloved Margaret to a relief pro.

Not even Sister Margaret was able to shake my pleasure in working in her ward. I began to agree with Jones about Sister. I did not go all the way and consider Sister restful; but, although she might—and generally did—bark at me, her bark was fair; Sister never found fault for the sake of finding fault. If you made a mistake she was on to it—and you— immediately; but she had no 'things' and no 'little ways.' After a week I decided I preferred working under Sister Margaret to working under either Sister Francis or Sister Casualty. Sister Francis' gentle personality in retrospect struck me as ineffectual, and she was quite overshadowed by her highly efficient and dominant staff nurse. Sister Casualty, even when pleasant, had always been something of an enigma to me; I never knew where I was with her. No staff nurse would ever be permitted to overshadow Sister Margaret, and she was no enigmatical young woman. She was a strong-minded, capable ward sister, who kept a tight hold on every corner of her ward, and who left you in no doubt of what she thought of your work. She either greeted me with a stern, " Never make your bed-corners—set your trolleys—rule up the admission book—in this way again, Nurse Standing. I like it done—so, and will allow no variation," or she gave me a silent nod. I started looking forward to those nods at the end of my night; they meant that Sister Margaret was satisfied with my work.

If it had not been for Jake Waring I should have been extremely happy at that time. I was not happy, because I missed his presence and thought about him in all my free waking moments. Sometimes, when I had to sit at the centre table alone at night while Jones was occupied out of the ward, I used to play games with myself. I used to pretend that I was a senior, that this was a surgical ward, and that I was waiting for Jake to come and do his night-round. I could imagine his formal " Good evening " and the quiet walk round the patients, and then we would come back to the table and I would watch him while he wrote up notes. Then, as a senior, I could offer him coffee. Jones often gave Dr Spence coffee in the kitchen while I sat at the table. And after we had had coffee, just as we left the ward and were well away from the patients, he would say, " When are your next nights off, Rose? Thursday and Friday? Right. I'll try and be free for a couple of hours at least. Can I call for you at the usual time? "

I lived through that little scene so many times that I half came to believe that it was true; it is easy to believe fantasies when all the world is asleep, and the only sounds are the different rhythms of breathing and the hiss of the various oxygen cylinders that were in constant use in Margaret. Sometimes, just before dawn, I would go out on the balcony at the end of the ward for the quite legitimate purpose of putting something into the wet-linen bin. Despite the cold on my bare arms, I often lingered out there for a few minutes, looking down on the street-lights that were strung like ropes of diamonds over darkened London, and watching the sky-line on the far bank of the river standing against the night sky like black lace. Dawn seems to come slowly when you wait for it, but when you watch it it happens in front of your eyes. Those January dawns were seldom pink or red, they were grey—all shades of grey from gun metal to off-white, and often when the morning came and before the smoke and

dirt rose to cloud the sky with smog the sky was the colour
of pale parchment, the air clear and clean and smelling slightly
of salt, and the buildings all around grey and white and
etched with the dirt of generations or centuries, merged into
the soft parchment background, and looked like those old
prints of London you find stacked in the dust behind the
shelves in an old bookseller's shop.

Then I would go back into the ward that seemed hot and
stuffy, and I would wonder how anyone could sleep in that
heat, until Jones rushed at me, "Shut that door, Standing. It's
freezing in here. Don't let any more cold air in, please."

But, although I lived privately in a dream, I knew that
dream could have no reality. Night after night, as I sat at the
table, I played my game; but when I looked down the
darkened ward towards the door no tall, fair man in a long
white coat came in. No man came in at all. Jones would not
have left me at the table if any of the men's rounds were
still to be done. The doorway and the ward remained empty;
yet my imagination, stimulated by fatigue, was so strong that
there were occasions when I stood up quickly, thinking I
must be seeing things—that couldn't really be Jake waiting
by the sterilizers. I was right. It was not. And I would sit
down again, feeling absurd and childish and utterly lonely.
I loved him so much, and, because of all these damned conventions and restrictions, we were never even going to get
on a first-name basis.

There were other complications, too. The night pros. were
all firmly convinced that Jake was only waiting to leave the
hospital to announce his engagement to Sister Casualty. They
said he had to wait to do that as it was an accepted tradition
that sisters did not become engaged to be married to members
of the resident staff. "They have to see so much of the men
that an official engagement would give rise to too much talk,
and sisters aren't supposed to cause talk. In the past one or
other party has resigned and then got married, stat. Sister
Verity left to marry Dr Mackenzie-Brown last year—no one
even suspected they were friends; and Sister Theatre resigned
and then got engaged and married in a couple of weeks to Mr
Old. And even Dr Spence waited until he stopped being a

registrar here to propose to Sister Agatha—she's Mrs S.M.O. now—six years ago."

I said I had not appreciated this fact.

My informant, Ellis from Henry, said I should have. "Take your Jones. She didn't get officially engaged to her Robert until he stopped being surgical registrar here. They announced it when he got that job at Martha's. Matron prefers it that way. Of course, people don't always wait, but those sort of people are generally junior men, like housemen. The senior residents, being more responsible, take their responsibilities more seriously. It can't really matter to them. They just get engaged under the counter and work until the wedding day is fixed, then resign."

"You think that's what the S.S.O.'ll do?"

She nodded. "Certain of it. We all are. It's too simple for him, as he's leaving soon in any case."

I smiled brightly and agreed it was very simple. To change the subject, I asked after Dingle. "How's her romance progressing?"

Ellis said, as far as she could tell, not too badly. "Her Bill's been behaving himself lately. He took her out to dinner on her last nights off and she's been so happy since that she's even appeased Sister Henry. Long may it last! I only hope she goes on being happy until I come off nights at the end of the week."

I had not seen Bill since that night in the plaster-room. He figured so little in my thoughts that I seldom recollected his existence and frequently forgot that he was the cause of Jake's being so annoyed with me that night. I wondered if that episode had bothered Bill at all. I doubted that it had, and felt very sorry for Dingle. She had a sweet face.

Mrs Simmonds and Mrs Yates both died during the first week of the New Year. They died in the daytime within a day of each other. On the night following Mrs Yates' death Margaret was subdued and sad; it was always a quiet ward, but that night a silence which was truly the silence of death hung over the ward. We had expected poor young Mrs Simmonds to die, and, although Jones and I were genuinely saddened by her premature death, we were not shocked as we were when we arrived on duty and found Mrs Yates' bed empty. The old lady had had another coronary thrombosis while lunches were being served and died in a matter of seconds. Mrs Simmonds' bed was already filled by a new patient, but as I did the drinks that night I found myself avoiding looking at the one empty bed and the neat sterile locker that still smelt of carbolic from its recent scrubbing. While I cleared the used cups I heard the phone go; a couple of minutes later Jones came in and told me to put hot-water bottles in the clean bed. "Another pneumonia, Standing. Usual setting. Get going."

I stared at her blankly for a moment, then said, "Yes, Nurse," took my tray to the kitchen, and went to the linen-room for hot-water bottles.

Jones followed me back into the kitchen. "Give me one—I'll fill it for you." As she unscrewed the top of the bottle she asked, "What's the matter, Standing? Don't you think we ought to use that bed?"

I hesitated. "Well—it was only this afternoon—and——"

She said slowly, "And a woman died in it? That it?" I nodded. "Now, you listen to me," she went on steadily, "I know all that, and so do all the patients. But that bed has had its iron frame and springs carbolized; it's got a new mattress, new pillows, new bedding. The locker's been scrubbed too, and the curtains are clean. That's all done automatically after every death. We can't just leave a bed empty for sentimental reasons, and if we left it empty it would be for no other reason. It's all new. And, as for some one dying in it"—she gave a slight shake of the head—"my good girl, I doubt if there's a bed in the hospital, and certainly there isn't a bed in Margaret, in which some one hasn't died. People do die in hospital. But you mustn't let your mind think about that; you've got to think of the patient coming in. She may be dying, and may live because poor Mrs Yates dropped dead this afternoon and so we've got room to take her in at once. Hospital beds," she reminded me, "are scarce—even nowadays. And one thing we don't do in hospital is mourn; regret—yes; mourn—no. There's no time for that, because there's always some one else coming in. Here, put this in the bed quickly, then get the rest of the things while I go and get some history sheets for her."

The next night the new patient had become an old patient. Margaret was full but comparatively quiet, and I took longer than usual with my first drink-round, because the women, being more cheerful, were feeling talkative. Jean, in particular, had a lot to tell me, and I stayed by her for several minutes, listening to her personal problems. When I eventually returned to the kitchen Jones was cutting the breakfast bread for me. We always cut that bread early in the night and left it on top of the refrigerator, covered with a clean damp teacloth, until it was needed in the morning.

I thanked her for starting the bread and apologized for being so slow. " I'm afraid I've been chatting too much."

She said she had noticed the long heart-to-hearts I had been having with the women. " I'm glad they are feeling up to chatting again. It's a bad sign when a woman's too ill to have a chat over a cuppa. There's nothing I must do just now, so I thought I'd get on with this bread in case something crops up later." She stacked the bread she had cut into a neat pile and started on a fresh loaf. " How's Jean? I thought she was looking rather down in the mouth when I went round. I saw her having a long talk to you. Did she tell you what's on her mind? "

" Yes, Nurse. I was just going to ask you about it." Then, remembering how irate Bennings had been when I chatted with the patients, I thought it best to add, " I hope you don't mind my staying so long with her? It wasn't easy to get away."

" I'd mind far more if you hadn't stayed put. It's as much part of our job at night to listen to the patients' talk as to rush round making beds and doing washings. It helps the patients enormously if they can get things off their chests, particularly in a women's ward. Women," she went on thoughtfully, " generally have a lot on their minds at night. They lie and fret about little things far more than men; but isn't life made up of little things? It may seem stupid to work yourself into a panic about what the old man had for his tea or if the nippers really did have a hot meal after school without Mum being there to make sure of it. It may seem stupid,"

she repeated, "but, personally, I don't think it is. And I consider any nurse who copes with that sort of problem by saying
briskly, 'Well, my dear, you can't do anything about it—so
stop worrying and go to sleep,' is a lousy nurse and entirely
lacking in imagination." She made another stack of bread,
then cut on methodically as she added, "I think the best
plan is to let them chat it out, and then, if I can, to offer a
constructive suggestion." She grinned suddenly. "You can't
conceive how many women I've put to sleep with fish-and-
chips."

"Fish-and-chips?" I echoed, wondering if I had heard
right.

"Yes. It solves so many problems. It's a good, hot, high-
protein meal, and there's hardly a street in this part of London
without a fried-fish shop. When one of our women gets in a
state about her family eating cold meals out of tins I tell her
to tell her husband to drop in at the fish bar on his way back
from work. Every one likes fish-and-chips; most kids adore
it. So all Dad has to do is shove the lot in the oven while the
kettle boils—and it probably cuts out washing-up, too, as, ten
to one, Dad'll dish up out of the grease-paper. Very hygienic
and far cleaner than a half-washed plate. So Mum, on thinking
this over, reckons it's a good plan, turns on her side, and goes
to sleep. Problem and insomnia solved. Now, what's worrying
Jean? Her young man?"

I nodded. "She tell you too, Nurse?"

"No. You're her great pal, not me. You made friends on
Christmas night, didn't you? I thought you would—and I
thought the poor girl looked in need of a friend, which was
why I told you to stay where you were."

I said I had guessed that. "It was very bright of you,
Nurse."

"Not bright at all. When you reach your fourth year,
Standing, you'll recognize sheer, blind panic when you see it.
It's not difficult; you get to see a lot of it here."

"How did you know Jean was worrying about her young
man if she didn't tell you? Is that something else you pick
up with experience?"

"More or less. People tend to worry about the same things

at the same age. Jean's not married; she's young—fairly pretty. If she has something on her mind, almost inevitably it's a man. If she was a man in the same circumstances it might be her job. What's up? Doesn't he visit her? "

" No. He's on shift work and his free time doesn't coincide with any visiting hours."

" How about Sundays? "

" He works Sunday afternoons for the overtime. They are saving to get married. Jean had a letter from him to-day telling her all this. He apparently said he didn't want her to think he hadn't come because he didn't want to come."

" And, having had that idea all the time, his letter has merely underlined it? She thinking he's just using shift work as an excuse to break off with her? "

" Yes."

She covered the bread with a clean cloth and rinsed the bread-board. " I'll have a word with Sister in the morning. Can you find out his name and where he works? We won't have it, as a fiancé is not a next-of-kin. Do it tactfully, so that she doesn't catch on, in case he really doesn't want to come. But I expect he's telling the truth: hospitals scare the daylights out of lots of people; they seem to think we go behind the Iron Curtain in non-visiting hours. Sister Margaret is very good about things like this. She'll probably contact him at work and see if something can be arranged. Sister knows patients can't sleep unless they've got quiet minds." She smiled at me. " Sister Margaret does not allow her patients to have unquiet minds. She'll fix something."

Jean's young man was called Sid Thomas. Sid arrived to see Jean before lunch next morning; when we went on duty that night, Jean was still glowing with pleasure.

" I never was so surprised in my life, Nurse Standing! I looked up and who should I see walking up the ward but my Sid! And he brought me a lovely bunch of roses. Hot-house ones. Yellow and red. Ever so pretty they are! They got taken out for the night, but you take a look at them outside, dear. But talk about surprise! Know what I said, Nurse? ' Sid,' I said, ' you can't come in here now—it's not hours!' And what do you think he said, dear? "

"Tell me, Jean."

" 'I've got the Sister's special permission to come, I have,' he says, 'and I'd like to see anyone try to stop me seeing my girl again after all this time.' " She smiled ecstatically. "And to think there have I been thinking maybe he didn't want to come and he was just making excuses! I can tell you, I feel ever so much better to-night, dear. I'd like to tuck down and get to sleep real early, if it's okay with you, Nurse? "

When the ward was settled to sleep I went out to the clinical room to have a look at Jean's roses. I knew she would ask in the morning what I thought of them, and I wanted to be honest in my admiration. The clinical room in which were kept the microscope and specimen glasses housed the flowers at night. The vases were labelled as in Francis Adams, and I found Jean's number immediately. The roses were very lovely. I smelt them, then counted the flowers—twenty-four. Good for Sid! And good for Sister Margaret too! I smiled at the flowers. Obviously Sister Margaret did not allow a romance to break in her ward. That thought inevitably reminded me of my personal affairs, and I stopped smiling. I did not want to waste time in foolish depression, but I could not stop loving him even if that love was folly, and at quiet moments like this, particularly when surrounded by flowers, it was difficult not to lapse into my favourite what-might-have-been-if-only-I-had-been-four-years-older day-dream.

But I had my routine to do, and that routine I knew very well was the specific antidote for depression. I was on my way out of the clinical room when I noticed that some one had deposited a fresh bunch of flowers on top of one of the empty dispensary baskets on the floor under the china shelf. I took up the bunch incuriously; the flowers must go into a vase or they would wither in the night. I looked over the outside of the tissue-paper wrapping to find a label or pinned-on envelope. Some one was due for a pleasant surprise when I delivered her flowers in the morning with her early tea. The flowers were carnations, and they had a glorious scent. I stopped my search for a label momentarily, and put my face down among the blooms. As I was smelling them the outer ward door leading into the main upstairs corridor opened.

Dr Spence appeared in the doorway, noticed me in the clinical room that was just inside that outer door, and bounced in to join me among the flowers.

"Evening, Nurse. Busy in the ward to-night?"

I lowered the carnations. "Good evening, Dr Spence. No, we are very quiet. Shall I fetch Nurse Jones for you?"

"Don't trouble yourself," he replied amicably; "I won't do my round yet if you aren't busy. I'll be back later. I merely thought I'd look in as I was going past." He glanced over his shoulder, as if he had some one waiting for him in the corridor outside. "I'm on my way to Francis to look at a chap there with the S.S.O. Just let Nurse Jones know that I'll be back at about eleven unless she needs me earlier, will you, Nurse? Much obliged." He had been gazing fondly at the flowers I held as he talked. Now he added impulsively, "I say, those are nice. Have they just arrived?"

"One of the visitors must have left them. I've just found them."

"Some one's saying it with flowers very late," he remarked with a friendly smile. "Let's have them a second." The S.M.O. never stood on ceremony; he was too intelligent and too well respected to need to do that; also he was known to be very happily married, which last fact enabled him to behave far more normally than he could ever have done in his bachelor days. He took the flowers to the outer door and pulled it open. "Jake, step inside and have a look at these. You remember I told you my wife was good at growing these chaps? Well, these are the exact type she grows. Good, aren't they?"

Jake stepped inside obediently, acknowledged my cap with a mumbled, "Evening," ignored my face, and admired the carnations. "They are good—and, yes, I do remember your sporting buttonholes of these last year." He touched the blooms. "I like the petal formation very much—or, sorry" —he apologized, as he inadvertently dislodged the white envelope I had been unable to find. It dropped to the floor by Dr Spence's feet. The S.M.O. stooped, picked it up, glanced at it casually, then gave it a second look.

"I've got a problem here, Nurse," he said, still looking at

the envelope. "I thought I knew all your ladies, but this foxes me. Who's Miss R. Standing? Can't be Jean—she's what? Maston?"

"Mason, doctor." Like an idiot, I blushed. "As a matter of fact, doctor——"

He was too curious to leave well alone. "Perhaps they belong in Martha or Agatha? We're going that way; we'll deliver them for you. Or how about you, Jake?" He looked up at his taller colleague. "You got a woman called Miss R. Standing?"

Jake put his hands in his pockets. "No. I should say they belong to Nurse, here."

"You Miss R. Standing, Nurse?" demanded Dr Spence. I nodded weakly, and he thrust the flowers at me, beaming like a middle-aged Puck. "I do beg your pardon, Nurse. And there was I trying to wrest them from you! There." He stood back and tilted his head to one side. "They become you very well, Nurse. I like to see a young woman holding flowers. I expect you're glad the S.S.O. discovered that note for you before I had taken them round the hospital, eh? Very well, Nurse. My compliments to Nurse Jones, and I'll see her later. Better push off to Francis now."

Jake had been watching me all this time. From his expression it was not apparent that he admired the prospect before him. He reached for the door without looking away from me, opened it, murmured drily, "It might be an idea to push off," nodded at me, but went off without bothering to say good-night.

As Dr Spence hopped out after him he said something that made them both laugh. I heard their laughter fading down the corridor, then closed the door they had left open, leant against it, and considered the carnations which I still held.

I was not surprised to recognize Bill's writing on the envelope, nor was I interested in his motive for sending them. I was only sorry that the wretched Dingle should have to be upset again; Bill sending flowers must mean Bill straying. I cursed Bill. Why did he have to keep upsetting people? Why could he not leave well alone?

I went into the kitchen, stuck the flowers in a jug of water, sat down on the bread-bin, and opened the envelope. Inside was a sheet of paper of the type used for Path. Lab. requests. It was closely written on both sides. I thought dispassionately: he probably wrote this in Henry while poor Dingle thought he was writing notes, and grimaced at my own horrible pun. Then I thought, What now? Several possibilities flashed into my mind; none of them were right.

Bill wrote:

I owe you an apology, Rose. Two apologies, did you but know it. To get on with the first, I really am sorry about that affair in Cas. I know I didn't ought to have done it, but a character can't always do just what he ought. I gather my boss got tough with you. My humble apologies. If it's any consolation he tore me into little pieces and threw me all over the H.S.'s sitting-room. From now on Uncle is going to behave himself—and, my God, Rose, how boring that is going to be! Must be, as I daren't put up a second black— certainly not while Jake remains with us. Talking of which brings me quite easily to my second apology. I only throw this in as I know you're a girl who enjoys a good laugh and feel in fairness I may as well give you the chance to laugh your head off.

It's this way: for some time now I've had a sort of hunch that a certain senior character had a soft spot for you. I've seen the way he looked at you, and so on. I even indulged in a little cloak-and-dagger stuff once and nipped you to Bert's when I knew he was going to be there. I thought it might be amusing to watch his reactions while I whispered sweet nothings into your ear. Far from admirable but with comic possibilities. Only you wouldn't play. How dumb are you, Rose? Not quite so dumb as you care to make out, I suspect. And how wise you were, seeing how things are working out. So please have your good laugh and accept this small floral token from a reformed character who is fast becoming exhausted by all this virtuous living, and who is also very shaken at having a hunch proved fallible for the first time in his life.

Regards, love, BILL.

There were two postscripts. The first read, " When are your next nights off? Doing anything that I can't do with you, too? "

The second read, " Have you heard that Sister Cas. is leaving too? How wrong can a character be? "

# 13

## *A Pro. turns Patient*

I SAT very still on that bread-bin. I did not drop the letter and burst into tears, feel sick, want to faint. I did not feel anything at all. I thought quite calmly, the night girls were right—she's resigning to get married; that's the accepted form. In my ice-cold, academic frame of mind I considered the possibility of Bill being mistaken; maybe she wasn't leaving? I answered myself at once. She must be. Bill was not talking about hunches but facts. As a Casualty Officer he would be very well up in all the Cas. news, and Sister Cas. resigning was big news indeed. That position is rated very high in the nursing world. Young women of Miss Mercer's age and experience did not throw up such a post lightly; only promotion to perhaps Night Sister or one of the Office Sisters would tempt her away if she was remaining in her profession; both those posts are stepping-stones to becoming a Matron. No. The only possible reason for her chucking up her job here at Martin's must be marriage. Women will chuck up any job for marriage, I had always heard. Until I met Jake Waring I had not been able to understand that attitude. Now I understood it very well.

Jake. I could no longer postpone thinking of him—and I ceased to feel academic about Bill's news. And the first sensation that broke through the numbness was anger. I was furious with myself for being such a fool, for believing in fairies, for wasting so many secret moments in wishful thinking. Why had I not had the sense to face from the start that the whole set-up was impossible? Why had I let matters get out of hand?

Why? Because I had had no say in the matter. I had seen

Jake, and, although not at first sight, it had not taken many brief meetings for me to recognize what he was—the man for me. But first-year pros., I reminded myself drearily, are not meant to be young women. They are just timid or irresponsible—what? First-years. Scruffy, always harassed, generally with caps flying and some sister or staff nurse glowering in the background. They were not young women who fell in love—the hospital would laugh its head off, as Bill had said I might—at the mere idea. It had never happened. There was not even an exception to prove the rule. And so I might as well accept this at last, step mentally back into the uniformed figure sitting on the bread-bin, and get on with my night's routine.

I stood up stiffly, took out a couple of long loaves, reached for the bread-board that was propped on the dresser, took the bread-knife from the drawer, sharpened it automatically on the rim of the sink, and began to slice the first loaf.

But cutting bread is not an occupation to occupy the mind. So I made myself think about Bill and Dingle and the open invitation he had offered me in his first postscript. Bill Martin, I decided fiercely, was a two-timing bastard. The word gave me genuine satisfaction. I normally never used it, even in thought, but it was Hector's second-favourite condemnation, and to-night I felt it was justified. Bill was just that; even if he was not officially engaged to Dingle he had no business to run two strings at once. And I was one string that he was certainly not going to run. Which, I now saw clearly, was precisely why he had bothered to send me those carnations and ask me out again. He simply could not conceive that I was not interested; I must be—every one else was; so I must have some deep reason for playing hard-to-get. Never in a hundred years would it dawn on a Bill Martin that he simply did not appeal to me. There was one great consolation; it had obviously never dawned on him also that Jake was important to me. So much for his hunches. And so much for his watching Jake looking at me, too. I had watched Jake constantly when he and I were in the same room or hall; I had longed to see some warmth in his expression when he glanced my way; I never saw any flicker of expression that could give me the slightest grounds to hope he even liked me. He simply looked and talked at and to the top of my cap.

I finished slicing the first loaf and began on the second. I could not stand any more thoughts of Jake, so I thought instead about Cas. without Miss Mercer. Who would take over? Of course—Davis. I knew that already. I should have taken heed of that warning. I wondered what kind of a sister Davis would make, and what Cas. would be like without Miss Mercer; she was so much a part of her department that it was hard to visualize it without her; but not as hard as it was to visualize Martin's and my future life here without Jake in the physical background and mental foreground.

I cut the loaf fiercely. Why did I have to come to Martin's now? Why not a year later when I would have missed him, never known him—and never known what I was missing? I closed my eyes involuntarily, thinking how much I was going to miss him and how long it would be before I could laugh at myself and the painful folly of loving a complete stranger. I had not closed my eyes like that for some time; a succession of sisters, beginning with Sister P.T.S. had come close to lecturing me out of the habit. It was a pity there was no watchful sister to disapprove of that habit in Margaret kitchen just then, because when I closed my eyes I was still slicing the second loaf with the sharp bread-knife. Instead of the loaf, I sliced the palm of my left hand.

Jones, coming into the kitchen a few minutes later, found me holding my hand under the running cold tap. " You stupid child, why didn't you call me? You can't deal with this yourself—it's really deep. And sit down, Standing." She pushed me back on to the bread-bin (the only seat in our kitchen). " You're pale green. Keep your hand up and your head down while I get some sal volatile." She vanished and returned instantly with a medicine glass. " Drink this." When I had drunk the liquid she examined my hand carefully. " This is more than a simple gash," she said soberly. " What were you doing to let the knife go so far in? Didn't you feel it? "

" No. It just—happened. I wasn't thinking, I'm afraid, and it was done before I realized it."

" Poor kid." She tightened the bandage round my wrist. " I

expect you had a touch of night-nurses' paralysis. I've had it a few times myself. Didn't you sleep well to-day? Hey—hold that hand right up, it's still bleeding. Just a moment." She tied another bandage over the original one. " I'll have to get this really tight, like a tourniquet. We won't stop it otherwise. Sorry if I'm hurting, Standing," she grunted, pulling the two ends of the bandage as tightly as she could, " but I can't let this bleeding go on. It's not arterial, but you must have hacked your way through rows of capillaries. I don't think you've done more than that. There." She straightened her back and held my hand up for me. " Now prop your elbow on the table while I phone Night Sister."

I sighed. " Oh, dear. Some one ill in the ward? I'm awfully sorry to have held you up like this, Nurse."

She said kindly, " The women are all right. I'm going to ring Night Sister about you. You'll have to have something more done to that hand."

" Oh, Nurse, must you? I'm sure it will be all right. The bleeding's bound to stop soon, and I always heal quickly. Honestly, it's only a cut."

She shook her head slightly. " Sorry, Standing, but I have to report this. You'll need some stitches, I'm certain. You can't work on with a cut like that. Sit here; I'll come back at once."

Night Sister arrived in Margaret kitchen ten minutes later. She was sympathetic about my hand, but impatient with my carelessness. " Surely, Nurse Standing, you are used to cutting bread by now! Could you not have noticed the knife was slipping? " Jones undid the bandages, and Sister clucked over my exposed palm. " You will certainly have to have this stitched. No two ways about it. I will ring Mr Waring immediately. He is still on his rounds." She turned to Jones. " You must have a relief, Nurse. I will send Nurse White to you for the rest of the night, and Nurse Jamieson will have to manage alone in Martha as best she can."

Sister went into the duty-room to do her telephoning; Jones had to return to the ward; and I remained alone, sitting on the bread-bin and feeling even more miserable at the prospect of seeing Jake again than I had felt half an hour ago when I had been convinced he was lost to my sight for ever.

Night Sister returned. "Nurse White is on her way and Mr Waring wishes me to take you to the minor surgical theatre at once." She looked at me, and her manner altered. "Poor child, you look thoroughly shocked." She slipped her arm through mine. "Do you feel too giddy to walk? Would you rather I fetched a chair? Perhaps that might be as well. Wait here while I fetch one."

"I can walk quite well, thank you, Sister," I replied quickly and uncomfortably. Her concern worried me more than her previous impatience; then I suddenly realized why her attitude had changed, and with the realization felt less embarrassed. I was now off duty and an official patient. Our sisters might be stern disciplinarians to the nurses, but they were uniformly kind to the patients. Night Sister was a different—and very much nicer—woman as she escorted me to the M.S. Theatre.

Jake had changed too. "You have got a nasty gash here, Nurse Standing," he said gently. "I'm afraid it will need quite a few stitches. Will you mind stitches? Ever been stitched before?" His expression was so sympathetic that I could not suppress a wild thought about cutting myself in pieces. Why hadn't I done this before? "I'll try not to hurt," he went on, "but you're bound to feel it. What do you say?"

"They won't worry me—I think, Mr Waring. I've often been stitched up before—truly. I didn't mind them at all."

He smiled at me as he took off his white coat and rolled up his shirt-sleeves. "Would you be in the habit of cutting yourself into shreds, Nurse Standing?"

Night Sister defended me magnificently. "Nurse Standing has never injured herself on duty previously, Mr Waring."

He caught my eye. "Splendid." His tone was dry but not unkind. "So you had these previous stitches in your pre-hospital days?"

"Yes. Some here." I showed them the white scar on the inside of my right fore-arm. "I had nine in there, three in my left knee, and—I believe—four in my head. Round the back."

He traced the scar on my arm with one finger. "You clearly are in the habit of cutting yourself to shreds. This was another nasty gash. How did you do it?"

" Climbing over a barbed-wire fence. I slipped."

He looked at me and raised an eyebrow. " And the others? "

" My knee was the same fence. My head was when one of my brothers hit me with a cricket bat. Accidentally."

" I see." A muscle twitched in his left cheek. " Did you hit your brother back, Nurse? "

" No. I couldn't."

Night Sister, who was growing more maternal with every second, said that was highly forbearing of me. " It is not easy to control one's temper even when accidentally provoked."

I said, " Well, as a matter of fact, Sister, he knocked me out. That's why I couldn't hit back."

Jake's muscle twitched again. " From what we are gleaning of Nurse Standing's childhood, Sister, I find it not at all surprising that she should take stitching in her stride."

Night Sister was placidly laying a stitching trolley. In our hospital sick staff were only treated by the most senior residents and sisters, which was why I had this exalted couple to deal with a very minor hospital emergency. Sister said, " I expect that to anyone who was still a child during the War barbed-wire fencing must have seemed only a tiresome obstacle to play. I remember we had a constant stream of such injuries to children when I was in Casualty. Will you use silk or nylon, Mr Waring? "

" Nylon, please, Sister." He looked at her and then at me as he went to the sink to wash his hands. " Yes, you must have been a very small child in those days, Nurse." He glanced over his shoulder at Sister and added pleasantly, " How well I remember your days as a staff nurse in Casualty, Sister— and how well you guided my first faltering steps as a C.O. Do you remember how often you saved me from incurring the wrath of old Sister Casualty? " He smiled at her as he soaped his arms. " I do not remember any sister in my entire hospital career who could so quickly reduce the medical staff to abject small boys as old Sister Casualty."

Night Sister wagged her befrilled head reminiscently. " She could be a terror," she agreed with simple pride, " but I've never known a better sister. We sisters are not the same these days."

"Sister! You mustn't say that! That is a sure sign that you and I now belong—as, indeed, we do to Nurse here—to the older generation. But I have to admit I find myself doing that myself. I have not infrequently heard my voice telling my housemen that housemen are not what they were in my young days. No doubt about it "—he shook the drips from his wet arms and hands into the sink and came towards us with his hands upraised as if in prayer—"that attitude of mind is a bad sign, and unavoidable. It's only a question of time, Sister, before you and I meet again and shake our greying heads sadly over the ways of modern night sisters and S.S.O.'s. Not what we were, we'll say."

She smiled at him as if they shared a private joke about this. "I shall look forward to welcoming you back, Mr Waring."

He said he looked forward to that moment too. "Possibly by then I shall have got used to not wearing a white coat." He picked up a sterile towel. "Just raise your arm from the table, please, Nurse. Thank you." As he spread the towel on which my arm was to rest he gave a small grimace. "What have I forgotten?"

Sister looked concerned. "Have you forgotten something, Mr Waring?" She considered her trolley setting. "I believe I have everything here——?"

I had been wondering whether he was not wearing a mask intentionally. I had never known him do any stitching without a mask. As they both looked over the trolley I said quietly, "Is it your mask, Mr Waring?"

"It is, indeed. I'm obliged to you, Nurse."

Sister, clucking at her own absent-mindedness, tied one on for him as his hands were clean. "I cannot conceive of what I was thinking."

He said, "I think we've both got rather a lot on our minds, Sister," and they exchanged another private smile.

When he was half-way through his stitching the theatre telephone rang. It was Casualty needing Night Sister. We heard her say, "I will be with you directly, Nurse." She came back into the small white theatre and explained why she was needed. "I will be back as soon as I can, Mr Waring, but I must go and see this man. Will you be able to manage alone? "

" Of course, Sister. Don't disturb yourself, we are doing very well. Won't be long now." He watched me. " How are you feeling, Nurse? "

I managed to raise a smile. " Fine, thank you."

Sister gave me an approving nod. "You are doing quite nicely, Nurse." Which was high praise from her. " If Mr Waring has done with you before I return, will you sit quietly in here until either I or my Night Assistant come to take you to Nightingale."

" But, Sister—can't I go back on duty? I am sure I could do quite a lot with one hand."

Jake replied for her. " Under no circumstances," he said, and bent over my hand.

He was silent when Sister left us. Occasionally he glanced up at my face to see how I was taking it, but he said nothing until he knotted the last stitch. " Move your fingers again, Nurse." I did so, and he touched each in turn. " You felt all that? Good. Now close your eyes and tell me which finger I touch as I touch it." He tested all my fingers, not in rotation. " Right. You can open your eyes again, Nurse Standing."

I could not open my eyes, because I had suddenly started to weep. I was not sure why; tiredness, shock, his going, the pain of that needle going through—any of them or all of them. All I was sure was that I had never wept in front of any man in my life, and I was not going to start now—and certainly not with him.

He asked gently, " What's up? Very tired? Did I hurt much? I tried not to, but I know I must have done."

I nodded dumbly, still keeping my eyes screwed shut. Better he should think that I was tired and my hand sore.

" Want to cry? " His voice was so kind. " Then why not go ahead? Here." I felt a handkerchief being thrust into my good hand. " You go ahead and don't mind me. I see quite a few tears in my day's work. They help one let off steam." He touched my shoulder lightly, then I heard him move away.

His gentleness was the last straw. If he had told me sternly to pull myself together I might have managed it. As it was, I wept into his fine clean handkerchief.

He spent a long time washing his hands at the sink. He turned both taps full on, and the sound of running water drowned the sound of my weeping. When I had mopped my face he strolled back and stood in front of me. " Better now? "

" Much." I sighed the way you do sigh after a crying-jag. " I'm so sorry. Thank you for your handkerchief. I'll send it to the laundry, then give it back to you."

He put on his white coat. " Don't give that another thought. Now "—he hitched a high theatre stool closer with one foot and sat down on it—" I want that dressing and strapping to stay on until I see you again. Try to keep it dry. I'll look at it in three days' time."

" Will I be able to go on duty to-morrow night, Mr Waring? "

He took his stethoscope out of his pocket and swung it over one hand. " You can't go on duty until I take those stitches out, Nurse."

I said weakly, " Oh, no."

He raised his eyebrows. " Oh, yes. Don't look so crestfallen, Nurse. I appreciate that Margaret is a perpetually busy ward, but Matron will find a substitute. We are none of us indispensable."

I said nothing. I just looked at him and thought how idiotic were those words. He was, and always would be, indispensable to me.

He was watching me more closely than I guessed. " You seem to disagree with me, Nurse? "

" No." I was too miserable to care about truth. " I don't disagree and I don't think that I'm indispensable. I was only thinking how busy we all seem to be at night and how much difference even the lack of one junior pro.—that is, probationer—can mean to Night Sister."

" I say ' pros.' too, Nurse. Every one in Martin's does. And I do understand your anxiety. But let me reassure you, if only on one count. You will not be inconveniencing this present Night Sister, since this is to be her own last night on night-duty."

I stared at him. "Night Sister coming off?" I forgot his senior position in my genuine interest at this bit of nursing gossip. "I didn't know that."

"It's quite official knowledge—from 9 P.M. to-night. So you haven't heard yet?" I shook my head, and he followed his first announcement with the equally staggering one that Night Sister was going back to Casualty to help Nurse Davis. "Nurse Davis is taking over as Sister Casualty very shortly, at which time Night Sister is moving to Matron's Office here. The present Sister Casualty's plans have altered slightly, and she is resigning a little earlier than was originally expected. No doubt you heard Sister Casualty was resigning?"

I looked at the strapping on my hand. "Yes, I heard that." He was silent. As I could not face seeing the happiness I was so sure must be in his expression, I asked my hand who was taking over the hospital at night.

"The present Night Assistant, Nurse Dulain. And Nurse Bennings is being promoted from Francis Adams to become Night Assistant. Nurse Bennings," he added thoughtfully, " is an excellent nurse. The surgical side will be reluctant to lose her, but no doubt the hospital in general will benefit by her new appointment."

I said, "Yes, Mr Waring." And if I sounded doubtful I was beyond caring. Bennings on nights was simply too much! I still had two more months to go. Nurse Jones stood between Night Sister and myself; no one, with the possible exception of Sister Margaret, was capable of standing between Bennings and her juniors. Life on nights was going to be sheer murder.

He climbed off his stool. "If you feel all right, Nurse, I think perhaps I should leave you. I still have several wards to visit. Sister will be back shortly for you."

"Yes, thank you. I am quite all right." I looked up and saw he was watching me again. I did not mistake the concern in his expression. Jake was a good doctor and he cared about his patients; I had seen that previously. I was now his patient, and temporarily he cared about me; that is, he cared if I fainted, felt sick, pain, or burst into tears—until my stitches came out.

"I must beg to differ, Nurse. I think you are very tired and rather shocked. The sooner you get to bed the better." He stood straight, squared his shoulders, and put his hands in his pockets. His stethoscope was now dangling round his neck. He was standing directly under the cold, bright theatre light, and the remorseless, shadowless brilliance of that light illuminated every line in his face and exposed the weariness in his eyes. He had said I looked tired; he looked desperately so himself to-night. I did not know his age; I guessed it to be round thirty-five. He looked years older. The years of constant work and responsibility had left their mark on his face; the harsh theatre light, turning his fair hair to white, added to the score. I thought, This is how he'll look when he's old, but I won't be about to see it. And then I thought, I will always remember him as he is now in this neat, silent theatre, which seems so much a part of him and where everything is white and still and the only sound is the beating of my own heart, which was making such a noise that I feared he must hear it. And above all, I thought, I'll remember his kindness to-night, the gentleness of his touch, and the concern with which he was still watching me.

I had to say something, so I said I would be fine after a night in bed.

He nodded absently. "Sister'll fix you up in Nightingale. They've several beds." He roused himself. "I'll take those stitches out in ten days' time. They will very possibly"—his lips lifted in a small smile—"be the last surgical job I do in this hospital. My contract terminates nine days from to-night; but, as I've put those stitches in, I'd like to finish off the job myself. But I should add"—his tone altered and became formal—"that you do not have to accept my services for that if you prefer otherwise. Mr Embry will then be S.S.O., and you are quite at liberty to ask that he do the job for you."

I said, "I—don't mind who takes them out. Thank you."

He inclined his head. "I did not imagine that it would be material to you. I'll arrange a time with Home Sister and see to it myself."

"Yes, Mr Waring. Thank you very much."

He did not answer. He merely nodded again at my automatic response, then walked out of the theatre. I sat and waited for Night Sister. There was nothing else I could do. In a short while she returned and took me to Nightingale Ward.

I spent only one night in Nightingale and the next morning was allowed to return to my room in the Night Nurses' Home. I was able to be up, had to wear a sling, and became officially a 'Home Patient.' That meant that I was free to wear mufti, wander where I liked in the hospital grounds, but must not go out of the hospital without permission. I was also expected to go to bed early and take reasonable care of my health. If I had not been so utterly wretched because of Jake I should have enjoyed those ten days. Home Sister was kind and fussed over me, her one patient, like a motherly old hen with one chick. She took me over to Casualty to see Jake on the third morning, shepherding me across the road to the hospital as if I was two and a half. I was not in Jake's presence for more than five minutes. He said he was satisfied with the condition of my wound, ordered a fresh dressing and strapping, which Sister Casualty applied. As Home Sister and I were leaving the Hall we ran into Night Sister, now an Office-Sister-elect. She gave us an amicable smile. " You and I are playing truant, Nurse Standing. How's the hand? "

When I had replied Home Sister asked Night Sister how she was enjoying returning to her old post.

" Very much, thank you, Sister."

Home Sister said she was pleased to hear it. " I am spending this coming week-end with old Sister Casualty. She will be so interested to hear all the news about her beloved department and that you are temporarily back, Sister. I shall be sure and tell her. And I know she will be as delighted as we all are to hear of Miss Mercer's new appointment."

I gaped openly at Home Sister, wondering if she was being facetious, but the old lady seemed to be talking seriously. We said good-bye to the ex-Night Sister and walked on. As we reached the Home a Mail van drew up at the door and a postman followed us up the steps. He was carrying two large parcels. Sister turned. " I am sure you are very busy, Postman. Shall we take those from you here? "

The man grinned. " Much obliged, lady. Ta."

Sister accepted one and offered me the other. She read the name on her parcel. "Miss Mercer—how exciting. Whose is yours, Nurse?" I twisted it round with my good hand. "Miss Mercer too, Sister." Wedding presents, obviously, I thought gloomily. No wonder Home Sister looked so thrilled; she took a motherly interest in all of us and was clearly enchanted by this romance.

She said happily, "I expect this is Sister's new uniform. She said she expected that it would arrive to-day."

I had to question her now. I had been longing to do so for the last few minutes and waiting for an opening. "Uniform, Sister? For Sister Casualty?"

"Naturally, Nurse. St Martha's sisters wear a totally different uniform to our own."

I asked carefully, "St Martha's, Sister? Is Sister Casualty going to St Martha's?"

She beamed at me. "Is it not splendid, Nurse? We are naturally sad to lose such a brilliant young sister, but we hope to have her back later. This is the most wonderful promotion, and our Matron was consequently only too pleased to assist Sister by releasing her from her contract here. Sister Casualty is a very young woman for such a post, but she has a Diploma of Nursing, and this," added Home Sister rather sadly, "is a young woman's profession nowadays. And rightly so. Rightly so. Hospitals need young Matrons and Assistant Matrons, and we must all move with the times. I do not have to tell you how proud we all are that one of our sisters should be chosen from so many applicants to be the new Assistant Matron at St Martha's."

I looked at her blankly—and dropped my parcel.

"Nurse! Careful!" Her expression relaxed as I picked it up. "But you have only one hand. I mustn't scold you for doing your best."

My best! I was not sure what I was doing. As soon as Home Sister told me I was free to visit any of my set on day-duty I went up in the lift to my old floor. I found Angela off duty.

"Oh, good, Rose! I hoped you'd drop in. How's the hand? Jake Waring going to save it for you?"

"So they tell me. Angie—have you heard about—— "

She cut me short. "Bennings? So help me, have I not! Talk about insult to injury. Here I have just had her for the last three months in Francis and now we'll be on nights together! Seen Josephine? "

"Not yet. Why? She off too? " I had not seen either of them until this meeting with Angela. They had both had days off on my first sick day, and yesterday had not been off until evening when I was in bed in the night home.

She said Josephine was off in more ways than one. "She's with Matron now. Resigning. Bennings has been the deciding factor. She and Gus fixed up another wedding date last evening."

"So she's going after all." I sat down on her bed. "Angie, how the old place is changing! "

"I don't know about that. No one else is leaving."

"How about Sister Cas.? And the S.S.O.? "

She rocked with laughter. "Dearest Rose, what does it matter to the likes of us if high-powered sisters and surgeons quit? We're still in our first year, remember? Just a couple of juniors. And we won't really miss Josephine, because since the return of Gus we haven't seen her off duty. No, dearie. You and I will stagger on up the years, growing older and wiser —and who knows? One of these fine days we may even take Bennings with a smile. A girl can get used to anything."

I said flatly, " I suppose so."

She looked at me curiously. "What's the trouble, Rose? You don't sound your usual mad self. Hand hurting? "

I had to have some excuse so I said, yes. " It aches—all the time." Which was true of my heart if not of my hand.

By the end of those nine days I had worked myself into an absurd state of anticipation. At least I was going to see him once more. I was going to make the most of that meeting. I was going to say good-bye to him properly, and if possible— if I had the courage—I was going to thank him for the times he had helped me. Times like that afternoon in the surgeons' room, when he never told anyone I had gone into the wrong room; times like that evening in Cas., when if he had reported me it would have meant my discharge. Somehow I must show him that I was grateful. Even if Home Sister was with me, I decided, I would find some way.

Home Sister went with me to have my stitches out; I had endless little speeches ready, which I had rehearsed in my room, and I was filled with the courage that accompanies desperation. Neither my speeches nor my courage were needed. When we reached the Hall Nurse Davis said, " Mr Waring has asked Mr Embry to take over Nurse Standing, Sister. Mr Waring left the hospital last evening. He asked me to be sure to give you his best wishes."

The wishes were for Home Sister; no one sends messages to first-year pros. I did not bother to acknowledge them, and Sister and Davis would have been shocked if I had. Mr Embry, the new S.S.O., removed my stitches efficiently and fairly painlessly, told me that I might have the rest of the day and night off, and could return to Margaret on night-duty the following night.

Home Sister told me to go out. "You have been in the hospital for far too long, Nurse Standing. You need a change. Have you friends in London? If so, pay them a visit. But do not ask one of your friends here to come for a walk with you; you will only talk hospital shop and you need to get right away for the day. I know your hand is better, but I consider you look very peaked and pale. If you know no one in London go to the Zoo, have lunch out, or go for a long bus-ride somewhere. Do not let me see you back in the hospital until this evening."

I had no desire to go anywhere, but, not having the energy to disobey, I went back for a handbag and a hat, made up my face with more than usual care to boost my flagging morale, and left the Home. And then I did not know where to go. I climbed on to the first bus, rode for an hour or so without being conscious of where I was or what I was doing. When the conductor bellowed, "All change, here! " I got out and took another bus back. It was only midday when I was back in the shadow of Martin's. I did not dare go in after what Home Sister had said, and I was wondering vaguely where to go for lunch when I recollected Bert's invitation. I certainly needed a ' cuppa ' and a quiet sit-down. I would go to Bert's.

# 14

## *A Visit to Bert's*

BERT recognized me at once. "Hallo, miss! Not seen you for quite a while. How you been keeping?"

"I've been on night-duty. Then I cut my hand and had a few days off sick. I've got a holiday now until to-morrow night, so I thought I'd take myself out to lunch. You do do lunches as well as morning coffee and supper?"

He mopped his counter and said I was dead right, I was. "You couldn't choose a better spot for lunch, miss. Care for another mixed grill? I mind as you fancied your grill the night your young gentleman fetched you in here. And how would Dr Martin be keeping, miss? Not seen him lately either."

I said I had enjoyed my previous grill very much and would be delighted with another. "Dr Martin's very well, but very busy, I gather." I saw the inquiring look he gave me, and smiled. "Dr Martin isn't my young man, Bert. He's just a—well—friend of mine."

Bert slapped his cloth down on his counter. "You don't say, miss! That Dr Martin's a one an' all. There's a cheerful young gentleman for you, and no mistake! The things he'll say! Always a smile and a bit of laughter when that Dr Martin's around. So he's settling down to the work now, is he? I can tell you, miss"—he leaned confidentially on his counter and began maltreating his ears again—"I see it happen so often. These young student gentlemen come in here as wild as you please, and then they make 'em doctors, and the next thing you know they've turned quiet and serious-like. But he was a one, that Mr Martin," he repeated reminiscently. "Never seen the like of him when it comes to having a bit of a lark! Ready for anything, he was! An', for all that, he got a good head on his shoulders; always knew what he was doing, he did. Dead crafty, he was, miss. I can tell you. He'd come in here of an evening, full of it all. He'd say, Bert, this, and Bert, that; and sometimes I'd say, 'Never!' But he always turned out to be dead right. I often tell my missus, 'That young Mr Martin,' I'd say, 'can see further into a brick wall than many who'd reckon he was just a card!' Never knew that Mr Martin tell me something as was wrong once, I didn't."

I thought, didn't you? I did. But I merely smiled again and agreed that Dr Martin was an amusing companion.

Bert said he was keeping me too long. "You take a seat at one of them tables, miss, an' I'll see to your grill. Care to look at a paper while you're waiting? Help yourself, miss Got some of the dailies there and a few books if you'd prefer. You young ladies like to look at one of them glossy books, I understand."

I thanked him and took the first magazine off the pile he was offering, not because I wanted to read it, but because I did not want to hurt his feelings. The café was half empty. I walked down to the table at which Bill and I had sat, then, on an impulse, turned back and sat in the one behind. I chose the seat which Jake had used. Then I opened the magazine and stared at the pages without seeing one word. So he was gone, without even troubling to say good-bye. Well—what did I expect? We were strangers. Our lives had only touched professionally, nothing more; all the rest was in my imagination. The only thing to do was to take a grip on my imagination, to push all my thoughts of Jake into a mental pigeon-hole marked 'Jake Waring,' and close the small door. I sat back in my chair and closed my eyes. That was all that was left for me to do. That, and weep the tears I had been resisting all morning. I could control them no longer. I half opened my eyes and squinted around. There was no one sitting in front of me, and through the window at my side I noticed the street was empty, except for a coster's horse and barrow. The horse's face was buried in a nose-bag.

The tears were pouring down my face now, and I reclosed my eyes automatically. I brushed my cheeks with my fingertips, then felt in my handbag for a handkerchief. I was still fumbling blind, when I heard footsteps coming by my table; I sat still and bent over the magazine pretending to be engrossed with it. The steps stopped, the chair beside me was drawn back, some one sat down in it, then for only the second time in my adult life I felt a handkerchief being pushed into my hand.

" I should use that, Miss Standing," said Jake's voice softly, " and don't bother to return it either. I carry an inexhaustible supply! "

I turned and looked at him, too surprised to remember my appearance. " What are you doing here? " I asked rudely. " You've gone."

He looked very unlike his normal self this morning. He was wearing a dark well-tailored suit, a white silk shirt, and a Martin's tie. He never used that tie in the hospital. I wondered in the abstract way in which you do wonder about trivialities when your mind is unable to accept the present happenings whether he wore that tie because he was feeling cut off from Martin's.

He laid his hat on the table. " I've gone from the hospital. I've got another day in London. I do apologize for breaking in on you now, but as I came into Bert's I noticed you through that window and I saw you were crying," he added honestly. " I wondered perhaps if something was very wrong—if there was anything I could do? "

I scrubbed my face absently. " Thank you. No, no, there's nothing really wrong. I was just crying because—I felt like crying."

" I see." He took up his hat as if to move on. I would have given everything I possessed to keep him beside me, but I could not think of the means of doing that or even of a word to say. All the fine speeches of thanks and farewell that I had rehearsed in my room last night had vanished from my mind like last night's dreams.

He did not move off at once. Instead he asked after my hand. " All well? "

I took off my glove and showed him my palm. " Yes, thank you."

He glanced at it. "I thought it would save complications if I handed you over to Embry."

I said, "Yes."

He asked if I had ordered lunch.

I said, "Yes."

"Would you object if I joined you?"

I said, "No. Please do."

"Thank you."

There was a small, strained silence. He broke it. "Our meeting like this," he said conversationally, "is rather coincidental. I—er—have just been ringing your Home. I rather wanted to speak to you."

"Me?" I demanded ungrammatically. "Why?"

The somewhat grave expression he had worn during this brief conversation relaxed. His mouth remained serious, but his eyes smiled. "You—er—don't beat about the bush, do you, Miss Standing? I rang you because, as I've said, I rather wanted to speak to you. There wasn't much time left, and if I was to contact you before I left London I had to do it to-day. I would still"—he did not take his eyes off my by-now quite unpowdered face—"like to have a talk with you if you could spare me the time?" He made that request in the tone he would have used had he asked me to pass him the salt. "Are you very hungry?"

I had been wondering if I had heard right, if I was dreaming, perhaps been knocked down by a car and was dead. This kind of thing did not happen to me. Never in my life had I been in the right place at the right time. But his final question made sense if nothing else did. I said I was not hungry.

"Nor am I. So would you mind if I suggested——"

But Bert was brooding by our table, wearing a large smile and carrying a plate heaped with steaming food.

"This'll suit you, miss!" He deposited the plate in front of me.

"And what can I get you, Mr Waring? Same again?" He shook a finger at Jake. "You didn't half give me a surprise when I see you walk in just now. My missus was looking out of the kitchen window and she just called to me, 'Bert, isn't that your Mr Waring a-coming in?' And there was I saying,

'Give over, Jen—that doctor's left us.' And there you were large as life! So what'll it be, sir? The usual?"

Jake stood up. "Bert," he said, "you aren't going to like this—but do forgive us. This lady and I have got to have a talk before we eat. We just have to talk," he repeated, looking at me. His expression was questioning and—incredibly—anxious. He reached for my plate and handed it back to the outraged Bert. "Shove that in the oven or somewhere, there's a good chap. Don't chuck it out; I'll eat it when we get back, and you can fix up a fresh lot for Miss Standing. We won't be long."

Bert grumbled that he didn't know, he was sure. "Food's going to be ruined, doctor! Ruined—that's what! But if that's how you want it," he shrugged grandly "you leave it to me. I'll save your table for you."

"Thanks, Bert. Thanks very much." Jake waited while Bert made his disgruntled progress back to his counter, then turned to me. "I am afraid I'm being very arbitrary. I hope you are not too annoyed, but I haven't a lot of time. I expect you have to be on duty to-morrow night?" I nodded. "I thought as much. And I have to go north to-morrow night. I was going to have three weeks' holiday before taking over my new job, but the man I'm succeeding had a coronary yesterday, and they've asked me to make do with a couple of days off now and have the rest later. It doesn't leave me "—he touched his collar as if it was too tight—" much time. Which is why I had to see you this morning, if possible. So shall we go outside and walk round somewhere, anywhere, while we do our talking?"

I stood up and was surprised to discover my legs could carry me. My bones felt as if they had turned to water. I heard my voice reply calmly, "I should like to go outside," and for an absurd moment wished that Sister P.T.S. could have been there to hear me. Sister had told us frequently that a good nurse should be able to control any situation. Her teaching must have gone deeper than she or I realized; superficially I was quite composed. Inwardly I was far from that. My heart was beating so loudly that when we reached the street I wondered how I would be able to hear anything he said over the noise in my chest and temporal arteries; not that that mattered. Nothing mattered beyond the glorious fact that I was with him because he wanted to have me there.

We walked towards the river; we talked about the traffic; the chances of another war; the weather. We walked a little apart from each other and looked at everything but each other. We went down a succession of small streets that grew smaller as we came closer to the water. Once we crossed one of the great traffic-congested roads of dockland, then we were back in the alleys again. The air smelt of salt and tar and coal-dust, and the skyline ahead showed a forest of masts of different sizes belonging to ships anchored in the docks.

Just before we reached one of the smaller entrances to the docks he stopped and felt in his pocket. "I think I've got my pass on me. Yes." He flicked it open. "It's valid until the fifth of next month. I know most of the chaps on the gates; let's go over and see if they'll let me take you in and show you round.

"Yes, let's," I agreed weakly. I was not clear what I had been expecting; but I was quite clear that I had not expected to be taken for a conducted tour round the Pool of London.

My surprise must have shown in my expression, because he said mildly, "The embankment is a shade crowded at this time of the day; the nearest park will be intolerable; we can't have a reasonable conversation in the street, and I can't take you to my club, as the ladies' room there is like a morgue. We could perhaps have got in a taxi and driven around, but I'm afraid I simply did not think of that until now. My car's being serviced "—he smiled at me—" so it's docks or nothing. If my conversation bores you you can always watch the ships. I expect you like watching ships."

Very dimly some understanding of what was going on lit my mind. He was trying to show me that we were out of hospital, on equal terms, two ordinary people. To make certain that I was right about this, I said, " And train engines. I spend all my off-duty watching the engine-drivers."

His smile deepened. " I see I should have taken you to Waterloo. I apologize. Now let's see this cop."

The policeman at the gate recognized him at once. " Hallo,

Doctor. Not sent for you, have they? I wasn't informed."

Jake explained that he was on holiday. "In point of fact, I'm on holiday for good as far as this place is concerned. I've finished my time in Martin's. I go north to-morrow night."

"You leaving us, sir?" The policeman seemed honestly sorry. "You don't say. We'll miss seeing you around. Been in and out of here many a time you have."

Jake said he was right there and would like to come in once more. "I'd like to take a final look round. And may I take this young lady in with me? We're only taking a walk. We won't go near any gangways or loadings; we merely want to look at the locks."

The policeman looked me over shrewdly. "The lady'll be your wife, I expect, sir?"

Jake said smoothly, "No, not my wife. Miss Standing is a nurse at St Martin's.

The policeman relaxed and hitched his thumbs in his belt. "The lady from the hospital, doctor? Right. That'll be all right. Which gate were you thinking of leaving by?"

"We haven't any specific plans. Like us to come out this way?"

"If you would, sir. But if you get lost—and there's a good many who know these docks and still do that—get the man on the gate you find to ring me up." He told us the number of his gate. "I'll mention that you're in to the Sergeant. Not that I reckon he'll worry, seeing as you are both from the hospital. Miss Standing, wasn't it, sir? Right. I thank you."

When we were a few yards inside the gates Jake said, "Martin's name is an open sesame in this district."

"So I'm discovering. First in Bert's; then here."

He did not answer directly. He was returning the wave of one docker, who was ambling by with a coil of old rope slung over his shoulder. "How's the back, Dan?"

Dan grinned, exposing a mouthful of nicotine-blackened teeth. "Mustn't grumble, doctor. Lasting me time out nicely."

As we walked on I asked, "Do you have to come here often? Don't they have a Port M.O.H.?"

"Oh, yes; and a surgeon to every so many ships in port. See that chap there." He pointed to a large blue-and-white flag on one of the ships. " That's the M.O.'s flag. They fly it to show where the surgeon is. It moves with him."

" Then why do you have a pass? "

He said slowly, " For official and unofficial reasons. Being the nearest general hospital, we get called in officially to take all emergencies; accidents major and minor and so on. For no really good reason beyond tradition, the Port M.O.H. is generally an old Martin's man; the present chap qualified when I did. He often rings up and says, ' Come on down—I'd like a second opinion,' and some one goes down. The S.M.O. and S.S.O. get official passes automatically; it saves a lot of fuss and bother on occasions when there is time to do neither. As most of the cases down here are straight accidents, I've probably been here more frequently than Spence. Wait a moment."

We waited as he said, while a small file of open trucks rolled past us on one of the many sets of railway lines, then crossed over to the road on the far side as he continued. " I thought we might go over to that far lock. There's a seat there some philanthropist built for the dockers, but none of them would ever dream of using it. They much prefer to hang around between ships by their braziers drinking tea. Good tea, too. Often had some."

The stone seat was built to the right of one of the long line of sheds. It directly overlooked the water in the now half-empty lock. As we sat down Jake looked round nostalgically; he looked as if he was taking a photograph in his mind.

I asked, " Are you going to miss all this? "

Slowly he turned to look at me. " Yes."

I could not look at him while he watched me. I looked at the water. " Have you worked in the north before? Do you come from there? "

" No to both."

We were silent. The silence was agony. I had to say something. He seemed to have forgotten that he had torn me from my grill because he wanted to talk to me. I asked more about his new job. " Are you going to work in a hopsital? "

" Several hospitals. I've got the job of Consultant Surgeon to a Group." He mentioned which one. " It's a good job and

I was very lucky to get it. The competition for such jobs nowadays is cut-throat."

I said I had heard that was the case. I glanced at him again, and this time I could not look away. We seemed to be having two conversations; the unimportant one was the one we spoke aloud. "And you start the day after to-morrow?"

"Yes." He removed his hat and laid it on the seat between us. "And you go back on nights to-morrow night?"

I felt breathless. "Yes."

He said abruptly. "This is where we came in." Then he seemed to have run out of words. He took out his cigarettes, shook one from the packet, lit it, and inhaled hurriedly as if he needed the nicotine in his blood-stream, then realized that he had forgotten to offer me one, and did so apologetically. "I'm afraid I didn't know that you smoked."

I accepted gratefully. I too needed a cigarette. "I don't often."

He shut the packet carefully. "I didn't know that," he said again, as if the matter was vital, "but then I don't know very much about you, Rose. I do know that on occasions you can be idiotically scatter-brained, and on other occasions highly intelligent. I know that you are good at drawing, very gay, very pretty—and so young." He looked down at the cigarette in his hand. I noticed that his cigarette was shaking slightly as he added quietly, "Does this worry you? Or can I go on?"

"Please—go on."

His grey eyes looked into mine, and I wondered how I could ever have thought them cold. "If I go on—I have to tell you the rest. I have to tell you what I have wanted to tell you since you scooted down that basement last summer like a child scooting on a toy pram. I have to tell you"—his voice was very deep and nearly inaudible—"that from the moment that I picked you up I have not once ceased to want to hold you in my arms again. It did not take me long to realize that I loved you, Rose—and I love you now. I also realize how absurd all this must sound to you. I am so much older than you; we work in different spheres. You've got your own friends, your own life; and that you enjoy that life to the full is patently obvious. Even if it had not been obvious that you had no need of me I could not have told you this while I was S.S.O., as hospital etiquette completely tied my hands. I had to wait."

He sat back and dangled his arms over the back of the seat. "Normally I am a moderately patient man. I have not been at all patient about you. You see, I thought after first meeting you last summer that, as you were so young, there was plenty of time; and if I got an appointment in or near London when my time ran out I could do something tangible about getting to know you after I left. Then this northern job cropped up. It was too good to ignore. I applied—and as I did not particularly want it—I got it. Then I thought, I've got three weeks. Yesterday those weeks narrowed to three days and two of them would be useless, as you were technically my patient. You don't," he added a little grimly, "tell your patient you love her unless you want to be struck off. Rather absurd under our given circumstances, I agree; but Martin's is in many ways an absurdly conventional world. Which was why I made a point of handing you over formally to Mike Embry. You do follow that?"

I nodded. I had no breath to spare in speech.

"Having got that fixed up, I waited for this morning. The time was running out. You'll have to be in bed by midday to-morrow, so it was getting down to twenty-four hours. That isn't very long. I told you about ringing your Home. I did not tell you I rang you five times. And I could not get hold of you. They said you were out for the day on the last time I rang, so I gave up. Being careless and from force of habit, I wandered down to Bert's. I often took refuge in Bert's when the job got on top of me. Then, when I got there, I saw you through the window sitting at my table. It was almost —as if you were waiting for me. I felt——" He stopped and looked at the lovely lines of the great ship waiting at the far lock gates. "I can't describe how I felt. Then I saw you were crying." He looked round at me. "Why were you crying? Martin's upset you? Or Sister Margaret?"

I simply sat and looked at him for several seconds. It was so wonderful to know I could answer honestly. I could not

take in all he said, but I could and did believe him. I said,
" No."

The lines on his forehead deepened. " Then—why? Your
hand? Let me see it," he asked, forgetting his fine sense of
ethics.

I removed my glove again and held my palm upward. " It
doesn't hurt at all."

He touched the scar. " Good union there. Looks all right."
He handed me back my hand as if it was a parcel. " Then,
why? "

I said, " Because you had gone and hadn't bothered to say
good-bye."

" Because—I—had gone? " He sounded as incredulous as I
had been, and in a way still was. " Why? "

I could not answer that. I shook my head stupidly.

" Rose," he said gently, " I've told you—I haven't much
time. I can't deal with this sort of thing in letters, and I
can't say yet when I'll be able to get back to London again.
We must get this straight now. Why, when you have clearly
disliked me for all these months, should you bother to weep
because I'm going away? "

Surprise helped me recover my powers of speech. " I—
disliked you? "

He nodded. " You probably don't recall an occasion outside
Eyes, but I certainly do. You were remarking loudly to some
friend what little interest you felt in whom I took to the
Rugger Ball. " He ground his cigarette on to the concrete
round the seat and lit a fresh one. " There's a touch of irony
about that. I only bought those tickets in the hope that I
might somehow manage to get a dance with you."

" But how could you know I was going? Bill hadn't asked
me when you bought those tickets."

He said suddenly, " Oh, God. We shouldn't smoke here. I
forgot that." He stubbed out his new cigarette, then turned to
me. " How did I know—or think I knew? Because I know
Martin tolerably well. I knew he was running that show, and
I was pretty certain by the way he was behaving with you
that he would suggest you break with precedent and go with
him. Martin has made a hobby of breaking with precedent;

he doesn't do it so much now he's qualified. He's learning fast. He's an intelligent, if very adolescent, youth."

I said, "That's exactly what Hector would have said."

He raised his eyebrows. "Hector?"

"My eldest brother." I told him about the boys. "Bill Martin has tested all Hector's theories for me."

He smiled. "So that's where you picked up your wisdom. I wondered about that. I couldn't help overhearing what he said to you that night in Bert's; I heard your replies too. You seemed to me to be quite unimpressed by him, and I wondered why. He's pretty successful with women as a rule. But when you got outside, then I did get rather disturbed. You looked so very young, Rose. It's so easy to be taken in when you are very young; and you can get hurt."

"Was that why you looked anxious?"

"You noticed that? I didn't think you had. Yes, it was. I was suddenly afraid that you might take him seriously. He's not a bad lad, but—— "

I said, "Labelled 'not to be taken seriously.' I did see that. I don't believe anyone should take Bill seriously for at least another ten years."

He looked amused. "I haven't any sisters. I rather wish I had. They might have saved me as many growing pains at your age as your brothers have you. Did Martin send you those carnations?"

"Yes."

"I thought they were from him. I saw you guessed that too. You looked as displeased with those damned flowers as I felt. Why did he send them? Still persevering with his attempts to impress you?"

"Partly." I hesitated. "Partly because of—that night in Cas."

"I've been wondering about that, too," he said evenly. "You shouldn't have let him kiss you, of course; but now that's all past may I ask, did you know he was going to?"

"I should have guessed, but I didn't. I was annoyed with him about something, and I walked straight into that one. I really am sorry about it. It upset me a lot. Thank you for not reporting me."

" It upset me too; in more ways than one. But did you seriously imagine I'd report you? "

I could not pretend to him. I told him the truth.

He said he did not blame me for being uncertain about what he would do. " I was very angry—and not just because you were you. But, for the record, Rose, I wouldn't have reported any other girl. I don't care to report people. I prefer to deal with things myself. But I do not seem to have dealt with all this conspicuously well. I have talked a great deal, and you've been very patient in listening, but now it's time I took you back to have your lunch. If we delay much longer poor Bert'll possibly have nervous hysteria about his ruined grills. And in any event," he added slowly, " there really isn't anything else to be said. Thank you for not laughing. I appreciate that there must be some humour in my present situation, although at the moment it escapes me. Doubtless I'll see the joke later."

" Joke? " I asked sharply. " What joke? "

He put his hands in his pockets and hunched his shoulders. " You're twenty and I'm thirty-six. You're a girl starting your career, and I'm at the end of one career and the start of another. A career not open to very young men; and we are going to be working a couple of hundred miles apart. Just for to-day we're together. And here I am, late S.S.O. at Martin's, telling a first-year pro. I've only called by her Christian name this morning that I love her, that I love her very much, and that I would give just about everything I possess to have her as my wife. There's no denying that it's a good story, Rose; it's a damned good story. It'll rock the Nurses' Homes and residents' sitting-rooms. Don't you agree? "

He looked so utterly defeated and tired as he spoke that the last vestige of reserve vanished from me. I only knew that I wanted to help him. And now that I knew that I could I did not bother about incredulity or wonder; I was going to help him, and nothing and nobody was going to stop me.

I said, " The hospital is going to do without its good laugh."

" Thank you." He stood up. " I did not really think you would rush back and give the news. I was talking academically. Now, come along; I'm sure you're very hungry." He walked a few feet from me and stood with his back to me, looking across the lock. "I'm sorry to have delayed you so long."

I watched his back and remembered another saying of Hector's: ". . . and when a chap's serious he makes mistakes all the way along the line because he's so anxious not to do the wrong thing." Only a lunatic or a lover, I thought, could suggest that a woman would want to eat after having an honest proposal of marriage.

I closed my eyes, thought hard, opened them again. For once, nothing disastrous happened. Jake was still there with his back to me, watching the lock. I said quietly, "Jake, sit down."

He turned slowly and stared at me. "What did you say?"

I repeated myself.

He sat down heavily. "That's what I thought you said." He looked at me as if he had never seen me before.

I took a deep breath; not because I was breathless, but because I had a lot to say. "You talked to me, but you haven't asked if I want to talk to you."

"My dear girl, I do try to avoid asking obvious questions. Why should you want to talk to me? You've been very sweet and kind and considerate, but what could you tell me that I do not already know? Apart from the pleasant fact that you don't dislike me as much as I thought, I don't expect you to tell me more; you and I have scarcely met, and when we have I have either lectured you or picked you off the floor. You will," he said gently, "have to be more careful how you go on in future, Rose. I won't be on hand any longer. But, oh, my dearest," he said suddenly, "how I wish I could always be there—for you."

"Then I think you'll have to do something about it, Jake. I don't see how I can go on at Martin's without you. I just can't."

He looked at me now as no man had looked at me in my life. "Say that again."

I said it again.

"But—this is ridiculous. We've—just met. You don't know me—you can't—be in love with me?"

" Why not? If you can be in love with me? "

He stared at me as if I had gone quite mad, then a smile that started in his eyes illuminated his whole face. " Suppose, my darling," he murmured, " you—er—tell me all about it? "

And so I told him.

It took quite a long time. When I had finished he said, " I don't understand any of this, Rose, but I believe you. I always will." And then there was no more talk, and I was in his arms and he was kissing me, and if any of the dockers noticed us neither Jake nor I cared at all.

After some time he raised his head. " Where do you come from, Rose? Have you got parents or must I face Hector? "

" Not Hector." I rested my head on his shoulder and thought how right and proper it felt for me to rest my head there. " My parents live in Hampshire."

" We'll drive down there this evening, then I'll bring you back in the morning." He rubbed his cheek against mine. ' I told you there wasn't much time. Do you think they'll let you get engaged? Or will they say you are too young? " His voice altered as he said that. I tilted back my head and saw he was frowning.

I said I thought my parents would give three loud cheers. ' They never could manage me. Mother said she thought the hospital would subdue me into a normally well-behaved young woman; father said I was far more likely to subdue the hospital."

He smiled. " Then perhaps they'll be on my side." He stroked my hair. " There's one thing, dearest. Will you mind leaving Martin's after only one year? "

I thought it over; not for long. " No. It's been fun and shattering. I may miss it a bit, but I can bear to miss it. I can't bear to miss you." And he kissed me again.

We sat on, watching the lock that was now filling again. It was very cold, but we were impervious to cold, Bert, the immediate future when we would have to go our separate ways, the prospect of springing our engagement on my parents, the life in the docks around us. But the docks had not forgotten us. While Jake was telling me exactly what had been in his thoughts as he held my head over my knees that afternoon in the surgeons' room we heard a shout behind us. We turned and saw a man running towards us across the railway lines. "Hey—mister!" he shouted. "You a doctor?"

Jake disengaged his hand from mine and stood up. "Yes. Why? Some one hurt?"

The man came closer. "That's right, mate. Bloke's just been knocked down by a lorry in the road outside that there gate. The cop said to see if you was handy. He's rung for an ambulance, but he said if the tall fair bloke with the fair young lady was still around to get——"

He did not go on, as Jake had given me his hat and said, "Hang on to that, darling—right! By the gate?" and was already half-way over the railway lines.

The man walked with me to the gate. "Cor—can't that tall bloke move!" He gave Jake's retreating figure an appreciative nod. "Reckon you got to be able to move smartish in his trade." He touched his cap to me. "Sorry I had to interrupt you and your husband, ma'am. I'll be getting along now." He strolled away towards one of the loading sheds.

There was a small crowd on the far pavement. Jake was kneeling beside a crumpled figure in the road. The policeman saw me and told the crowd, who were nowhere near me, to stand back. "Let the lady through. She's a nurse."

The ambulance arrived as I reached Jake's side. He glanced up. "They've come? Good. Sooner he gets into Martin's the better."

I knelt down beside him. "Anything I can do?"

"Not a thing. He's got a fractured base. I can feel it. Only superficial wound, but it's right in. He needs hospitalization —stat."

I nodded and stood up, then moved back out of the way as the careful ambulance men lifted the unconscious man into the back of the ambulance. They recognized Jake. "You coming along with us, Mr Waring?"

"Yes." He jumped into the ambulance, looked round, and beckoned to me. "Rose."

I went to him.

"I'm not sure how long I'll be; not very long. Will you wait for me in Bert's?"

I looked up at him. " I'll wait for you," and for that brief moment he and I were alone in a private world. Then he closed the white doors in my face, and the ambulance moved off.

The policeman touched my arm lightly. " Best get out of the road, miss."

" Yes, of course. Thank you." I walked to the pavement with him.

On the pavement he stopped and surveyed the road which was now filled with traffic again. " Lucky the doctor was handy. Good when you can catch a chap on the spot. But bad luck for the doctor and him being on his holiday. 'Fraid he didn't get much of a chance to show you round much." He took off his helmet, mopped his forehead and replaced his helmet again. " Doctors—I dunno. Seems as if that's one job in which you can't ever be properly off, as you might say. Always some one needing you. But I reckon as you understand that, Miss, seeing as you're a nurse."

I said, " Yes, I do understand." We exchanged matey good-byes, and I walked alone back to Bert's. I walked slowly, thinking of the accident; of what was about to happen in Cas.; of the hospital; and above all about Jake and this fantastic and wonderful morning. I thought of what had been my first, and was going to be my last, year as a nurse; of the friends and the work and the laughter and occasional tears. I thought of Bill's uncanny perceptiveness and Jake's concern that I should not be hurt by Bill. And then I stopped thinking of anyone and anything but Jake: the man he was and the work he did and was going to do in the future, and how when that was done he would come home to me.

I sailed into Bert's and smiled and smiled at his woebegone expression. " You're not going to tell me, miss, as Mr Waring isn't coming for his dinner after all? "

I said, " He's been held up by an accident, Bert. He's back at the hospital. Don't worry; he'll come as soon as he can. And until then, if you don't mind, I'd like to wait."